A PORTRAIT
OF
Marguerite

A PORTRAIT
OF
Marguerite
A NOVEL

Kate Lloyd

RIVEROAK®
Good News in Fiction

COOK COMMUNICATIONS MINISTRIES
Colorado Springs, Colorado • Paris, Ontario
KINGSWAY COMMUNICATIONS LTD
Eastbourne, England

RiverOak® is an imprint of
Cook Communications Ministries, Colorado Springs, CO 80918
Cook Communications, Paris, Ontario
Kingsway Communications, Eastbourne, England

A PORTRAIT OF MARGUERITE
© 2006 by Kate Lloyd

This story is a work of fiction. All characters and events are the product of the author's imagination. Any resemblance to any person, living or dead, is coincidental.

Cover Design: Koechel Peterson & Associates, Inc.
Cover Illustration: Dan Thornberg

First Printing, 2006
Printed in the United States of America

1 2 3 4 5 6 7 8 9 10 Printing/Year 10 09 08 07 06

Unless otherwise noted, Scripture quotations are taken from the *Holy Bible, New International Version®*. *NIV®*. Copyright © 1973, 1978, 1984 by International Bible Society. Used by permission of Zondervan. All rights reserved. Scripture quotations marked KJV are taken from the King James Version of the Bible. (Public Domain.)

ISBN-13: 978-1-58919-056-6
ISBN-10: 1-58919-056-4

LCCN: 2005938002

Dedicated with love to my husband, Noel

I would like to thank my sons, Bryan Redecker and Chris Lloyd, for their patience while I pursued my creative dreams. Thank you, Chris, for helping me many times with my writing. Thank you dear sister, Margaret Coppock, and friend and realtor, Nancy House, for your encouragement and for proofing my manuscript, and Waverly Fitzgerald, my first critique group leader, for your wisdom and guidance. Thank you to my agent, Les Stobbe, and Jeff Dunn at RiverOak.

1

"This was a mistake," I said, peering down the hall of the art building at a display of framed watercolors and a bulletin board smothered with notices of upcoming events.

"Why?" Laurie asked.

I tried to untangle my thoughts, but found no explanation to give my friend. "Because it's bad luck to return to the scene of a crime."

"Marguerite, you haven't done anything wrong." She nudged me forward. "Come on. We're going to be late."

As I led the way into the shadowy stairwell, memories poured over me. Back in college I'd waltzed up these stairs with my paint box in one hand and a stretched canvas in the other. And in the painting studio I'd found my lover, Phil.

With Laurie on my heels, I reached the second floor and shoved open the door. I inhaled the smell of turpentine and oil paint, what used to be a sweet perfume. But tonight the biting odor assaulted my nostrils. Moving forward, I spotted our room, number 213. I slowed my pace and tried to settle my jagged breath, but a tornado of anxiety whirled through my chest, as if I were about to topple off a cliff.

Laurie swished past me and breezed through the classroom's doorway. Watching her angular silhouette disappear, I stood for a moment in disbelief. Why had I let her bamboozle me into taking this class? This was the last place on earth I wanted to be.

Get a grip, I told myself. There was no reason to come unglued. I could fake it through one evening; I was a master at camouflaging my emotions. Not even my parents or best friends knew the real me. And that was how it needed to stay.

I straightened my spine and widened my shoulders—the way I did when tackling a difficult real-estate client—and followed Laurie into the room where ten people sat at low worktables set up in a semicircle.

She and I found vacant seats off to the left just as a man standing at the front of the room said, "Good evening. I'm Professor Marsh, your instructor for this session of Beginning Drawing."

He wasn't what I expected. Judging by his thick peppered hair, he was probably fifty, about ten years older than I. He seemed muscular under his collared shirt, as though he worked out with weights. No wedding ring, I couldn't help but notice, and not bad looking. But I'd vowed to steer clear of artists. Once was enough.

Professor Marsh scanned the students, and his gaze settled on the woman in the seat next to me. "Please, call me
Henry," he said, the corners of his mouth lifting.

Behind him stood a chalkboard. On its greenish surface
in a bold, slanted hand were written the words: *Every child is
an artist. The problem is how to remain an artist once he grows
up. Pablo Picasso.*

"Tonight, we'll review some drawing basics." Henry's
baritone voice rang with easy confidence. "We'll explore how
our eyes perceive the three-dimensional world, then translate
those images onto a two-dimensional surface."

As he spoke about drawing techniques, I surveyed the
still life arranged on the table next to him: a dented brass kettle, a stack of weathered textbooks, three mason jars, and a
hideous-looking orange lamp with a crooked shade. Had he
brought this mishmash from home? I grimaced as I imagined
what the inside of this guy's house looked like. Probably a
typical artist's hovel, I thought, remembering my ex-husband
Phil's apartment the last time I'd seen it. His place was a
pigsty, and it stunk of cigarette smoke and stale beer.

Henry adjusted the lampshade, then stood back. "Regard
these objects as geometric shapes: cubes, cones, and prisms.
Nothing more than solid shapes sitting on top of other solid
shapes." His face brimmed with enthusiasm as he gave
instructions on cross-hatching and blending methods used to
create the illusion of shade. "Now let's get to work."

I watched my classmates sharpen their pencils and spread
out their drawing paper. At least I wasn't the oldest person
there. More than half of the students in the class were what
my eighteen-year-old son would call middle-aged, meaning
over thirty.

9

Out of the corner of my eye, I could see Henry standing at the far end of the desks chatting with a young redheaded woman. Our professor probably relished the attention of pretty, naive students, I thought, and maybe even took advantage of their eagerness to please, if you catch my drift.

He moved to the next student and stopped to make a suggestion. I admonished myself to get busy and at least appear to be participating. Slipping my new notebook out of its bag, I opened the pad to the first page and stared at the gaping white surface. When it was time for Henry to view my work, what would I show him? I couldn't remember how to draw anymore. It had been twenty years.

My slacks pinched me around the waist, and I felt cool dampness gathering under my armpits. The desire to jump up and escape seized me—almost lifting me off my chair. But I couldn't leave; Laurie was my ride home. Anyway, I wasn't the type to skitter away with her tail between her legs. I was my father's daughter, the eldest child, a single mother who had made it on her own.

Quite honestly, it required all my willpower to force my attention back to the blank page. Focusing my eyes on the kettle's wooden handle, I pressed my pencil tip to the center of the paper and started drawing. What an odd sensation, almost as if the pencil had a mind of its own. I quickly filled in the dark area and was soon working on the spout.

I looked up to see Henry wandering down the line of students observing their work. Laurie, her eyes sparkling from behind frosted bangs, giggled when he came by her desk.

"I haven't drawn since grade school," she said, one shoulder lifting into a coy shrug.

"You're doing fine," he said. "Have fun, and don't worry about making a finished product." He stepped behind me. My shoulders hunched and my hand gripped my pencil as he glanced at my work. I held my breath and braced myself for his critique, but instead of addressing me he said hello to the older woman on my other side.

"Emily McBride, I'm honored to have you in my class."

Emily's beautifully wrinkled face bloomed. "When I saw your name in the Extension School catalog last week, I couldn't resist," she said. Her silver hair was combed back into a loose bun and secured by two wooden picks. "And I've missed you. We haven't seen you at church for a while."

"I've been trying something new. Smaller fits me better right now."

"That's fine, dear. Just know you're missed."

"Thank you." He patted the back of her speckled hand, then strolled to the front of the class.

So, he's religious, I thought, which told me a truckload about him, and none of it good.

Laurie leaned over to me and bumped elbows. "This is fabulous, don't you think?" she said. "I've already learned so much."

I managed a smile. "I'm glad you're having fun." At least one of us was.

"Good work, everyone," Henry said. "That first forty-five minutes flew by." He unbuttoned his sleeves and rolled them up, revealing a splotch of yellow ocher paint on one forearm. "We've explored how the eye perceives objects as solid masses. Now let's look at the same grouping as nothing but lines. Extending one arm, use your index finger as a pointer and visually define the contour of each item on the table." He demonstrated with his hand as he spoke. "Take that finger around the edges and through the shapes."

I don't know if I was being obstinate, or maybe grumpy, but his instructions annoyed me. I kept my hands in my lap as the other students, their arms reaching out like children playing Simon Says, followed his directions.

"Continue studying the contours," he said, "and without looking down at your paper use a pencil to record what you see. Let your eyes tell you where to move your hand."

The others turned the pages of their notebooks. The rustling of paper prickled my eardrums, and my stomach clenched into a fist. Once more, it took Herculean strength to position my pencil on a new piece of paper, then I fastened my gaze to the still life and began outlining a jar. A moment later, much to my surprise, my pencil glided across the paper in a flowing line and captured the curve of the lamp.

Just as I was beginning to enjoy myself, I noticed Henry walking my way. I tried to look as though I were concentrating on my work and paying no attention to him. Again, he paused for a moment, glanced at my paper, and said nothing.

Was my drawing so awful it didn't warrant a comment? My throat tightened around a growing lump, but I swallowed it down and told myself I didn't need his approval. I was a grown woman, for goodness sake. Who cared what he thought?

"You're all doing beautifully," he said, striding to the front of the room. But I didn't feel included in his gratuitous compliment. If he thought I was doing well, he would have spoken to me directly.

He glanced at the clock on the wall. "Let's take a short break. I brought a thermos of decaf, and there's a pop machine down the hall for those who've heard how bad my coffee is."

The sound of chair legs scraping the floor and voices chattering filled the room. I watched most of the class stretch to their feet, then straggle over to the thermos and Styrofoam cups.

"I love our teacher, don't you?" Laurie said, gushing like a teenager experiencing her first crush. "What a wise man."

I looked at her crude drawing—a jumble of squiggly lines—and felt a wave of fondness for my dear friend of eighteen years. "It looks like you're doing great," I said.

"I figure I can only improve."

While the other students mingled and inspected each other's sketches, Laurie and I talked about our kids.

"Day after tomorrow my Rob's off to college." I raked a hand through my shoulder-length hair and found a snarl. "It's hard to believe. Like the end of an era." Rob's choosing to attend school down in California had seemed like a good idea last spring, but not anymore. I couldn't imagine how I would fill the long expanses of my days without my only child close by.

"Are we even old enough to have children in college?" Laurie asked.

I coughed a laugh. "I'm afraid so."

"I can't believe I'm turning forty in six months."

"Welcome to the club." Not that sliding into another decade had hit me that hard. I liked to think I'd grown wiser. Although looking back now, it was plain to see I hadn't.

"Never mind. I've decided to stay thirty-nine for a few more years," she said, a grin fanning across her face.

I heard footsteps behind us, then recognized my ex-husband's voice saying, "Let me introduce you to the mother of my child."

He sounded like an elephant trumpeting in my ears, and my first impulse was to dive under my desk for cover. But I figured I was imagining things. Phil here? Impossible.

I inhaled a whiff of spicy aftershave, his favorite brand, then felt a pat on my shoulder, making me flinch. I turned around to find his baby blue eyes gazing into mine. Against all logic, a warm breeze buzzed through my chest as I examined his handsome face crowned by curly blond hair. I hadn't seen him for more than a year, but he hadn't aged one bit, which struck me as profoundly unfair.

I clenched my jaw and waited for this momentary attraction to Phil to pass. It always did. I reminded myself that he'd given me nothing but grief. And if I hadn't threatened to sue him two years ago, he never would have paid me the back child support.

Henry, several inches taller than Phil, stood at his side. "Hank, meet Marguerite Carr, my ex-wife," Phil said, as if he were introducing his two best friends.

"Margo," he said to me, "do you remember my talking about Hank Marsh? We go way back—shared studio space and did several shows together." His hand moved to Henry's shoulder. "You're in for a treat. This man's talented."

If I wasn't mistaken, Henry was avoiding making eye contact with me. I flushed with annoyance. "Nice to meet you," I said, and noticed his vision finally taking me in.

He replied, "Good evening," then pivoted his head to speak to Laurie, who said something about how much she was enjoying the class.

"This is just like old times finding you here," Phil said, smoothing his jaw line with his fingertips.

I got to my feet. "I wouldn't go that far." I looked him over and saw that a dusting of white plaster sprinkled the front of his ragged jeans and T-shirt. I sniffed the air for alcohol. He appeared to be sober. And I couldn't even detect a hint of cigarette smoke.

I crossed my arms and said, "I'm still not comfortable with you driving Rob to school."

"I thought we had this all settled. I'm the one with the passenger van, and you're the one who has a hard time taking a day off from work."

"Are you going to show up?"

"Of course." He raised his right hand as if being sworn in. "I'll be there. I promise."

I knew better than to believe what he said. I arched an eyebrow the way my father did to show disapproval. "See that you are." I couldn't stand having Rob disappointed again by his flaky father.

"I'm helping a buddy do some casting tonight and need to get back to work." He turned to Henry, and the two men began discussing a gallery opening as they strolled toward the door.

"I haven't seen Phil in years," Laurie said. She watched him shake Henry's hand, then leave. "He looks different somehow. Better."

I frowned as a thousand agonizing memories coursed through my brain. When we were married, I'd seen Phil crawl into the bathroom, hang his head in the toilet and vomit his insides out, and then get up and chug down another beer. I'd smelled marijuana and cheap perfume on his clothes after a night of partying with his buddies. And in the dead of the night, I'd felt his hot breath caress my ear, then heard him murmur another woman's name,

"Not that I'm suggesting you two—" Laurie added.

"Don't worry," I snapped. "I know way too much about Philip Carr to ever be sucked in again."

I watched Laurie zoom in on the display of best-sellers planted inside the doorway of Seattle's biggest Barnes and Noble.

"There it is." She scooped up a hardbound book with the title *Unearthing Your Childhood Dreams* printed across its jacket and handed it to me. I turned it over to examine the photo of the author, a woman in her early thirties with short permed hair and a pixie face.

"Are you sure this is good?" I asked. I didn't have extra money to waste on books I didn't need.

"I saw her on *Oprah*. She sounded fabulous." Laurie grabbed another copy and hugged it to her breast. "Let's both buy one. Please. Then I'll have someone to talk to about it."

As we headed to the cash register, I silently tallied my collection of self-help books. Most of the two dozen or so pertained to child rearing, a subject quickly becoming obsolete. I gave the cashier my money, careful to slip the receipt in the book in case I decided to return it.

Moments later, Laurie and I climbed the stairs to the café on the mezzanine. Up ahead I could hear an espresso machine blast, then sputter. On the final step, I felt exhaustion blanket me like a lead apron. I scanned the room, which overlooked the rest of the store, to see that only three of the dozen or so tables were occupied. I bought a single nonfat latte and plopped down at the nearest empty table.

Laurie picked up her order, then trotted over clutching a tall mocha latte and a scone. At five-eight, five inches taller than I, she seemed able to consume practically anything and remain her gorgeous trim self, while I needed to watch my calories. And she was a head-turning blonde—almost my opposite in hair color and skin tone.

She sat across from me, wriggled out of her red quilted jacket, and bit into her scone.

"Sorry if I'm not very good company," I said, recalling my depressing 8:00 a.m. sales meeting. It seemed like every other realtor in my office was enjoying a dynamite month but me. And the past few months hadn't been much better. "It's been a long day."

"Don't fade out on me yet," she said. "I'm too pumped to go home and watch Dave vegetate in front of the TV or deal with the kids' homework." She tasted her latte and left fuchsia lipstick on the cup's rim. "Mondays will be ladies' night out, okay?"

"I'm still not sure a night class is going to work for me." I had to find a way to get out of going again. "The real-estate market's hopping, and I want to be free to meet with clients." No need to mention I'd nearly run out of prospective buyers.

"You've got to keep coming. It would be terrible to miss even one class."

"Sweetie, I only went to keep you company. You'll do fine without me."

"But it wouldn't be half as much fun." She watched me rip open a packet of sugar substitute. "You're lucky you can already draw so well. How come you never do it?"

"I guess I don't feel like it." As I stirred the white crystals into my drink, my brain searched for the true reason. "No self-discipline maybe." The past twenty years whirred by in my mind like a one-star movie on fast-forward. "Somehow when Phil and Rob showed up in my life, I lost interest. It's just as well, because it's almost impossible to earn a living as an artist. I should have gone to the school of business instead."

"I love that painting in your living room."

"Thanks." My *Morning at Cannon Beach*, the only painting I still owned, hung above my couch. I supposed some might have called it well crafted or even quite good, but I'd completed the piece so long ago I felt as though someone else had painted it.

"I wish I had your talent," Laurie said. "But I had fun in class, and I think our teacher's a doll."

"I'd better warn you, any friend of Phil's is probably a flake."

"Maybe. But that older lady knew Henry from church. He might be a good Christian man."

Let me tell you, the word *Christian* grated in my ears. "Some very wicked people have called themselves Christians," I said, hearing anger amplify my words. I glanced around the room and was glad nobody at the surrounding tables had heard me. I lowered my voice. "That's the last trait I'm looking for in a man."

"There are worse things."

At that moment an orange-haired youth with a ring in his nose sauntered across the room.

Laurie chuckled into her hand. "Don't you agree?" she said.

"I suppose." I sipped my latte to avoid continuing our conversation. I knew she attended church every now and then, and I didn't want to hurt her feelings. But as far as I was concerned, religion served as a pacifier for the ignorant and the weak.

"Hey, what happened to the cute accountant you brought over for dinner a few months ago?" she finally said. "He looked like a keeper."

"He was boring. No sense of humor." I yawned with drama. "I fell asleep every time he opened his mouth. And he drove like a little old lady. I couldn't wait to get home."

She tossed me an exasperated look. "I've heard a list of complaints about every man you've dated."

"I don't care. I have Rob and my girlfriends and work to think about. Now, if I could find someone like your husband, Dave—a cute, successful businessman—I'd marry him on the spot."

"No way. I see you with an intellectual, a scholar."

"I tried that head-in-the-clouds type once, and we know how that ended. Since the divorce I've learned to rely on the logical side of my brain." I sighed as I remembered how innocent I'd been, and how stupid. "Phil told me right from the start his parents were supporting him, that he hated work, and all he wanted to do was hang out with other artists." I tapped my temple. "He was completely honest, and I married him anyway." Not that I'd had much choice.

"I was hoping after we had a child, his adolescent behavior would change," I said. "Like magic, Phil would grow up and metamorphose into my Prince Charming. Is that pathetic or what?"

"Don't think Dave and I haven't been through the wringer a few times. He's not perfect either." Laurie cupped her chin in one hand and leaned on her elbow. "About ten years ago, things were so bad I almost called it quits. Remember?"

I eyed her one-carat solitaire wedding ring. "I'm glad you two came back to your senses."

"Yeah, I'd hate being single in today's world." She must have seen my features sagging, because she added, "Oh, sorry, Marguerite."

"That's okay." I noticed a couple strolling by, their arms looped around each other's waists. "I'd consider marriage again if the perfect man materialized. But being single has its advantages too."

Although I couldn't think of any at the moment.

∞

As I mounted the porch and stepped inside my small two-story Victorian, I listened to Laurie's Lexus roll away from the curb, then purr down the street. I carried my new book to the second floor and tossed it on the bed. My work attire, a boring navy blue pants suit and white cotton blouse, lay draped across the back of the chair. I dragged off my clothes, tossed them on top of the suit, and slipped into my nightgown. Then I fluffed my pillows against the headboard and slid between the sheets.

My hand found the book. At first I just stared at the jacket and contemplated the title: *Unearthing Your Childhood Dreams.* I wondered if I had the strength or desire to dig up anything. Not really, but I opened the book to the first chapter and started reading.

"As we grow to adulthood," the author wrote, "we become our own worst enemies, our most ruthless critics. Kind and encouraging to those around us, generous in our praise, we recognize ability only in other people's creations. When we hear our own unique voice or see our own pen on paper, it seems somehow meager and inadequate."

The first step toward achieving one's lost childhood dreams, the author claimed, was to recall them. A lengthy exercise with numerous questions made me sleepy. I got stuck when I couldn't remember my favorite food or teacher in elementary school. And my favorite toys? Surely I had some, but all I could recall were my art supplies. I'd always longed to be a famous artist.

I clapped the book shut and set it on the bed table next to a ten-year-old photo of Rob cradling our cairn terrier, Charlie, then a puppy the size and color of a russet potato. I remembered Rob begging for a dog, as if his world would snuff to an end without one. Charlie, a squirming bundle of energy, was my son's best friend for more than a year until my boy discovered lacrosse, a sport, he informed me, originally played by Native Americans. Then, when not in school, Rob often skipped out the door carrying his lacrosse stick in search of someone to throw him the ball, something I couldn't do worth a hoot.

I remembered how Rob—who'd once snuggled on my lap with his knees tucked under his chin—started shrugging off my embraces as if I were a stranger with bad breath. By age eleven, he couldn't fit in my lap anymore, his giant feet reaching the floor and ready to escape. Almost overnight he towered over me and had to lean down to receive an obligatory kiss on his cheek. Then the girls started calling.

I yawned, but my lungs refused to expand all the way. Maybe I should have bought a book on empty-nest syndrome,

I thought. Is that what I was going through? My father always said a midlife crisis was an excuse for not taking responsibility for one's obligations. Well, I was sick of acting responsibly.

I flicked off the lamp and sank into the mattress, its spongy softness comforting my stiff back. I tugged the covers up around my neck and drifted into slumber.

After what seemed like a few seconds, I awoke in a cave of darkness. I instructed myself to fall asleep again, but my brain thrummed with activity. In a few hours I would help Rob pack for college. I wondered if I'd collected enough cardboard boxes for all his clothes and his sound system. Would he have too much to fit in Phil's van? I dreaded Rob's leaving. I couldn't imagine life without him.

Hoping to doze off, I forced myself to lie in bed for another hour, but visions of my son kissing me good-bye swirled through my head like snowflakes scattered by an icy wind. Finally, I flipped over and read 5:30 on the clock's illuminated face. I staggered to my feet, put on my chenille robe, and padded downstairs. Charlie watched from his basket in the corner of the kitchen as I poured water into the coffeemaker.

"Too early for an old guy like you?"

Charlie moaned a lengthy response and stayed put.

I opened the canister and breathed in the nutty aroma of Italian Roast, then scooped grounds into the paper filter and switched on the coffeemaker. When the urn stood half full, I poured myself a cup of the syrupy liquid and headed to the living room. As I eased down onto the couch, my eyes turned to the window. I expected to behold nothing but dismal blackness, but instead saw a huge, glowing moon staring back at me. The porcelain sphere, so brilliant it seemed to produce its own light, was framed by a halo of mist.

Feeling dazzled, I almost dashed upstairs for my camera, but I knew the sky's splendor would appear insignificant on a three-by-five snapshot. I gazed at the moon like a child staring at a Christmas tree, trying to affix every detail in my mind. Then without thought, I took a piece of scratch paper lying on the coffee table, grabbed a pencil, and began sketching the moon. First with a heavy hand I drew a small circle, then a paler one around it to depict the ring of fog. Finally, blurred lines described the wisps of horizontal clouds partially covering the moon.

For several moments I looked down at my finished drawing. When I glanced back to the window, I saw a bank of clouds had taken over the sky, completely masking the moon. Only a piercing shaft of light shone down to the earth like a dagger.

I watched the morning sun tint the clouds smoky-pink, and the vague shapes of my garden transform into shrubs and bushes. A robin warbled up the scale, then another bird answered.

I felt a pleasant tightness in my throat. Many years earlier, I'd experienced those same sensations when I gazed upon my new baby boy wondering what to name him. Even before his birth, Robert Laurence Carr had been a part of me.

This drawing was my new infant. And it begged for a sibling.

2

Listening at Rob's bedroom door, I heard nothing. I had plenty of time to dash out for my weekly stroll with the Mom's Brigade—a group I named years ago when we four women were all pushing strollers shoulder-to-shoulder— before night-owl Rob got up. Laurie, Susan, and Erika would be greeting each other at the usual spot on the corner in less than twenty minutes, but I chose to stay home because I didn't want to miss one precious moment with my son. In twenty-four hours he would be moving out, leaving—gone.

Heading down the steps to the basement, I gathered the empty cardboard boxes I'd amassed all month, hauled them upstairs, and stacked them outside Rob's room. In his usual "Not now, I'm busy" fashion, he'd done nothing to prepare for his departure. The night before, I'd finally cornered him in the kitchen, not letting him escape for his date with Andrea Walker until he agreed to spend the morning packing.

An hour later, Rob rattled open his door and clumped into the bathroom.

"Good morning," I called, hurrying to the bottom of the stairs to ask him what he wanted for breakfast. But before I could open my mouth again, the doorbell jingled.

Charlie scrambled out of his basket; his nails clicked across the kitchen floor. Standing sentry in the front hall, he yapped, his stubby tail wagging frantically. I opened the door to find Rob's girlfriend, Andrea, holding a McDonald's bag.

"Hello." I tried not to stare at the swatch of bare skin peeking out between her hip-hugging jeans and her clingy knit top.

"Hi." She rarely said more than two words to me and, to be honest, she wasn't my favorite of the girls Rob had dated.

I noticed purplish circles rimming the girl's eyes, and her normally squared shoulders were stooped. "Are you okay?" I asked, wondering whether she was coming down with something or if she'd been crying.

"I didn't sleep very well," she said.

"That's too bad." I remembered hearing Rob come in late the previous evening. He and Andrea were probably lamenting their impending separation. I gave her arm a gentle rub as she entered. I did feel sorry for the girl, but it was for the best. In my opinion she and Rob were too young to be this serious.

Rob appeared at the top of the stairs. With his wavy hair mussed and unshaven whiskers darkening his chin, he looked like a college-aged Phil, only taller.

"Come on up," he said in a manly voice that still surprised me. "Hey, McDonald's. All right!"

I watched Andrea's beige ponytail sway as she jogged up the stairs. Trying to ignore a twinge of jealousy, I followed in her wake.

Rob's room looked as though a troop of monkeys had cavorted through it—sheets and bedcovers hanging halfway onto the floor and clothing flung everywhere. I stood in the doorway with my arms folded across my chest. It required a good dose of self-control not to start straightening as I watched Rob jam his CD collection into a box that threatened to explode under the pressure, then stuff a tangle of stereo wires into a plastic bag.

Andrea, her hands capping her knees, perched on the edge of his bed.

Rob glanced up at her and said, "We'll be fine."

Her lower lip quivered as she blinked back a tear.

"I'll e-mail you every day." He stood, gathered an armload of clothes, and shoved them into a duffel bag.

"Oh, honey, you're not going to throw your dirty laundry in with your clean, are you?" I asked, imagining the locker room smell that would erupt from his bag when he opened it. "I'll run down and do a load." I grabbed several T-shirts, a pile of questionable underwear, and a pair of jeans with a grease spot on the knee.

By the time I returned to his room, it had lost its personality. His prized posters, which used to spring to life under a black light, lay rolled and secured with rubber bands. Most of his belongings were boxed, the tops folded down. The room resembled a tenement with patches of missing paint on the faded walls and a stain on the carpet that I never could get out. Only his bed, its covers yanked up halfheartedly, his desk and chair, and his bureau, supporting his collection of dragon figurines and lacrosse trophies, still remained. It was eerie how quickly he'd taken away so much of himself.

During the next few hours, I wandered by Rob's open doorway several times to see him and Andrea sitting on the floor, leaning against the bed, and locked in conversation.

I finally planted myself at the kitchen table. I pushed aside the piles of work-related papers, to-do lists, and coupons that littered the table's oval surface, and kept busy sorting through a stack of bills. Hadn't I just paid my electricity, gas, and water bills? I wondered. It seemed the moment I sent them off, another round appeared.

As I ripped open my mortgage statement, I heard footsteps on the stairs. A moment later Rob and Andrea walked into the kitchen.

"We're going," Rob announced.

"Wait a minute." I jumped to my feet, barring their exit. "How about having dinner together?" I asked. "We could go out somewhere nice."

"Sorry, Mom." Rob stared at a speck on the floor. "We already have plans. Dad's new opening is tonight. He wants me to be there." His gaze rose to meet mine, and he flashed me a crooked smile. "You could come with us."

I couldn't contain a scowl. "I don't think that's a good idea."

"Come on, why not? Aren't you curious about what Dad's up to?" He swayed back and forth as he spoke. "I know you think his paintings are bad news, but he told me he's doing something different."

Like the sand candles at the University District Street Fair every year, Phil's paintings had yet to evolve out of the psychedelic sixties. *Different* probably meant he was remembering to sign them.

"I said they weren't my style, that's all." I was satisfied with my tactful reply. "I wanted to take you out somewhere special tonight." I decided not to add, "just the two of us," knowing it would be futile to try to shake Andrea. "Tell you what, I'll go with you if you'll come out to dinner with me first."

That evening, the kids decided on Italian food. I took them to the newly opened restaurant Il Gattopardo with its checkered tablecloths, votive candles, and recordings of The Three Tenors crooning in the background. I tried to keep the conversation going while my son wolfed down lasagna and Andrea picked at her chicken parmesan.

Even when seated across the table, Andrea towered over me. The girl's fair complexion, the horizontal cut of her bangs, and her long eyelashes that fluttered when she spoke to Rob all reminded me of what I'd coveted in my rivals in high school. As I speared a square of ravioli, I thought about the popular crowd, the cutest girls in the senior class, and the cheerleaders who dated the football players. Apparently my son liked this type more than the short, dark-haired ones who were funny and smart. In other words, the girls like me.

"Want any of this?" Andrea asked Rob as she nudged her plate in his direction. They traded plates, and Rob polished off her chicken.

I lingered over the dessert menu. "We could order one spumoni ice cream and one tiramisu and share them," I suggested.

"I'm too full to eat another bite," Rob said. "Besides, we need to get going." He tossed his napkin on the table. "I don't want Dad thinking we're not going to show."

"Like he didn't show up for us?" I wanted to say, but instead I pursed my lips. I knew putting Phil down would only hurt Rob.

"I'm tempted to ask you kids to take me home on the way to the gallery," I finally said.

"Mom, you promised."

I rifled through my purse and found my wallet. "I wonder who'll be there." I placed my credit card on the table, even though I'd promised myself to pay off the balance before I charged any more.

"You mean Dad's new girlfriend?" Rob said.

Using my best poker face, I shrugged. "I couldn't care less about your father's social life." The man always had some woman prowling around, but Rob had hinted that this one was something special. I hated that I cared who she was, or what she looked like. I finally convinced myself my interest was mere idle curiosity.

"Okay," I said. "I'll go, but only to spend time with you."

Rob pulled open the door of the bustling Vanguard Art Gallery to let me cross the threshold first. I was surprised to see so many people—men in suits, women in evening attire—all conversing merrily as they drifted around the packed room. For one silly moment I wondered if this crowd had gathered to see Phil's paintings. No way. A renowned artist must be displaying his work here too.

With Rob and Andrea following, I inched my way along the wall.

A man wearing a tuxedo shirt and black slacks glided up to me and offered a tray of champagne. I waved him on. When I turned to speak to Rob, he and Andrea had disappeared into the crowd.

I crept further, expecting to see one of Phil's unsightly works. But the first painting I came upon was unlike anything I'd ever seen. The artist had depicted a gnarled tree, its limbs dominating the canvas. As I looked closer, I realized the branches were merely frames for bold pieces of sky, the vacant shapes themselves becoming solid forms. Fascinating.

I examined the next painting. A Rubenesque girl reclined upon a bed of grass as she gazed up to a heaven of magical clouds that seemed to float in an endless universe. I stepped back to view the painting better, but couldn't see over the heads crowding in front of me.

"Hey, Mom." Rob grabbed my arm. "We found Dad's exhibit. Come on. You won't believe it."

I followed the kids to the next room, and saw Phil, dressed in a neatly ironed shirt and khaki slacks—not his usual attire—standing among a group of sculpted figures.

"Look at these," Rob said with pride and excitement. "Wait until you see them up close. You'll love them."

He was right. The grouping of life-sized bronze statues— three men, two women, and an infant spanning several generations—were quite remarkable. I strolled around the sculptures to view the unusual faces with their whimsical expressions. It was difficult to stop looking. They reminded me of mime actors, ready to burst into action at any moment.

"The old gentleman has so much personality," I said, making note of his walrus moustache and bushy eyebrows. "And I love the mother and child." As far as I knew, Phil hadn't sculpted since we were in school together. I glanced his way to make sure he wasn't pulling my leg.

"You made these?" I had to ask. I knew the grueling labor required for such a project.

"Yes." He stood tall, his hands jammed in his pockets. "Honest."

I reached out to touch the statue of the woman cradling an infant in her arms. My fingers brushed the metal's burnished surface, and I felt a wave of goose bumps on my arms.

"They're wonderful," I said. *Marvelous* would have been a better adjective.

"Thanks. Coming from you, that means a lot." As the room's volume expanded, he stepped closer. "For a long time I couldn't afford to cast anything. But, with my new job at Microsoft, things are looking good."

"Way to go, Phil," said an attractive blonde in a miniskirt as she strutted by.

"Thanks, Val," he replied, then turned back to me. I hadn't seen him look so alive in years. Maybe ever.

"I had no idea," I said. "How long have you been doing these?"

"I started with smaller pieces a few years ago. Pretty scary at first. I mean, I wasn't sure if they were any good."

"They're good, all right," I assured him. "I didn't know you had it in you."

He chuckled, shifting his weight to one leg. "The truth is, I was getting nowhere with my painting—something I don't need to tell you. I needed a drastic change. When you get to be our age, you want your life to matter. You know, to create art that outlives you—for the next generation."

I took in his words. For years I'd considered Rob my only legacy.

"Hey, the city just commissioned me to do a piece for a park on Lake Washington," he said. "I'm actually selling."

"That's great," was my automatic response, but the words sounded artificial.

"Did you see Hank's work?" He pointed across the room.

I eyed the paintings I'd admired earlier. "Those were done by Henry Marsh?"

"Yeah, I told you he was gifted."

Three more people gathered around Phil's work—all raving about his talent.

"Come on, I'll show you my other piece," Phil said. He guided me toward another room.

"I hear you have a new girlfriend," I said, trying to sound blasé.

"Darla? She'll be here later." He scanned the room briefly. "By the way, it was fun seeing you drawing up a storm the other night. I never know where I'm going to run into you."

I tried to ignore his comment but felt my cheeks warming.

The man carrying champagne stopped to offer us a glass. Phil's hand swung out, as if to ward him off. "None for me, thanks." Then he said to me, "Did I tell you I haven't taken a drink for over two years? Boy, it feels good to say that."

"Really?" Staring into his elated face, I wondered if he was being straight with me. Phil dry for two whole years?

Unlikely, but I supposed anything was possible. "I'm glad to hear that."

"Not half as glad as I am."

We approached Phil's other work: two lovers caught in the tension before an embrace.

"Wow" was all I could say. The almost life-sized bronze woman wore long, corded hair and a peasant dress. It had to be a coincidence, but the woman looked somewhat like me when I was in college. My hair had been longer, and I'd drawn it back to one side in the same fashion. And I'd owned a dress similar to that one.

I examined the athletic young man, who had been executed with spontaneity yet precise attention to detail.

"Isn't Dad's stuff awesome?" Rob reappeared, holding hands with Andrea.

"Yes, honey, it is."

Rob tugged impatiently on my arm. "Hey, Mom, Andrea and I want to go."

"Okay, just a minute."

As he and Andrea said good-bye to Phil, I took time to inspect the paintings on the back wall, none of which could compare to Henry's. I turned to see Rob and Andrea wandering toward the exit, and Phil speaking to several members of what my father would describe as upper crust, who were questioning him about his project for the city and a dedication ceremony at the park. Being happy for Phil's success felt surreal. I tried to picture him sober, working at a great job, and becoming a successful artist. Why couldn't he have done all that when we were married?

I gave him a wave.

"I'll see you in the morning," he said.

The thought of Rob's leaving the next day sent a shudder through my upper body. Maybe I should have agreed to drive with Phil and Rob after all, I reflected. I might change my mind and do that.

As I wove my way through the crowd, I spotted Henry Marsh talking to an intense little man who was scribbling on a pad of paper. Henry's eyes widened as he noticed me.

I slowed to a halt and said, "Hello."

His mouth lifted on one side. "Good evening." Then his lips flattened into two parallel lines, and he looked right past me, as if I were a fly too small to be noticed. He spoke to the man, who jotted something down, then asked Henry a question about canvas preparation.

I didn't appreciate being ignored. My hands moved to my hips, and I stood for a moment glaring at Henry. He didn't look back, but rather rotated, forcing the other man to move in order to continue their conversation.

What a snob, I thought as I marched toward the door. I couldn't remember anyone acting so rudely. Was Henry ignoring me, or had I become invisible? I'd looked in the mirror before leaving for dinner and thought I looked quite respectable, even pretty.

But as I plunged ahead, I found it impossible to ignore the man's paintings, his startling use of colors and design.

On the drive home, with my son behind the steering wheel and me sitting in the backseat behind Andrea, Rob's voice rang with pride as he described Phil's creations. I was grateful he had a father he could admire, but somehow I felt Phil's victory detracted from me. I knew I was being petty and attempted to sound enthusiastic.

"Your father's an amazing guy." Which was true. He'd amazed me many times.

"What did you think of Henry Marsh's stuff?" Rob said.

"They were exceptionally good." Even if I'd painted every day since college, I wouldn't have been able to create anything half as wonderful. What Henry possessed went beyond technique, study, and practice. The paintings exuded an energy that practically pulled me across the room.

"Did you see how much they cost?" he asked. "Dad says his paintings sell as quickly as he finishes them."

I hadn't noticed the prices, but had seen the red dots on several title cards signifying the pieces were sold. I caught Rob's eyes in the rearview mirror. "What do you know about him?" I asked.

"He and Dad have been friends for years." His voice turned serious. "His wife died of cancer a few years ago."

"How very sad." For a moment I felt sorry for Henry. Still, that didn't give him the right to treat me like a nobody.

As I lay in bed the next morning, I speculated when Phil would arrive. No need for me to hurry, I thought. It could be hours. Phil loved lounging in until noon, but maybe not anymore, with his new job at Microsoft, of all places. How was it possible for a man to improve so radically? Or was it all a masquerade? What Dad would call a put-up job? I pushed back the covers and swung my legs over the side of the bed. Imagining Phil in a twelve-step AA meeting was a stretch. Yet, Laurie was right when she said something was different about him.

I tossed my nightgown over the chair, then pulled on some sweats. I splashed water on my face and applied taupe shadow to my lids to accentuate my brown eyes. I could find no reason not to ride with Rob and Phil to California, really. Phil's passenger van had plenty of space. It would mean an overnight stay along the way, but Phil and I could easily get separate rooms. Of course, we would. Only my pride, my harbored anger at him—which was futile after all these years—had been stopping me.

I brewed a pot of coffee and brought out the half-dozen cinnamon rolls I'd purchased especially for the occasion.

The toilet upstairs flushed, meaning Rob was awake. Then I heard Phil's familiar rapping on the door. Charlie romped to the front hall; the dog's body wiggled with anticipation. It always irked me how Charlie adored Phil, as if he were the alpha male of our pack. The man had charisma: a way with animals and women.

I hauled open the door, and the dog charged out, leaping against Phil's legs. Hair tousled and eyes sleepy, Phil looked like he'd just crawled out of bed.

"Hi, Margo," he said in a froggy voice.

"Good morning. I wasn't expecting you so soon."

"I figured we should get an early start." He bent down to give Charlie's wooly head a scratch, then stood tall again. "Is our college student ready?"

"He'll be down in a couple of minutes." I felt the cool autumn breeze brush against my cheeks. I filled my lungs, smelling the aroma of dew-covered grass laced with drying leaves.

"Come on in," I said, touching his arm for the first time since our divorce. "You look like you could use a strong cup of coffee." I imagined us sitting together in the kitchen. The bond of parenthood that still united me to Phil would comfort both of us this day.

"That's okay." He tipped his head toward the street. "Darla brought along some Kona Coffee, straight from the Big Island. You should try it." I glanced past him to see a woman who looked barely twenty-five opening the back of his van.

"Darla?"

His gaze followed mine. "I thought I told you she was coming," he said without hesitation. Then he bounded up the stairs, leaving me to meet his attractive companion. At first, all I could see were tight jeans and big bosoms swelling under a tank top.

Darla waved hello with her fingertips. I wanted to shut the door and never open it again, but felt obligated to step into some shoes and go down to the sidewalk. Darla greeted me with a show of straight white teeth.

"Hello," I said, extending my right arm. "I'm Rob's mother."

She clasped her hands together as if I carried leprosy. "I adore Rob," she said.

I withdrew my hand. "Thank you."

She scrutinized my face as though she were examining a lab specimen. "He looks like his father, doesn't he?"

"Yes, he does."

Phil, with Charlie tailing him, appeared with the first box. "Darla's a genius at packing," he said. "I'll let her figure out how to fit everything in." He gave her a leisurely wink, then loped back into the house.

"Would you like a muffin?" she asked. She leaned into the van and lifted a pan out of a picnic basket. "I baked them for Philip this morning." Clad in her sleeveless top, with sculpted biceps curving down to slim forearms and dainty hands adorned with silver rings, she looked like she worked out in a gym seven days a week. She even cooked. I tried to remember if I'd ever baked muffins for Phil. Probably not, but I didn't think those things mattered to him.

The tantalizing aroma of warm blueberries and bran tugged at my stomach, but I said, "No thanks, I've already eaten."

Charlie began sniffing at Darla's pant leg. "Go away, bad dog," she said, her lip curling. "I'm a cat person." She spun around to set the muffins back in the basket.

"Go inside," I told Charlie. He pawed the ground, then stalked away.

"I'm glad we got a chance to meet," Darla said, her voice downright surly. As she edged closer, like a jackal sizing up its victim, I inhaled a cloud of harsh perfume that burned my nasal passages.

"Philip filled me in about you," she said.

My breath caught in my throat. "What do you mean?"

"Why he married you in the first place. What you threatened to do if he didn't." Her eyes narrowed, chiseling a line across the bridge of her pert nose. "Don't worry, I'll keep it to myself. As long as you stay out of my way."

Speechless, I stared back. This can't be happening! was all I could think.

A look of satisfaction suddenly brightened her face as Phil and Rob each lugged out a carton.

"Sugar, you're the greatest," Phil said. He shoved in a box and his leg bumped up against Darla's. She turned to him, her lips forming a flirtatious pout.

I felt anger brewing in my gut. Phil used to call me sugar, I fumed. Not that I should care anymore—but the words stung.

Within half an hour, only a few items still sat at the curb waiting to be wedged in. I watched Darla instruct the men to put a box here or a bag there, as if she were their queen and they her adoring subjects. With each reach into the van, out stuck her trim little derrière, stuffed into her Calvin Klein jeans. I'd always cut the designer labels off my pants. I disliked labels on clothes. Didn't Phil? He used to.

My face aching from the tension, I tried to appear gracious—no small task, I assure you. I heard the back of the van close with a metallic clunk.

"I'm ready," Rob said. He strode around the side of the van and opened the rear passenger door.

"So soon?" I asked. "But you haven't had any breakfast."

"Don't worry, Mom. I had a muffin, and Darla knows places to eat along the way."

Our farewells sped by like a wave splashing against a rock. My face buried in Rob's sweaty T-shirt, I embraced my towering son. He gave me a quick hug in return. Then he dove into the back seat, as if he were just dashing off to a Mariners baseball game, and left me staring into Darla's open window.

"It was nice to meet you," I lied.

"Same here," she said, saccharinely.

Phil started the engine and cranked the transmission into first gear. "Bye, Margo," he said, while checking for other vehicles.

As the van rolled away, I heard a burst of laughter. I waved, but no one waved back. In a moment the van rounded the corner. I stood there, almost expecting them to return after circling the block. Everything had happened too quickly. I thought of significant things I should have said to Rob before he left. Words of wisdom. Life-changing advice. My son was gone, and I hadn't really said good-bye.

I plodded up the front steps and trudged inside. The house felt like a morgue, cold and lifeless. I kicked the rumpled rug back into place so the door would close, picked up several fragments of leaves that had been tracked in on dirty shoes, then followed the trail of debris up the stairs. Rob's empty bedroom drew me in like a vacuum.

As a teenager, I remembered, Rob had become more and more private. His door was usually clamped shut while he slept, listened to music, or talked with friends on the phone. It was odd to enter without knocking first, as if I were trespassing into forbidden territory.

I felt a tear form in one eye, then trickle down my cheek. The small stream expanded to a river, then gushed into an ocean. Bending forward, I wept without control, the convulsive sobs hurling through my torso, shaking me like a rag doll in the hands of an angry child.

"God, help me," I cried out.

The room hung heavy with silence. I shook my head. When had God ever stepped in to help me? Everything I'd learned in church was a lie. It was embarrassing to think how gullible I'd been in my youth, and frightening how alone I was now.

Standing in front of Rob's mirror, I saw a twisted mask with squinting red eyes. Blinking, I staggered into the bathroom, yanked out an arm's length of toilet paper to blot my face, then glanced into the mirror above the sink. A stranger, someone I didn't even want to know, stared back. I tried to change my expression to one of dignity, but saw only ugliness and despair.

41

The banister supported me as I descended the stairs to the kitchen. Charlie waited by the back door and watched with wary eyes from across the room.

"It's all right, little man." Not true. Nothing about my life was all right. I dragged open the door and let the dog out into the fenced yard.

The uneaten cinnamon rolls still sat on the counter. I slid them into a plastic bag, careful not to damage the frosting. A sudden torrent of nausea surged through my stomach. In one swift movement, I shoved the rolls into the garbage can under the sink. I pushed down with all my weight, crushing the soft dough. The icing squished against the plastic bag under my palm.

My knees buckling, I sank to the floor. New tears welled up from a lifetime of unresolved sorrows. I leaned against the cupboard door and allowed the floodwaters to flow.

When I was a miserable teenager, my mother had assured me I could trust in God. "All things work together for good for those who love the Lord," Mom had said many times.

But this sadness was a long, dark tunnel with no light at the end.

4

I spied Laurie and Erika milling on the corner one block from my house. I waved, then used a hand to cover my yawning mouth. Had I gotten any sleep? Several times during the night my dreams were shattered by strange clomping sounds. Once, I'd thought I heard Rob rummaging through the refrigerator for a snack, and I'd yanked myself into consciousness. Rob was at school, I remembered in a fog of confusion. Had someone broken into the house? No, Charlie would be barking—unless he was going deaf. No, he'd heard a dog trot by the house this morning and raised a horrific racket. The noise was probably the neighbors wheeling out their garbage cans for tomorrow's pickup. I was safe—as safe as I would ever be.

Charlie pranced ahead, yanking on his leash, and I lengthened my last few strides. My gaze swept ahead to the lake, which glittered through the trees like thousands of little suns. The September morning was splendid, but it brought me no joy.

Laurie looked snazzy in a periwinkle blue jogging suit I'd never seen before. "Have you heard from Rob?" she asked once we'd greeted each other.

"We've spoken a few times. He said his room's tiny, and his roommate listens to rap music all night." Our conversation the day before had lasted less than three minutes. Rob had hung up with a quick "Gotta run, I'm late." When the line went dead, I'd stood with the receiver in hand, feeling glum. In an effort to elevate my spirits, I'd reminded myself how independent I was at his age. My parents had seemed like old codgers. Now I realized how wise they were. And how foolish I had been.

Erika, her straw brown hair hanging limply, stood with her hands on her hips. "Did Phil show up to drive him?" she asked with a slice of sarcasm.

"Yeah, and he brought his new honey with him." My voice cracked, unexpectedly. "Meeting her was quite an experience."

Erika's eyes narrowed, generating a web of crow's-feet on her otherwise smooth face. "I already hate her," she said playfully.

I tried to laugh, but it sputtered out a dry hack. "If I never see that woman again, it'll be too soon." The thought of Darla's farewell smile still made me cringe. It came to mind that she and I were both north poles, our forces repelling each other. With any luck I would never see her again, which would probably suit her, too.

"I can't believe he brought his girlfriend to your house," Laurie said. "Men can be so dense."

"Not all men," Erika said.

"Yeah, I know," Laurie said. "Your Jonathan's a prince."

"Yes, he is."

Susan, who lived a half mile away, swerved her minivan up to the corner. A moment later she hopped out—a giant stretch for her short legs. "Sorry I'm late," she said, slogging over to us. "The phone rang just as I was running out the door." Panting, she dropped her keys in the pocket of her baggy jeans. "How was everyone's week?"

"Great," Laurie said. "Marguerite and I started our drawing class." She aimed her grin at me. "I can hardly wait until next Monday, can you? Have you been doing your drawing assignment, twenty minutes a day?"

"I haven't had time. I've been swamped at work. If you're a realtor, you have to jump whenever a client calls." The truth was, I hadn't been busy, nor had I given the assignment a second thought. "How about you?"

"Yes, I've done three drawings."

"Good for you," Susan said.

Charlie tugged in the direction of the lake. I loosened my hold on his leash and allowed him to lead me. Erika and Laurie fell in on either side of me, and Susan walked next to Erika.

"Our teacher is outstanding," Laurie said. "Marguerite, you should go out with him."

The corners of my mouth drew back. Remembering my encounter with Henry at the gallery, I felt like using the words *arrogant* and *stuck-up*, but I wanted to forget about the incident. "I don't like his type," I said.

"What type is that?" Erika asked.

"He's extremely good-looking." Laurie said.

"I wouldn't go that far," I said, although I could see how some women might find him attractive. "And who could get past his personality?"

Laurie paid no attention. "Henry's got dreamy eyes that make you forget what you were thinking about. His hair's graying a little, but even that looks good." She bumped against my arm. "You should definitely go out with him."

Laurie had a habit of talking me into things, but this was one hook I wouldn't bite. "Let's change the subject," I said, whining in a way that would have made my father grumble. He never did spank me as a child, but I would have done anything to avoid his frown. I guess it took a crisis for me to get over that.

We reached the paved walkway around Green Lake, then merged into the pedestrian lane. I'd walked the almost three miles around this lake so many times, I felt like a train coasting along on a track. Ahead of us two women pushed strollers. From the other direction, a youth on rollerblades, who probably should have been in school, skirted past us. I noticed the breeze kicking up the water's inky surface, then felt it stroke my face and lift my hair off my forehead.

"I love September," Susan said. Her swinging arms bobbed against her wide hips. "It feels good to have the kids back in school."

Laurie and Erika jumped into the conversation. The three of them still had kids at home; their words mingled together in my ears like a distant radio with fuzzy reception.

Overhead, geese honked. I glanced up to see a V-shaped formation of black wings pounding against the sky as a dozen Canadian geese migrated south in search of warmer weather. I thought about Rob as a little boy. How happy I would be if he were still in grade school.

"Just think, in a few years, all our kids will be out of the house," Laurie said.

I slowed my pace to watch mustard-colored leaves flutter across our path. "After eighteen years, maybe we've outgrown being a Mom's Brigade," I said. "Do we need a new name?"

"No way." Laurie wrapped an arm around my shoulder, and I leaned into her. "We'll keep walking this lake, even when we're using canes."

"Oh, no," I gasped as I recognized Bill Sullivan sprinting our way.

"Hi, Marguerite," Bill yelled out. He shortened his steps. "How goes it?" He started jogging in place, sweat streaming down his ruddy face.

I'd met him through a coworker at the office, and we'd dated for almost three months. We had little in common, really, other than we both sold real estate and liked Mexican food. Once, over dinner, I decided he was the most boring man I'd ever met. But I still went out with him again. I was that lonely.

I didn't feel like revisiting the past. "Just keep walking," I instructed under my breath with a horrified snicker that started the women laughing.

"You're looking good," he said, giving me the once-over. "Call me if you want to go out again."

"I remember that guy," Laurie said. She turned her head to appraise him from the back. "He's kind of cute."

"Cute ain't everything," I said.

"Well, if I were single—"

I lifted an eyebrow.

"It's not against the law to look, is it?"

Twenty minutes later, we stood on the corner saying good-bye. We hugged each other, then split off into our different worlds.

"Go home and draw," Laurie called to me.

I gave her a dismissive wave but carried her words with me.

Charlie lagged at my side as I entered the yard and closed the gate. I unsnapped his leash, and he moseyed over to his water dish by the back step. Lately, I'd noticed the dog's hair was thinning in spots, and his eyes were clouding milky gray, probably dimming his vision. I knew he was getting old. But the thought of losing him was more than I could contemplate at the moment. I unlocked the glass-paned kitchen door. Ignoring the dirty breakfast dishes congregating on the counter, I sauntered down to the basement, a large cement-sided storage room with a washer and dryer in one corner.

In a bookcase crammed with Rob's favorite childhood books and board games, I found his old sketchbooks. The first one was filled with his drawings from third grade. Hoping to catch the scent of his young fingers at work, I flipped from page to page to examine each picture, and inhaled the musty smell. The next pad, yellowing around the edges, was blank inside. Which made sense. Once Rob discovered sports he'd lost interest in art.

As I carried it upstairs I could hear Charlie scratching at the kitchen door. I let the dog in, and he began snuffling the floor under the table hunting for dropped morsels of food.

I checked the clock on the microwave. Henry Marsh had instructed us to draw anything we liked for twenty minutes. But what did I like? It had been ages since I'd observed the world through an artist's eyes. I contemplated skipping the homework. Twenty minutes was a valuable chunk of time I could use to call a client or check new listings. Henry would never know the difference—especially if I didn't return to class. Most likely he wouldn't even notice my absence.

When Charlie found nothing under the table, he cocked his head in my direction, no doubt hoping I'd forgotten I'd already fed him two hours earlier.

"Okay, little mister, you're going be my model," I said. While I sharpened a pencil, he minced over to his bed, a wicker basket with an orange pad. He gyrated in a circle, then flopped down like a stuffed animal and closed his eyes.

As I sketched my snoozing pooch, the time zipped by. I put the pencil aside and groaned. The finished drawing looked like nothing more than a chaotic mass of fur.

"That's awful." In college I could draw so well. But over the years, the inkwell had gone dry.

Charlie opened one eye and glared at me with annoyance. I swear, I could almost read his mind. And that went both ways.

"You really are just a fuzzy mass, you silly old thing." I realized I should have chosen a subject with more lineal definition. I gazed out the window at my neighbor's maple tree, its leaves flashing rust and burgundy, and imagined what it would be like to execute the finest drawing Henry had ever seen. This vision lightened my mood for a moment, but when I glanced down at my real drawing again, I was flung back to reality.

5

I double-checked the address as I pulled my Toyota up in front of a dingy cottage perched on a steep hill in the Phinney Ridge neighborhood. I peered out the window to see a flesh-colored house with paint peeling back to reveal layers of turquoise blue and murky brown. Its unkempt lawn looked like it had been mowed several weeks ago, but no one had raked up the matted grass clippings. A laurel bush grew in unruly globs, and a hawthorn tree had been pruned back to stumps.

"Not much to look at," I told Susan, who'd asked to see the property. I tried to remember what I'd read on file and the scuttlebutt around the office. "The same couple lived here for forty years. It was remodeled in the fifties and hasn't had a thing done to it since. When the husband died, the wife moved into assisted living."

While turning the front wheels against the curb and firmly setting the parking brake, I thought of my aging parents. My folks had talked about moving to a smaller place some day. That is, if they stayed married long enough.

As I scaled the uneven porch steps, I warned Susan, "Be careful, and I wouldn't use that hand railing." I removed the key from the lock box and worked open the door.

She passed through the front hall without seeming to notice the curling wallpaper or the warped flooring. "I love it. She proceeded to the kitchen at the far side of the house. "Look at that view of the Olympics."

Following her, I caught sight of pale mountaintops jutting above Puget Sound out the window. "You already have a nice view where you live now," I said.

"Not this good." Susan opened empty cupboards, then looked under the sink and found a baited mousetrap.

"That's a bad sign." I sniffed the stale air and detected rancid cooking oil and mold. "This kitchen's awful."

"But it has potential." A fan of the Cooking Channel, she'd renovated her present kitchen into a chef's paradise, while my idea of updating was purchasing new dish towels and pot holders, and decanting the liquid dish soap into a glass bottle.

"I wish I had your energy," I said.

We climbed to the second floor, and she counted the two bedrooms. "The upstairs is much too small," she said, her voice sinking.

"Not to mention only one bathroom." Earlier, when waiting in front of Susan's colonial, with its fluted pillars standing on either side of the front door and shutters framing each window, I'd wondered why anyone would want to leave such a charming home. Four years ago I'd sold the house, then a fixer-upper, to Susan and her husband, Bob. And, several years earlier, the couple had purchased another rundown place from me, extensively remodeled it, and then decided they needed something bigger.

"You don't need to say it. I should be content where I am," she said. "I have everything a woman could want: a terrific husband and three kids and a beautiful home. Is it wrong for me to want more?"

She was living the life I'd always dreamed of—the kind my parents enjoyed when I was a child. "Are you talking about a change of locations or a change of lifestyles?" I asked.

"I'm not sure. I seem to get restless every fall when school starts. I think I'm going to utilize the free time, but all I get done is the grocery shopping and laundry. Then the kids come home, and I'm busy fixing snacks and helping with homework."

"What else would you want to be doing? You're welcome to take the drawing class with Laurie and me. In fact, you could have my spot and keep Laurie company."

"It sounds like fun, but I'm exhausted by seven o'clock. After I've fixed dinner and cleaned up the kitchen, I'm ready for bed."

"You're a wonderful mom," I said with sincerity.

"Thank you. I'm glad someone thinks that matters."

"It does. It's the most important job there is."

Her dark eyes grew somber. "When I go out to dinner with Bob's associates or clients, they ask me what I do. When

I tell them I'm a stay-at-home mom, they can't wait to change the subject."

I wondered if I'd ever written off housewives the same way. I wouldn't do it again, that was for sure. "If it weren't for women like you, working moms wouldn't have chaperones for school parties or drivers for field trips. When Rob was young, I rarely had time to help. I wish I could have been like you."

"But there has to be more to life than taking care of kids and vacuuming the house." Susan leaned against the wall. "I feel guilty saying it, but I'm sick of being home every day at three, waiting for the bus to show up. With Rob away, you can waltz out the door whenever you want. You're completely free."

"Yeah, I've told myself it's going to be great," I responded blithely. I swallowed the lump that had been lurking at the bottom of my throat ever since Rob's departure. Again this morning, thinking I'd heard him, I almost called out his name, only to feel the immediate stab of disappointment.

"No one tying up the phone or playing loud music," I said. "And I could use Rob's room for an office, so I won't pile papers on the kitchen table anymore."

"I'd love an extra room in the house. When Brandon decided to go to junior college for two years, I told him he should stay at home and save up his money. Now, I sort of wish he was living in a dorm."

"Hang on to him as long as you can. I miss Rob so much, I feel like I'm going through withdrawal. Like I'm shriveling up." Putting it into words only made me feel worse, which she must have read on my face.

"You'll probably get over it in a few weeks," she said.

"Maybe." Holding in tears, I fixed my eyes out the bed-room window and stared at the brick house next door.

She took my hand. "When I'm down, I try to keep busy. Just about any diversion can do the trick." Her voice turned merry. "I like eating best, but your drawing class sounds less fattening." She chuckled when I cracked a smile.

A clattering racket suddenly erupted on the roof above us. She cowered, her hands balling under her chin. "Birds?"

"I hope so." I dove into my purse to find my keys. "Let's get out of here before the roof collapses."

I dropped Susan off, then jetted off to my next appointment on time. I arrived at the Henricks' home with two minutes to spare. I had already shown Sherry and Wayne seven houses and had tried every tactic to get them to choose one, without success.

They were such nice people, I thought as I rang the doorbell, sending the first eight notes from Beethoven's Fifth Symphony through the fifties bungalow. But were they just another name on my list of lost causes?

I could remember plenty of similar incidents. Clients who looked and looked. Pleasant people, who insisted they liked me, said I was the greatest agent they'd ever met, then evaporated like a drop of rain on hot pavement. Sometimes, I'd find out later they'd wandered into an open house and bought from another agent without even contacting me. Didn't they know I could have sold that house to them? Didn't they know I worked on commission and had bills to pay just like everyone else? Maybe I needed to be more assertive. That's what Dad would have told me.

I knocked several times, then stabbed the bell again.

Finally Sherry, clad in a pink terrycloth bathrobe, came to the door.

"Oh, it's you," she said. Her button nose and small intent eyes reminded me of the Beanie Baby piglet I'd given my four-year-old niece on her birthday.

"Am I early?" I asked, knowing I wasn't.

"No, I'm running late, just got home from tennis. Come on in and make yourself comfy." Leaving me standing in the family room, Sherry ambled off to the back bedroom.

A stack of fashion magazines lay on the coffee table. I grabbed the top one and sat on the overstuffed leather couch. Across the room, an expansive TV set, its volume just audible, caught my attention. As I opened the magazine, I glanced over at the screen and noticed an attractive black woman interviewing several teenage girls, about fifteen years old, all holding babies that looked to be their own.

Seeing them filled me with a self-righteous indignation I had no right to own. Hadn't young women learned anything in the past twenty years? Were they just as easily fooled as ever?

Then I remembered how at age twenty my own resolve to remain a virgin floated out the window the night Phil invited me to his one-room apartment. "I'm flunking out of psychology," he'd said. "Could you come help me study for an exam?" But when I arrived, I didn't see a single book.

The TV show was too painful to watch. I found the remote and clicked off the set. I congratulated myself for having a son. There was so much less to worry about with boys.

Fifteen minutes later Sherry meandered into the family room and started transferring items from her mock crocodile purse into a navy blue one that matched her shoes.

"Wayne and I drove all over Ballard after lunch yesterday," she said, squinting into her compact mirror to apply lipstick. "We saw lots of cute houses down there."

I shaped my face into a cheery facade. "You poor thing, you must be exhausted by now." I knew I needed to put the brakes on. I didn't intend to show this couple every house on the market.

"Aren't you feeling overwhelmed with options already?" I said. I'd heard top saleswoman Lois Grimbaldi from the office talk to clients this way, and they always came around with a little persuasion. "I can give you several reasons why we shouldn't even bother checking out Ballard." I stiffened my voice, sounding more like an attorney than a realtor. "It's miles away from the freeway, which would make Wayne's commute longer."

Sherry's round hand grasped the doorknob. "We already figured that out. Wayne could hop on Highway 99. It would be a straight shot into town."

"What about your kids?" I stalled, my mind floundering for a new approach. "You and Wayne said you wanted to live within walking distance of a good elementary school. And I thought you loved Wallingford Center. It's so much fun to browse around in."

"There must be good schools in Ballard, too. I love the quaint main street." She tugged open the door. "Let's at least swing by."

After a hurried drive, I coasted up to a sprawling two-story residence. The unappealing structure, with its added second floor, a garage that had been converted into a bedroom, and a makeshift carport, towered over its neighbors. The architect, if there was one, should be ashamed of himself. Most likely the owner came up with the design himself.

"That's it." Sherry craned her short neck to gawk out the side window. "What do you think?"

"Now, Sherry." I killed the motor without removing the key. "Right off the bat, you need to understand that the size of this house enriches the values of the smaller ones around it, but receives no monetary advantage from them."

"I don't care. Let's go in. Looking is such fun."

Of course, I would do whatever she wanted. The situation reminded me of my father's old Pontiac. Once he'd invested in a new engine, he felt obligated to spend whatever it took to keep the automobile running.

After I dropped off Sherry, I headed to the office. Now that my sales had slackened, all the workdays seemed to blend into one another. I thought about the past year. Even when I'd jumped through every hoop set before me, most of my promising deals had trickled away. Several buyers were unable to obtain adequate financing. Others frightened themselves with their own self-doubts. Then calling me with what sounded like a fabricated excuse, they'd demanded their earnest money back.

I could recall beating myself up over every lost sale. But that only made the losses hurt more, as if dollars had been stolen directly from my own billfold. After each defeat I contemplated switching to a dull, predictable nine-to-five job. But the next day I returned to the same old thing. What other skills did I have? None, really. I should have learned to type back in high school when my mother suggested it. But I was determined never to work in an office.

I cruised around a corner and into the office parking lot, which sat adjacent to the one-story brick building. By the time I got to the receptionist's desk to check for messages, I felt myself slipping into the doldrums. My little desk, surrounded by three movable burlap-type fabric walls, was no place to liven my spirits. On the other side of the building, I thought, before a glorious picture window, which looked out onto a tree-lined street, Lois Grimbaldi was putting together million-dollar house deals at her mahogany desk.

6

I strolled into the Monday morning sales meeting bringing with me the kind of jubilance only a sale can produce. I waved across the room at Lois, the woman who'd made my achievement possible. As I found a seat, I remembered how she'd persuaded me to hold an open house at her listing the previous Sunday, while she and her husband flew to Palm Springs for a weekend of golf. At first I'd resented spending the day in that dreary little home no one seemed to like. That is, until Bev and Bill Avery showed up. The sale had seemed too easy. Bill was being transferred to the area in two months. The Averys' only question was "When can we move in?"

It had been a mediocre month in the real-estate market, and after the meeting several colleagues congratulated me for selling the property. I thanked them. Maybe things were starting to turn around for me after all.

That evening, I ate a quick meal, then stretched out on my living room couch. I sank deep into the worn velour cushions; my heavy lids blackened the room.

I was startled back to consciousness by Charlie's barking, followed by the shrill ring of my doorbell. I stood up too quickly, and watched the room do a spin, then staggered to my feet and yanked open the front door to find Laurie standing on the porch, rubbing her arms to keep warm.

"You ready yet?" she asked.

"I totally forgot about the class." I checked my watch and realized I'd slept over an hour. "Maybe I'd better skip tonight." All I was good for was watching TV, then diving into bed.

"No problem, I'm early." Laurie sashayed into the living room, her hips swinging. "I had to leave before Dave and the kids needed something." She plunked down on the wingback chair, which stood perpendicular to the couch. "I'm not cooking on Monday nights anymore. No way. That's my artist's evening."

I took note of my sadly wrinkled work clothes. "I can't leave the house like this."

"If you're not going, I won't either." She crossed her legs at the knee, then selected a fitness magazine and started reading the table of contents.

I knew that escaping Laurie's grasp was like attempting to fly out of a spider's web, so I caved in without a struggle. "Fine, give me ten minutes to get ready." I changed into chestnut

61

brown corduroy slacks and a matching sweater. There was no reason not to look nice, I thought. Soon I was being chauffeured through the darkening streets toward campus.

Once in the art building, we found our seats while the other students straggled in. Henry arrived with a cardboard box in his arms.

"Good evening." He opened the box, removed half a dozen wooden blocks, and arranged them on the table. "Everyone did beautifully last week. You seem like a group that can take on any challenge."

He spoke about ways to incorporate sketches with other projects. "In Emily's case, perhaps her weaving." All faces turned to the woman sitting on my left. He paused, his gaze moving to me for a moment. "Some of you may have studied art in high school or college."

Had Phil talked to Henry about me? My chair grew harder, and I squirmed to find a comfortable position.

"You don't need to take classes to be an artist," he continued. "Rousseau and other Primitives painted without formal instruction. But for most people, it helps to learn the basics." He repositioned a block. "Tonight we'll explore perspective."

Several students groaned.

Chuckling, he stood back to assess his arrangement. "For thousands of years, artists drew without using perspective and got along quite well. Creating an illusion of depth wasn't necessary to making fine art."

I watched Henry's animated features as he spoke. I half-listened, wondering how it felt to harbor such an intense yearning for anything. The man was obviously passionate about teaching and about art. Long ago, I'd felt a similar craving for my painting. I remembered myself as a young woman standing before an easel. My hand boldly directed my brush, and images emerged from the untamed color.

A pencil dropped to the floor. My shoulders jerked, and I realized Henry had stopped speaking.

"What do you think of our still life?" my neighbor asked. The woman leaned closer, bringing with her a delicate aroma of lilac. Her face, framed with snowy wisps of hair, was at least as old as my mother's.

"I'm Emily McBride," she said.

"Nice to meet you. I'm Marguerite Carr." I searched my purse for a pencil, then opened my pad.

"Are you enjoying the class?" Emily asked. She wore an olive green, loosely knit sweater and a silky floral skirt. A tiny gold cross hung from her neck on a chain. "I came away from last week's lesson with so much good information. I've already seen my work improve."

"Professor Marsh said you're a weaver." As I spoke we both began drawing.

"For most of my adult life, but recently I've been writing children's poetry, and now I want to illustrate it." She softened her *r*'s like someone who grew up somewhere on the East Coast. "Maybe it's a foolish notion, but I thought I'd give it a try." Her lips formed a crescent. "I don't have much drawing background. How about you?" She glanced at the beginnings of my sketch.

"I studied art in college." I decided not to mention the endless hours I'd spent in the painting studio, or that I'd carried paper and pencil practically everywhere I went.

I outlined the blocks in quick, easy lines. My hand seemed to remember the fundamentals of perspective like recalling the words to a childhood rhyme. I executed the correct angles to make my flat drawing pop out into the third dimension.

"Cool," Laurie said. "How did you do that?"

"It's really nothing." Actually, I'd surprised myself with my accuracy. "Once you learn how, I guess you don't forget."

Henry suddenly stood behind me, staring over my shoulder. When would he say something? Did he think I had learned perspective from his lecture, or could he tell I'd studied drawing before?

He moved behind Emily. "You might work with this angle here," he pointed out. "Otherwise that looks quite respectable."

"You mean I'm not too old to learn new tricks?" Her laughter fluttered like a rippling brook; her slender fingers intertwined.

"In my eyes you're a young woman." The rich timbre of his voice vibrated against my back as I shortened a line, then lengthened it. Again he passed behind me without a word. I felt my pulse quicken and heat radiating up my throat. Why was I submitting myself to this torment?

After the break Henry asked us to get out our smaller sketchbooks. I'd forgotten mine. It contained only my one miserable attempt at drawing Charlie anyway. If anything, I was relieved no one would see it.

"How did you all do?" he asked. "Not an easy assignment, was it?" Several students shook their heads.

"Making yourself draw each day can be a daunting task. You'll remember that I asked for quick, information-gathering sketches, the way a person might take a few notes if a speaker said something useful. A short phrase so the note taker could later recall the whole presentation."

Addressing a plump woman with an anxious expression, he added, "Don't worry, Toni. I'm not going to look at your work." Relief swept across her face. Then he asked us to take the rest of class time to draw a new piece. "Use one of your sketches to inspire you."

Again, the rustling of paper and quiet chatter filled the room.

"What's up?" Laurie asked when she noticed me sitting motionless.

"I forgot my pad. Not that it would have done me much good. I don't feel like drawing my dog again."

"Who cares? You're a good artist. Make something up. He said he wasn't going to look at our original sketches. Besides, what's he going to do, flunk you?" She opened her pad, then tried to decide between a sketch of a carnation and another of an apple.

How can a grown woman feel so insecure? I wondered about myself. I'd always encouraged Rob to jump in without caring what others thought. I stared at the rectangular page hoping for a brainstorm. I'd never been able to draw things off the top of my head. I'd always needed a subject sitting right in front of me. My mind grasping for ideas, an image formed itself like a pearl in the back of my mind. I began to sketch the oak tree near my house. Up sprang the giant, knotted trunk. Out stretched its arms, heavily laden with foliage. The massive tree became a home for robins and sparrows. It waved its hands at the cumulous clouds swimming by, and the earth beneath it took shape. Deer and rabbits came to wander and graze around it.

I put in more detail, more life. Only the drawing existed.

"Hey, that's great." Phil's voice sounded like a machine gun beating into the back of my skull. I twisted around to see that he and Henry had both been watching me draw. It was as if they'd seen me dancing around the house to Kool and the Gang's "Celebrate Good Times" the night I sold a duplex following a bidding war that skyrocketed the sales price up ten thousand dollars. In other words, I felt exposed.

"I like what you're doing, Margo," Phil said. He was wearing a polo shirt and clean jeans, not plaster-room attire. Had he come here to bug me?

"Don't you have somewhere else you need to be?" I said, and, thankfully, he drifted toward the door.

Laurie leaned over to get a clear view of my drawing. "That's awesome," she said.

"It's that big tree on the corner," I told her. "You know, the one we meet under for our walks. I guess I got carried away with the rest."

Emily looked over and said, "How lovely."

Henry addressed the class. "Our time is up for the night. If your drawing's not done, finish it at home." He strode to the front of the room and began tossing the blocks back into the carton. "Your perspective studies were quite good. We'll go over it again next week, but I promise not to bring these back."

He paused for a moment to glance at me. "Drawing, like everything else in life, needs review and repetition. And compassion." I felt as though he were addressing me, alone, but then his stare moved to Laurie. "Show the child within you compassion."

Again, our homework was to draw twenty minutes every day. "About ten years ago, when I gave up watching most television," Henry said, closing the box top, "I had much more time on my hands. Window-shopping, cross-word puzzles, talking on the phone, can fritter the day away. I'm not suggesting that you forgo dining with friends or watching the Mariners on TV, but make sure to invest twenty minutes a day in yourself."

When he'd finished speaking, Laurie turned to me and chortled. "I'm not giving up my favorite soap," she said. "I know—I'll stop house cleaning. That's a bunch of wasted time. I'm sick of picking up after Dave and the kids." Delighted with her own humor, she added, "Hey, want to stop for a little snack on the way home?"

Laurie and I found Starbucks humming with activity that evening. The aroma of coffee beans and warm milk permeated the air. Frank Sinatra's swooping words, "I did it my way," mingled with the whooshing of the espresso maker.

Laurie and I stood in a slow-moving line to purchase lattes and scones. Then we scanned the crowded room and found one empty table in the back against the wall. Laurie forged ahead, tugged two chairs together, and motioned me over. I scooted in next to her, so we both faced out. I thought about my evening, recalling the exhilaration I'd experienced as I sketched the oak tree. In spite of Henry's lack of praise and Phil's unnerving intrusion, I felt hopeful, as though my life might change for the better.

"What's Emily like?" Laurie asked between sips. She licked frothy milk off her upper lip. "I haven't had a chance to talk to her."

"She's wonderful—the kind of woman I want to be when I'm her age." I thought of Emily's sophisticated style, yet her childlike excitement each time she drew. "She probably has a husband to support her, so she can dabble with whatever she likes." As I said the words, I realized I had also described Laurie's situation.

"I'm not putting that down, mind you," I added, wishing I'd chosen my words with more care. "I'd love to have that kind of setup." I gnawed off a chunk of currant scone, and savored its sweet taste.

"It doesn't always work that way. I have all the time in the world, but no talent. Anyway, being a housewife may come to an abrupt end one of these days. I haven't decided yet."

I washed my mouthful of scone down with a gulp of latte. "What are you talking about?"

"I've had it with Dave."

I remembered her making similar proclamations before, and it never came to anything. I knew she liked to vent her frustrations every now and then. Who didn't? As she grumbled about his lack of communication, I noticed a young couple studying at the next table. Rob, a late-nighter since the age of ten, was taking an 8:00 a.m. math class. I wondered if he was sleeping through his alarm every morning, the way he often did at home. And without me there to keep after him, was he bothering with his homework?

"This time I mean it." She spoke with precision, her volume building. "He loves work more than life itself. Certainly more than me and the kids."

My fingers wrapped around my warm cup. "That's not true. He's crazy about you."

"Be glad you're single. If I had to do it all over again, I'd never have gotten married."

"Come on. Sure you would." Her spats with Dave never lasted more than a day or two, and then I'd be hearing about their joyous reunion.

"Well, I wouldn't have hitched up with Mr. Work-Eighty-Hours-a-Week. You've done perfectly fine being single, Marguerite, and I'm sure I could too."

"What did he do this time?" The din around us was growing, and I found myself catching phrases from other conversations.

"One more vacation cancelled at the last minute." She shook her head in a quick rhythm. "This was the weekend we were going take the Clipper to Victoria and stay at the Empress Hotel. My parents were all set to look after the kids. Today the jerk told me he's too busy. He claims he has to fly to Baltimore to see a client and can't get out of it. It's probably some bimbo's bed he can't get out of."

In all the years I'd known Dave, I'd never seen him ogle a woman other than Laurie, let alone come on to them. "I agree that Dave works too much. But he isn't the kind of man to have an affair. He loves you."

"That's not good enough. I need someone who's really there, listening to me, not waiting for some phone call or fax. He's always late—sorry, can't make it, tied up, maybe next time—always something more important than me."

I didn't know what to say. For eighteen years I'd jealously watched Laurie's lifestyle and tried to be happy for my friend's good fortune.

Her voice dropped an octave. "There's something else I want to tell you. Now, try not to judge me. I haven't said a word to anyone, and I feel like I'm going to explode. Susan and Erika are way too serious. They'd give me some hysterical lecture."

Her face took on new life, as if she were about to unveil the solution to an ancient riddle. "I met this man at the driving range a couple of weeks ago. He's there every Wednesday when I go for my lesson. I've never met anyone like him before, and I can tell he likes me."

I almost choked on my mouthful of scone, but managed to swallow it down. Every soap opera I'd ever watched spewed through my brain like water through a hose nozzle. I envisioned Laurie's ship crashing into the rocks, sucking her family down with her. And why? Because some stranger made her feel attractive?

I needed to say something wise. Spouting ultimatums wouldn't work. Which of my many mistakes should I use to illustrate how women mess up their own lives?

Her eyes lit up and she waved across the room. "There's Henry Marsh with Phil."

Please understand, before my first drawing class, Phil's and my paths never crossed each other unless we were attending one of Rob's school functions.

Holding full coffee mugs, the two men were searching for an empty table.

"Laurie," I said, "let them sit somewhere else. This is serious, we need to talk."

Ignoring me, she beckoned them over.

"Mind if we join you?" Phil said above the clatter. He pulled up a chair and parked himself across from Laurie. "Hope we're not intruding, but there's nowhere else to sit."

Wishing he and Henry would disappear, I shrugged.

"Sure, no problem," Laurie said, her voice melodic. "There's plenty of room." Henry found a chair and positioned it opposite me.

"I adore your class, Professor Marsh—I mean, Henry," she said the moment he was seated. "I'd love to see your work sometime." She looked as happy as ever.

"Oh, he's quite a painter," Phil said, his gaze landing on me. "You were at the opening the other night, Margo. What did you think?"

"His paintings were beautiful." I looked at Henry straight on. I felt like adding a comment about his bad manners, but supposed it would only make me appear foolish. I would act magnanimous. If I could put up with Darla, I could tolerate anyone.

"Thank you," Henry said, then spoke to Phil. "Your statues were excellent as well." As he and Phil discussed the value of placing sculptures in public spaces, I scanned Henry's face. His eyes were nutmeg brown, speckled like the chest of a wren. Laurie was right about his good looks. There was something intriguing about the man. But who needed intrigue?

During a pause in the dialogue, Laurie asked Henry, "Did you always want to be an artist?"

"Yes and no," he said. "For as long as I can remember, I loved to paint. But my father, a cardiologist with dreams of my following in his footsteps, offered to pay my tuition if I studied biology, which I did the first two years in college. I received good grades and all, but found the subject boring. You can imagine my father's dismay when I announced I was switching my major to art in my junior year, even if it meant getting a job and supporting myself. He was sure I'd become another hippie dropout."

"You must admit," Phil said. "Not all of us have been as successful as you."

"Your time will come, my friend. Especially now that you have a day job to pay the bills."

"Life's getting good," Phil said. "I even got caught up on my child-support payments." He winked at me, as if he and I shared some amusing joke. "This woman's been more than patient."

"I'm not sure how patient I've been," I said, recalling the threatening letters I'd sent him.

"At least you didn't have me arrested. There were a few years when I would have deserved it."

I slurped the last drops of my latte. This was a crazy conversation. At one time I'd hated Phil so much I wouldn't have cared if he'd rotted in jail. Tonight we were chitchatting like old friends.

Phil checked his watch. "I'd better run, have to be at work early." He and Henry got to their feet. "It's been a pleasure, ladies," Phil said, bowing slightly.

"Good night, see you next week," Henry said, speaking mostly to Laurie.

"Bye-bye, this was fun," she said. As the two men worked their way toward the exit, she gathered her purse. "Let's go."

"Wait," I said. "We need to talk."

She stood and shoved her chair against the table. "Not now, I'm out of time."

Outside, ominous clouds bristled just above the lamp-posts. We made it to Laurie's car moments before the rain started lashing down. As we rolled through the darkened streets, I tried to rekindle our previous conversation.

"Flirting with a man, any man, other than your husband can only lead to trouble," I said.

She cut me off. "Give me a break. If I'd wanted a lecture, I would have called my mother."

She'd always described her mother as a manic-depressive busybody, but I was sure the woman and I would agree on this subject.

"Bingo," I said to myself as I eyed the Craftsman bunga-low from my car. This two-story dwelling—its wide front porch supported by stately columns of river rock and wood—would be ideal for Wayne and Sherry Henrick.

It was Broker's Open, the morning realtors previewed new listings each week, and I'd been driving from house to house—along with the rest of Seattle's hungry real-estate agents—pretending I had hot buyers ready to scoop up each one.

Trotting in on the heels of three other agents, I climbed the L-shaped staircase. I could smell the scent of cedar and mothballs, and I wondered if older people lived here.

I mentally ran through the Henricks' list of requirements. Sherry longed for a larger master bedroom and private bath. She found sharing a sink and toilet with their five- and seven-year-old children a nuisance. This place had a glorious master bedroom with a spacious bathroom, plus a small deck off the suite as a bonus. The two other bedrooms featured built-in bookcases and window seats.

I said hello to the listing agent as I surveyed the updated kitchen. Not perfection, I thought, but livable. I descended a flight of carpeted stairs to the daylight basement with its extra room that could be used as an office or sewing room. Standing in a quiet corner, I fished out my cell phone and called Sherry.

"I'm busy," she said, her voice sounding rigid. "I'm on my way to an important meeting."

Dad might have been proud of me because I refused to take no for an answer and was waiting out front when she finally arrived, dressed in tennis whites and looking aggravated.

"This is a fabulous house. I know you'll like it." I ignored her cool, almost hostile, demeanor. "I don't know why we didn't check out this neighborhood before."

Her mouth angled down as she glanced at her watch. "I have to leave in five minutes."

Doubt began worming its way into my mind, but I admonished myself to stand firm. "This whole area is being fixed up," I said. "See how cute the other houses and yards are?"

Her head rotated a few inches, and she sized up what she would view as she came out the front door.

I asked myself what else a top saleswoman would say. "Picture this house with a coat of new paint," I said. "Maybe taupe or cream." Sherry was now following me up the driveway, catching my every word.

I slowed my pace to admire the home's shingled facade. "Don't you love this old-fashioned front porch? You could put a planter on either side of the entryway and maybe paint the door a contrasting color."

Over the years of vanishing buyers and fizzled deals, I'd lost so much of my confidence that closing a sale made my heart race like I was running a marathon. When I was a girl, I remembered, a neighbor's German shepherd would sometimes charge out, snapping at my heels with menacing growls. While the other kids ran away, I would stomp my feet and yell at the dog to go home, and the animal would eventually slink back to its yard. I still wasn't afraid of mean dogs, nor of spiders, nor snakes. Why people?

You can do this, I told myself. What had my boss said? People are looking for the experience they think they will have living in a house.

I led Sherry to the living room. The owners' antique furniture—a Victorian sofa and two high-back armchairs sitting before the fireplace on an Oriental carpet—warmed the room.

"Imagine Wayne, you, and the kids hanging your Christmas stockings on that mantel, then waiting for Santa to come down the chimney."

She stood with her hands on her hips, her head tilted.

"Nice high ceilings too. The Christmas tree could go in that corner." Her eyes moved to the place I had indicated. "You want to be in your new home before Christmas, don't you?"

I moved closer, speaking into her ear. "This place has it all, and the prices in this neighborhood haven't quite caught up with the rest of the city. I must caution you though—" I paused and looked around to see who else was listening, then lowered my voice. "Other realtors have their eyes open for these jewels for their own buyers. This one won't be on the market for long. If you're interested, we've got to move quickly."

"May I use your phone?" Sherry held out her hand, and I passed her my cell phone. She punched in a number and scanned the room again as she waited for an answer. "Wayne, honey, I think I've found the house we want. Can you get right over here?" Her lips parted for a few seconds. Then, "Yes, I'm sure. Let Marguerite tell you how to get here."

Within the hour I was writing up an almost full-priced offer for the home.

"This should go through without a hitch," I said, sounding one hundred times calmer than I really was. "We're lucky to be the first ones. I'll call when the offer's been accepted."

"Most of us have allowed ourselves to become cemented into a job, a routine, a mode of life that is both unsatisfactory and boring," the author of *Unearthing Your Childhood Dreams* stated.

I was reading as I lounged on the couch with a tartan blanket draped over my lap and my morning cup of coffee nearby.

"Often, we blame our willingness to remain in limbo on our bosses, our spouses, our kids, or on not having the money or time to make a transformation." The author thought people stayed stuck in a monotonous, unfulfilling lifestyle because they were too busy being grownups.

"Oh, really?" If I hadn't been the adult around here, who would have? Laurie could flirt with whatever frivolous pastime she wanted, but I'd always been burdened with too many obligations.

A cool draft wafted across the room. I wrapped the blanket around the backs of my legs, but then felt trussed like a mummy. Was reading about a creative life a waste of time? I wondered as I kicked my legs free. What had all those years of studying art done for me? I earned a diploma, but I couldn't make a living from it. What was I supposed to do with a degree in painting: make billboards, become a manicurist, open a tattoo parlor? After graduation I'd had to jump into the work force and swim for my life.

Reading on for a page and a half, I resisted every suggestion. Why worry about taking the wrong path in life if there was no turning back? By my age it was just too late.

I closed the book and put on the morning news. The weatherman declared it would be blustery and wet all day, a fact I could see for myself. Then a fitness expert complained about what bad shape Americans were in. Looking down at my growing thighs, I thought about mounting my stationary bike, which stood in the corner of my bedroom, but decided to go to the kitchen for a snack instead.

My large sketchpad lay on the table. Examining my drawing of the oak tree, I stood back to view it from afar. Was it any good? Maybe, but it looked as though someone else had done it. My landscapes and still lifes had always been predictable and staid, while this composition bustled with motion and humor.

Opening my smaller notebook, I flipped to a blank page. I sat down at the table and scanned the room for a suitable subject. My gaze traveled out the window, and I saw bulbous clouds floating by like sailboats in a regatta. I picked up my pencil and began to draw. Soon my cloud shapes grew dense, grand, and alive. Consumed in creation, I was unaware thirty minutes had slid by. Finally, I paused to inspect my work, and my chest swelled with exhilaration.

I could remember taking a watercolor class in summer school at age nineteen. That July my classmates and I wandered around the almost deserted campus painting gothic buildings, trees in profuse attire, distant mountains, students sleeping on the grass. Our small group played with our paints like children. My only ambition was to satisfy myself with my art. Everything I did seemed to turn out right, even painting trees red and the sky orange, or zeroing in on a young woman reading and transposing her into a princess wearing a bejeweled crown.

In the fall, however, when I showed my bulging portfolio to my favorite teacher, Professor Jenkins, he wasn't pleased with my carefree approach. Instead, he steered me toward his own conservative style. Adoring my mentor, I tried to imitate him. By the time I graduated from college, though capable in my craft, I'd lost the spirit of that magical summer.

I escorted the Henricks to my desk at the office and offered them chairs. As I sat down across from them, my mind scrambled for the opening lines I'd rehearsed to myself moments before.

"I have good news for you," I said, sounding too cheerful. "The home inspector said the house is in good shape." I dreaded going on. Sometimes a repair could tip a whole sale into never-never land. "The only serious concern is the roof."

"How much will that cost us?" Sherry said, her words coming out like pellets from a shotgun.

"It probably won't need to be replaced for a couple of years. But we can get someone out there to give you an estimate, if you want."

Wayne, his suit a size too small for his chunky frame, nodded his balding head. "Absolutely. We're not made of money."

Sherry swiveled in her chair to face him. "Maybe this isn't the right house, after all. Maybe we need to keep looking."

I drew in a full tank of oxygen. "By the way," I said, as offhandedly as I could, "someone made a higher offer on the home just hours after yours was accepted."

Sherry seemed to grow an inch. "Does that mean they get the house?"

"No, it's still yours, as long as we don't start making new demands. The offer behind yours is full price."

"Really? They're willing to pay more, even with the roof?" Wayne asked.

"Well, they can't have our home," Sherry said.

A few minutes later, I walked the Henricks to the door. As they exited, Lois sailed in like she was stepping onto a runway at a fashion show. She looked flawless, as if a stylist had just given her black hair a final poof. Her understated but obviously expensive clothes matched right down to the mauve Feragamo shoes.

"Come back to my office," she said to me as if I were her secretary. As I followed, I listened to her three-inch heels clack-clack on the wooden floor. It was hard to tell Lois's age from looking at her. Maybe late fifties. But she wasn't the type anyone would dare ask.

Once in her private office, she sank into her desk chair and motioned me to sit across from her.

"I met with a new client who says she's an acquaintance of yours," she said. "Darla Bennett."

My scalp tightened so much my eyebrows must have raised an inch or two. "I've met her, once." I intended to keep my private life just that.

Lois tossed me a look of impatience. "In any case, perhaps you could keep an eye open for a condo for her. I've been so inundated with new clients this week I can't keep up." She paused. When I didn't respond, she said, "Darla wants a view, a hot tub, and enough room for her boyfriend. She's planning to get married in the near future."

"Married?"

"Yes. Apparently to someone you know."

Strange as it may seem, I felt like a car had just knocked me off my feet. "Did she give you his name?" It had to be Phil.

"No, I didn't think to ask."

Her phone rang. She swung the receiver to her ear, turned away from me to speak, and didn't look back.

At my desk, I tried to remove the image of Phil and Darla standing at the altar from my mind. But a moment later, I found myself picturing her in a white satin and organza gown looking as resplendent as a Miss America Pageant winner. I supposed it made sense that Phil would remarry after all this time. Divorced men often did so within a year. Not that I cared one way or another. I wouldn't allow myself to.

I glanced at Rob's photo, sitting on the shelf next to my file cabinet. It had been taken years ago, but remained my favorite. I picked it up, feeling the cool silver frame in my hands. Clad in his lacrosse jersey, twelve-year-old Rob was innocently radiant. His smiling face still beamed with soft preadolescence, before his voice dropped an octave, before stubble darkened his chin, before he'd dated a girl, let alone fallen head over heels for Andrea. That little boy didn't exist anymore, I thought. My son was a young man now, waking up in a bed far away, eating what he wanted, managing his own time.

I wished he would come home for the weekend, but he wasn't planning to return until Thanksgiving vacation. Last Thanksgiving, I remembered, he'd accompanied me to my parents', meaning this was Phil's year to have him. I hated that I had to share my son, but inviting Phil to family gatherings wasn't an option. Even if my father didn't nix the idea, as he had in the past, the dinner would be miserable for everyone, especially me.

Noticing a thumbprint, I polished the photo's glass surface with my sleeve. Over the years Phil had passed up many opportunities to spend time with Rob. Several times he'd asked to take our boy somewhere, then failed to show up. As long as I lived, I would never forget the afternoon Rob, age five, sat waiting on the front steps for his father to pick him up for an overnight visit. At six o'clock I'd begged my son to come in for dinner, but he'd sat listening as each car passed—none stopping. It still made my insides quake with fury when I considered how much Phil hurt our little boy. I'd wondered if he'd carry that sense of abandonment with him his whole lifetime.

But over the past few years, I'd noticed Phil changing little by little. He started taking Rob to baseball games, an occasional movie, or just out to eat. He even stopped by the house on Christmas mornings to drop off presents—last year with an unexpected box of chocolate truffles for me, which I thoroughly enjoyed.

I placed the photo back on the shelf. Thanksgiving was still a long way off. As I calculated how many months away that was, a pool of sadness gathered at the bottom of my throat, spilling into my chest. I leaned back in my chair and closed my eyes.

Was there any way for a single woman to feel anything but lonely? For a moment I considered calling Phil, just to have someone to talk to about Rob. But he'd be at work, or if he were home Darla might be there. Was he really going to marry her? That thought evoked a tidal wave of confused thoughts that scooped up all my neatly stacked emotions and tossed them into disarray.

Darla's biting words began whirling through my mind. Until that moment I hadn't allowed myself to contemplate the obvious: She'd threatened to expose me. Had Phil really told her the whole ugly story?

I felt like I'd ingested a vial of acid. My eyes popped open, and my hand rose to cover my mouth. No, I reassured myself, Phil promised never to divulge my secret to anyone.

A leaf floated by my face, skimmed the bill of my baseball cap, then zigzagged to the moist grass where its yellowing predecessors lay. The first to arrive for the weekly promenade, I watched puffs of moisture parachute from my mouth into the chill morning air. Charlie tugged on his leash to inspect his favorite fire hydrant.

I heard voices and noticed two women pushing infants in strollers on the other side of the street. Rob had been that age when the Mom's Brigade formed. It had been promoted as a playgroup, which would meet at the Community Center every Thursday morning. Within six months one of the original gang moved away, two went back to work full time, and one lost interest. We four remaining moms became sisters, the threads of our hearts knitting together through our common concerns, and we started meeting in each other's homes. While we busily fed, burped, and diapered our babies, our conversation often centered on weight loss and lack of exercise. Would we ever be able to zip up and fasten our old jeans? Would we be stuck with distended stomachs and colossal thighs forever?

Erika came up with the idea of walking around Green Lake—but only when the weather was good, she'd promised. My calves had complained the first few journeys around the lake's circumference. I couldn't believe people exhausted themselves for enjoyment. I would rather have camped out in someone's family room and nibbled homemade brownies. But I forced myself to continue. I didn't want to miss seeing the other moms, and I figured our get-togethers were saving my peace of mind. My endurance grew, and I was ecstatic when the unwanted inches began shrinking. When the kids finally entered school, we continued to meet, rain or shine.

My memories were interrupted when Erika rounded the corner and twirled once to show off her new haircut, which was highlighted and shorter at her neck and poofed out around the crown.

"You look great," I said.

Her fingers explored the blunt ends. "Are you sure?"

"Absolutely, you look five years younger." As I watched her flip several pale strands behind her ears, I recalled my dreary reflection in the mirror that morning. "Maybe it's time I cut my hair," I said. "I could use a drastic something. All of a sudden I feel old."

"Come on, you still look gorgeous."

Susan strode the last few feet to the corner. "Who's gorgeous?" she asked, out of breath.

"Marguerite is, but she thinks she needs a new hairdo. Or was that a face-lift?" Erika loved to kid around.

"Very funny. Be serious." I dragged off my cap to expose a mass of mousy hair in need of washing. "I admit I'm shallow, but please tell me the truth. Do I look as much like a schoolmarm as I think I do?"

"No, you look as good as you did on the day we met," Susan said.

What a kind thing to say—I didn't buy it. "Then how come I haven't been out on a date for months?" I'd settled into a rut of renting videos on Friday nights, eating dinner in front of the TV, then turning in early.

"I told you, Bob has that friend at work," Susan reminded me. "We could double date, or I'll give him your number. His name's Tim O'Brien. You'll really like him. Such a nice guy, dependable and hardworking."

Susan hadn't mentioned the man's appearance, meaning he was probably so-so, at best. I envisioned her sweet but homely husband, Bob. Was his friend a cookie-cutter version of him? As I ground my toe into the cement I reminded myself that being dependable and hardworking was more important than good looks and charm. And didn't I like nice guys? Still, I'd sworn never to subject myself to another night of torture on a blind date.

"Susan, I don't know—" I was saved from further discussion by Laurie's appearance. She wore body-hugging running tights and a red sweatshirt with the words "I'd rather be at the mall" written across the front.

"Hi, everyone," she said. "Let's get rolling."

I gave Charlie a yank to keep him from running across the tops of Laurie's white sneakers. Since last night she and Dave must have made up, I thought. She looked on top of the world. I'd called her the night before saying, "We didn't get a chance to finish our conversation."

Her voice had become muffled. "I can't talk now, I'm busy."

"Just promise me you won't do anything hasty. I've made mistakes in my life, and I still live with that guilt."

"You married the wrong guy," she'd said in a hissing whisper. "And you had the sense to move on. What's to feel guilty about?"

I'd felt like gushing out the real story, but I controlled my tongue. "Believe me, you can never erase your mistakes."

Susan and Erika started toward the lake, and Laurie and I fell in behind. The air felt cold, dry, and delicious. Smoke from a chimney drifted in the blue sky, and I could detect the aroma of burning cedar. Crisp leaves dotted the sidewalk. Dahlias still bloomed, but the hydrangeas had shriveled. Up ahead I saw Green Lake cloaked in white fog, as if someone had tossed a cotton blanket over the water's surface.

Susan spoke over her shoulder to me. "I'm not going to let you escape that easily," she said. "What movie do you want to see? Or maybe a nice dinner would be better, so you two could talk more."

"Blind dates never work out." I could list a half-dozen horror stories to prove my point, the worst being the evening I spent with a man I later described as The Groper.

"Not true. I know several happy couples who met on blind dates," Laurie said with authority. "I introduced Lorelle and Nathan. Gave Nathan her number, and he did the rest."

"It's the best way to meet men these days," Erika agreed. "I was lucky to meet Jonathan at the hospital. Most women don't work around eligible men all day."

"What have you got to lose?" Susan asked.

"I'll think about it. But don't give him my number yet." I wondered if my friends really had a clue what kind of a mate I needed. I loved them, but they didn't understand what I was going through. They all had happy, complete lives, with husbands who were their best friends.

As the day brightened, the pathway around the lake began to brim with activity. Three children coasted by on pint-sized bikes, followed lazily by one of their fathers. He was maybe five years younger than I, and robustly handsome. His gaze flashed right past me, without pausing even for an instant. I didn't usually inspect each man on the path, but that day I did. Few bothered to look back. Maybe Henry wasn't the only one to find me invisible.

"You're not getting out of this," Susan told me as we hugged good-bye. "I'm going to bug you until you cave in."

"Let me get back to you." That line always seemed to work for my clients.

∽

When I got home, I dove into the refrigerator to find it bare, except for a clump of shriveled lettuce, a carton of iffy milk, and a Styrofoam container of leftover teriyaki chicken.

With Rob gone, I hadn't felt like cooking. But I knew if I kept eating take-out food every day, I would inflate into a blimp. I'd already put on several pounds since he left.

Not bothering to change clothes, I drove to the grocery store. As I steered my cart down the bread aisle, I spied an older woman with a familiar face.

"Hello, Emily," I said. "Do you remember me from art class?"

"Of course I do, dear. Nice to see you."

"Good morning, Mrs. McBride," an employee said as he walked by with a box of celery in his arms. Emily greeted Sam in return, then asked if he'd recovered from the flu.

"I'm feeling better, thanks," he said.

I flung a loaf of French bread into my shopping cart, then followed Emily as she moved to the produce section, where she paused to examine the tomatoes. My style was to grab whatever vegetables caught my eye, without paying much attention to their color or firmness. I usually shopped for food on an empty stomach, and just wanted to get the chore done so I could go home and eat.

"These are vine ripened, so I splurge a little," Emily said, bringing the plump tomato to her nose and inhaling. "I try to buy things in season." She glanced into my almost empty cart. So far, I'd accumulated milk, yogurt, several frozen dinners, and bread.

"My son Rob's away at college," I said, sequestering a head of romaine lettuce and stuffing it into a plastic bag. "It doesn't seem worth the bother to cook a whole meal just for me."

"Less cooking must give you more time to draw. Have you been keeping up with your sketching?"

I bagged a handful of carrots, bending the crinkly leaves back so they would fit in. "Only twice. It's hard for me to get much done at home. I'm always so busy."

"That's understandable," she said with sympathy. "The world is such a hectic place." She slowed her cart and gazed up at me. "A lot of women put their personal goals on the back burner until their children are out of the house."

"You're right. Now that my only child Rob's in college, I can't use him as an excuse anymore."

A woman with a toddler in her cart strolled by. In a cooing voice, she spoke to the little boy, then offered him an animal cracker. I stood for a moment watching him gnaw on the cracker and then give his mother a toothy grin.

Averting my eyes, I started testing avocados for softness. I felt as though I were suspended in limbo, as if the tide were about to change, but in the meantime I was going nowhere.

"I need to start filling my days more constructively," I said, then placed an avocado into my cart, even though I'd been told they were fattening.

"You will. Give yourself time." Emily's sigh glided down through an octave. "Isn't it funny? First our children crawl away from us, then walk away, then drive away—then off they rush into the world." One hand patted her heart. "I remember how hard it was to let go, particularly of my last one. I must have cried for a month." She gave her cart a short push. "I bumped around the empty house like a zombie. The worst year of my life." Her smile returned, but her eyes were moist. "I finally joined a weaving group. At first I used it to fill my empty days. Then the pleasure of weaving became the end."

"I may have missed my chance." I spoke softly, my words catching in my throat. "As I mentioned, I studied art in college." I swiped at my nose with the back of my hand. "But as soon as I graduated, my painting screeched to a halt. You should see the pathetic drawing I did of my dog the other day."

"Don't be too hard on yourself." She touched my arm in a gentle way that showed she cared. "Like being a mother, art is a nurturing process. Not all my new creations are pretty, but I don't look at them as failures, but rather stepping stones to my next project."

"It's embarrassing," I said, unsure why I'd chosen her to be my confidant. "I can barely bring myself to draw in class."

"I'm sure you'll get over that with time." We reached the checkout counter. "Hello, Janice," Emily said to the cashier.

I got in line behind Emily and watched the checker double-bag her selections, then load the bags into the cart.

Emily turned to me. "So nice to run into you," she said. "Sorry if I slowed you down, dear. I don't walk as fast as I used to."

"I didn't mind, I enjoyed our conversation." Very much.

"And by the way," she said. "My youngest child's thirty-two now, and has his own kids. If you think your son was a joy, wait until you have grandchildren."

When I got home, I gobbled several cookies as I stowed the groceries. I folded the paper bags and stuffed them in the drawer. I needed to get ready for work, but noticed my smaller drawing pad, which I opened to my cloud sketch. Not bad, I thought, but I noted an area needing more definition. I erased a few lines and reworked them, only to find the drawing looked worse. I erased again, removing the top layer of paper and leaving a smudgy surface. Ready to scream, I reminded myself it was only an exercise and not a big deal. I patiently attempted to redo that spot. Completed, it looked too polished compared to the rest of the work. In thirty minutes, I'd changed my spirited sky to boring mediocrity.

Visiting my childhood home always made me feel eight years old again. Which wasn't all bad. My father answered the door with the sports section of the Sunday paper in his hand. As I crossed the threshold, he greeted me with a firm one-armed hug and a peck on the cheek.

"How's my girl?" he asked.

"Fine, Daddy." Gee, I thought I stopped calling him that decades ago.

"That's good." Then he headed into the living room where the TV droned.

I watched him shuffle across the shag carpet toward his easy chair. Once a tall man, his drooping shoulders and ample waistline made him seem shorter. In his younger days he could bench press 250 pounds, but these past few years I'd stopped asking him to carry things for me. His strength was waning.

I glanced into the glass-fronted cabinet standing in the front hall and spotted the Venetian glass paperweight containing purple-and-red swirled flowers I'd coveted as a child. When young, my little sister, Nicole, and I devised secret pacts deciding who would inherit what when our parents died, an occurrence that seemed a hundred years away to two young girls.

The succulent bouquet of pot roast filled my nostrils. I followed the thick aroma to the kitchen to find my mother mashing potatoes at the counter. The room looked the same as it had when I was a child. Against the wall sat the small table where my brother, my sister, and I nibbled afternoon snacks of cinnamon toast and lemonade. Over the table hung the brass lamp, which sent a golden glow across the yellow-flowered wallpaper. I still considered the Bentwood chair against the wall my seat.

I felt my muscles relax, as if I were sinking into a warm bath, swished back to a time when someone else made all the decisions, and life was safe and predictable.

Mom, wearing an apron with her grandchildren's names embroidered on the front, embraced me. Her short salt-and-pepper hair, usually neatly coiffed, needed a trim. And I noticed bluish shadows beneath her eyes and a new frown line between her brows.

"I'm glad you could make it tonight," she said. "Are you okay? You look a little pale."

"Just tired. I haven't been sleeping well." I shouldn't have told her. Now she would probably worry about me.

"Have you lost weight? You look awfully thin."

"I wish. If anything, I could lose five pounds. Stop worrying." I pulled flatware out of a drawer and headed to the dining room to set the table. An ecru lace cloth lay across the table's rectangular surface, and three napkins sat in the center. My mother always insisted on cloth napkins, never mind the bother.

A few minutes later, Mom called out, "Vern, dinner," then brought the sliced pot roast, mashed potatoes, and tossed green salad to the table. My parents sat at either end of the table, and I slipped into my usual chair, on my father's right side.

Mom ladled extra gravy on my potatoes. "Now that Rob's away, maybe we can do this more often." Her eyes filled with love, but I wondered if a lecture on how they never saw me anymore was soon to follow.

"Sure, Mom, that would be nice," I quickly said. I knew I got lucky in the parent department, and it wouldn't hurt me to show my appreciation. "I've missed your great cooking."

Dad cleared his throat. "Marguerite, any big sales in the works?"

"Things are picking up." I was glad I had something hopeful to report.

He spoke again before I could continue. "Did I tell you your sister and Gregg are putting in a hot tub and a pickleball court?" Mom tried to pass him the salad, but he frowned and shook his head. "Everything should be finished in two months. That new house is going to be a doozy."

"Yes, it is." I knew all about it. Nicole kept me abreast of her recent purchases: the three-thousand-dollar convection oven, the state-of-the-art surveillance system, and the forty-eight-inch-screen TV. The eldest of three, I had been revered by my siblings while we were growing up, but not anymore.

"You probably heard about Eric's promotion?" he added.

"Yes." I also knew of my brother's coup at work, but I tried to hear the three-month-old news with fresh ears. I sliced my pot roast and dropped a square of beef into my mouth. Dad was just sharing his happiness with someone he thought would be thrilled, I told myself as I chewed the meat, biting into a knot of gristle. Yet I felt uncomfortable, to put it mildly, when he gushed on. I'd been the child with great potential, a girl who could go far in the art world. What did my father think of me now? Was he as disappointed in me as I was in myself?

Half-listening to his words, I speared another piece of meat. I hadn't done much with my life and had produced only one grandchild. And I was the only family member to be branded by divorce. Seldom mentioned in the Marsden household, it represented failure. During that ugly ordeal, I'd sometimes thought it would have been easier to wear the Scarlet Letter than to live with my father's silent disapproval.

Mom served apple crisp for dessert, and I devoured a second helping, all the time telling myself apples were good for me. "No more, Mom, I'm going to burst," I pleaded when she offered me more.

"Good dinner, Dorothy," Dad said, then receded into the living room to finish the paper.

I cleared the table, stacking the plates into a dangerously high pile as I'd done as a child.

After several moments, Mom asked the dreaded question. "Are you dating anyone new?"

"No, but I may go out on a blind date," I said without thinking it through. Now, I realized, I would have to call Susan and set it up. Or I could just wait a couple of weeks, then tell Mom things didn't work out. That seemed the best plan.

"How exciting," she said. "I hope he's the right one." Meaning marriage material.

"Mother, I haven't even met the man."

She transferred the leftover meat to a smaller platter and stowed it in the refrigerator. "How's my oldest grandson?"

"Fine, and busy." I placed two glasses in the dishwasher. "We don't talk much. He turns off his cell phone most of the time so it doesn't ring in class. I leave messages, but he rarely gets back to me. And I've given up asking him to return my e-mails." I wedged the last glass into a tight spot. "You'd think he'd need me for something."

"I remember when you started college." She rearranged the glasses. "By the end of the first quarter, you acted as if you knew everything there was to know. You didn't ask our advice for the next four years."

"Sorry about that. I must have been a dreadful brat." I crammed silverware into the rack. "I'm also sorry you and Dad wasted your money on my tuition."

"Now, why would you say that? I'll bet you've used your education in a thousand different ways." She removed one of the knives, scrubbed its blade, then placed it back in.

"I haven't accomplished anything the past twenty years," I said.

"I don't agree." She sat at the kitchen table and patted for me to join her.

"You raised a fine son, didn't you? You were always there for Rob when you could be, and we loved covering for you when you were working."

I lowered myself onto my old chair. "I don't know what I would have done without you and Dad. And now, paying Rob's tuition …" I could barely afford to send him to a local junior college much less to an out-of-state university.

"We're glad to help."

Gazing into Mom's face, I noticed the fine, jagged lines around her eyes seemed to be etched deeper than the last time I saw her.

"So, what's up with you?" I asked. "Everything okay?" It was my turn to be nosy.

She pursed her lips, which I knew meant trouble.

"You're not still worried about Dad and Alice, are you?" I checked to make sure my father hadn't walked in. "They probably talk about gold crowns and gum disease." I visualized ever-grinning Alice, Dad's former dental assistant of thirty years, clad in a white smock, her bottle-blonde hair slicked back into a French roll. "She's way too old to be a threat."

"Thanks a lot. She's ten years younger than I am." She heaved an extended sigh. "Who knows what the two of them do now when they go out for lunch. But there was a time …" Her voice trailed off.

"Come on, Mom. Dad?"

"Sure. Dear old Alice—always so sweet at the office, standing at your father's elbow all day with that insipid smile on her face. Then he would come home at six thirty to find me with a crying baby on my hip and dinner burnt."

"That doesn't mean anything happened."

She hesitated, as if deciding whether to proceed, then said, "I walked in on them once. Alice was in his arms." Her eyes became two slivers of darkness. "He said it was the first time and that it would never happen again." A flash of rage swept across her face, hardening her features. "I was so dumb back then. I should have insisted he fire her. But I was afraid if I gave him an ultimatum he might choose her."

Dad and Alice? I didn't know how to respond. I stared back, wishing she would tell me she was kidding. But her expression showed no sign of humor.

She wiped the corner of one eye. "Every time he'd go anywhere after that, I'd panic, my imagination sending me into a tailspin. I was furious, then numb. Things were never the same. The one good thing that happened was I started going to church again. God saved my life."

"God did?" A twist of sarcasm curled through my tongue. "Exactly what did he do?"

She sat back and surveyed my eyes. "When did you get to be so cynical?"

"Listen, Mom, let's not get into this discussion again. We get along great as long as we don't talk about God."

"Just tell me, was it my fault?"

My eyes bulged as my aggravation flared. "It's nobody's fault." I remembered well the last time I prayed. The scene lay hibernating in the back of my mind. "What's the use of talking about it now? I've never seen God, never touched the hem of his robe, and he's never returned my calls."

She wrung her slender hands. "Honey, he will answer you when the time is right. We humans are always in such a hurry. What seems like an eternity to us—"

I contained a smirk out of politeness. "I'm happy for you, okay? You were worried about Dad, and you found a way to help yourself. That's great. Glad it worked."

She tugged a Kleenex out of a pocket and dabbed her teary eyes. "By the way, your sister and brother don't know about your father. I probably shouldn't have said anything to you. What's the use of burdening you with all this now?"

I gazed at her face and saw a frail sadness, and I realized what it must have taken for her to speak about this. "I'm glad you did," I said. My arms slid around her narrow shoulders, and I hugged her tightly. "I wish you'd told me sooner."

Charlie sniffed the residual scent of pot roast on my slacks, then demanded his evening kibbled dog food with a loud yap. After feeding him, I wandered through the house, flicked the TV on and off, then leafed through the newspaper.

Dad fooling around? Mom must have misunderstood or dreamed up the whole thing. Maybe women grew more insecure with age, I thought, in need of a hormone replacement or counseling. No, except for the God thing, Mom was the most levelheaded woman I knew. While I was growing up, she'd been my biggest supporter, the one person I could always count on to be honest, my ally.

My hand moved to my hair, and I combed my fingers through it. When I was a little girl, Mom had untangled my hair, then brushed it until it shined like silk. I could still recall the feel of the soft bristles against my scalp. She also sewed elegant evening gowns for my Barbie doll, making my friends jealous. And it was my mother who'd bought me the art supplies.

Later, I remembered, my high-school art teacher had encouraged me. He was the first to publicly acknowledge my talent, praising my projects before the class, encouraging me to major in art. When I entered the university, I knew I would be an artist. It was a natural progression, like the tide following the moon.

What happened after college? a voice sounding like Henry's asked. *What stopped you from painting?* I stared into space for a moment.

I didn't have any answers.

I felt a gaping hole—a deep cavern of sadness—expanding in my chest. It dawned on me: Everything in my life was a lie. No, my love for Rob was real. I ached for my boy.

I tried reaching him on his cell phone, but got no response. Was he avoiding me? No, I was slipping into paranoia. Picking up the phone again, I dialed Phil's number. After four rings, he answered, but I could barely hear his voice above the talking and music in the background. In an instant, I was flung back to my high-school cafeteria, where I sometimes sat alone pretending I was there by choice. I almost hung up without speaking.

"Have you heard from Rob?" I finally asked in my clearest voice.

"Not for a few days. Hey, Margo, I can't talk right now." His words blended in with a bluesy country-western song. A woman shrieked with laughter, and Phil's voice became muffled. "I'll give you a call later, okay?"

"Sure." The phone line went dead, the silence throbbing in my ears.

I thudded down in front of the TV and flicked through the stations until I found a schmaltzy old black-and-white movie. When the hero and heroine reunited, I began to weep.

10

I felt like a mother trying to corral her rebellious child as I followed Laurie into the art building on Monday evening. She'd barely spoken to me on the drive over, but I wasn't sorry I'd asked how she and Dave were getting along. Divorce was not a notion to be tossed about lightly. I was living proof.

Halfway up the stairs, she came to an abrupt stop. She swung around and glared down at me. "This is the last time I confide in you." She gripped her sketchpad like a shield. "I thought you'd see things my way."

"I'm your friend, and I care about you."

She began stomping up the stairs again. "Do me a favor, stop caring so much."

"But, Laurie—"

She shoved open the door to the second floor. "Conversation closed," she said, then marched into the class-room.

I entered the room and saw Henry standing near the doorway speaking to several students.

"My home's too distracting to get much work done, so my studio is my refuge," I could hear him say. "Like an athlete entering a gymnasium, I can get right down to business."

He strode to the front of the room to speak to the whole class. I noticed his denim shirt and his jeans bore smudges of paint. He must have come straight from his easel.

"I've started buying my paints through the mail and have them sent directly to the studio," he continued. "They're cheaper, and I don't waste a whole morning at the art supply store. I'm as easily distracted as anyone, but I've found ways to keep on track. Not that I don't give myself a breather every few hours. I need time away from the studio to explore and be rejuvenated. Every artist needs down time."

He erased the chalkboard with wide arcs. "I'm usually ready for a break around noon every day, and you're all invited to stop by my studio tomorrow—if you have the time or inclination." He wrote his address. "Several of you have asked about work space, and I'd be happy to show you around." It was located on the east shore of Lake Union, he said, not difficult to find.

∞

The next day, my car jostled down the rough, cobbled hill toward Lake Union. I turned onto Henry's narrow street to find it inundated with parked cars. Around the corner and halfway down the block, I wedged my Toyota into a parking spot, then walked until I found the weather-beaten, one-story structure. Was this the right place? The building looked old and neglected, its paint chipping and cracking. But the front door had been enameled a crisp malachite green, with the address neatly inscribed above it.

I checked my watch and realized I was five minutes early. Hoping to see someone else from class, I lingered on the sidewalk for a moment. Finally, I climbed the front steps and searched for the doorbell, but found none. I tried rapping on the door, but got no response. Maybe others had arrived already, I thought, and they couldn't hear me above the chatter. I turned the doorknob and pulled the door open several inches. I could smell the familiar odor of paint and thinner, which meant this had to be the right place. I gave the door another tug to see a small front hall devoid of any furniture except for a low wooden table supporting a telephone and a few scattered papers.

I heard classical music lilting around the corner. I followed my ears to discover Henry standing in front of a wide canvas. Engrossed in his painting, he hummed as he dabbed on colors—first burnt umber, then raw sienna. His arm moved like a branch being rhythmically propelled by gusts of wind. Except for two threadbare chairs in front of a spacious picture window and canvases stacked against the walls, the room was bare.

105

He continued painting, now in quicker strokes, and hummed a bit more loudly. Was it Mozart? I wondered. The piece ended, and another began. I decided to retreat, to wait outside until others arrived. At that instant, he noticed me.

"What time is it?" he asked, his words resounding off the bare floor.

I looked at my watch again. "It's not quite noon. I'm early." Sidestepping toward the door, I almost knocked over an empty easel. "I could wait outside."

"No, this is fine. I'm ready for a break." He'd probably started the painting this morning. So far, the surface was tinted with layers of muted colors, which I assumed would be the background for whatever he had planned.

Setting his brush in a can, he stood back to examine his work. "It's good for me to get a little distance." He grabbed a rag to wipe his fingers, then tossed the cloth in a corner on top of several others. "Sometimes I get so caught up that I forget to slow down and look at the whole composition."

He directed me to a thermos sitting on a wooden crate near the window. He poured two cups of coffee and handed me one before sitting on one of the armchairs. I stood for an awkward moment, then planted myself on the other, keeping my weight forward. Inhaling the heady steam rising from my cup, I stared out the window at the bay, ever changing as boats skimmed across its shimmering surface. Beyond the water, I recognized familiar buildings on Queen Ann Hill.

Neither of us spoke for several minutes. Finally, the quiet became oppressive, and I said, "I've enjoyed your class." But I hadn't, of course. I'd always felt too self-conscious to have fun.

"I'm glad."

"Except, I think I've forgotten how to draw," I added, hoping he would contradict me.

"I doubt that." He sipped his coffee.

Why was I nervous? There was no reason to feel ill at ease, just because he was some big-shot painter. I returned my gaze to the window to watch a seaplane landing.

"Does this view distract you from your work?" I asked, determined to get a conversation going.

"Yes, I could spend hours sitting here. In the morning I stand with my back to it. In the afternoon I often pull down the shade to cool the temperature and tones. Luckily, I also have that nice north window, which is a godsend. It gives the best light." Looking at me again, he said, "Now tell me about your work."

Was he asking about my real job? I didn't have any artwork to talk about. "As Phil may have told you, I graduated from college with an art degree," I started, "but that's as far as I got. I guess I needed a nasty old professor giving me assignments and cracking the whip." I slapped one palm over my mouth. "That didn't come out right. I mean, I'm lazy—or something."

"Your drawings in class are quite good."

These were the words I'd been craving—if I'd heard right. "Thank you," I said, wanting to ask if he really meant it.

His eyes grew intense as he studied my face. "Phil said you used to paint. What's stopping you now?"

I shrugged as though I hadn't given it much thought. "The usual. My job eats up most of my time." My words stumbled over each other, and I could feel my face warming. "I don't have a place to paint either. I mean, not a studio like this." I knew I sounded like an idiot. But why should I have to defend myself?

Glancing out the window, I saw a sailboat tacking into the south wind. Then, like a flash of lightning in a calm sky, a crazy notion gripped me. I was sitting close enough to him to touch his hand. I speculated about what would happen if I reached out and took it. Yes, it was a ridiculous idea, something I would never actually do, but I could almost feel the warmth of his skin. I turned my head to find him watching me as though I'd just said something captivating. He couldn't possibly know what I was thinking, I assured myself, but I felt trapped in what seemed like an endless moment.

The front door creaked, and I tore myself out of Henry's visual grasp as Emily and Roger from class entered the studio.

"Hello, hello," Emily called, curving the words into a melody. Roger followed, clad in a suit and a striped tie.

Henry and I got to our feet. "Welcome," he said. "Watch where you step."

"What a lovely work space," Emily said.

"It doesn't look anything like my office," Roger said, good-naturedly. I recalled his mentioning he sold advertising and worked downtown.

Henry laughed. "I imagine that's true."

"This one is marvelous," Emily said, pointing to a canvas sitting on the floor, propped against the wall.

"It sure is," Roger said. "Is it finished?"

"That's still up for debate." Henry placed the canvas on an easel. The painting portrayed an auburn-haired woman playing a flute. Her eyes half-closed, she seemed in reverie, as if mesmerized by the tune. On closer inspection, I saw she was standing before a lead-paned window, each square of glass mirroring an ivied garden.

"All my endeavors are in some state of transition," Henry said. "With each one I have to force myself to stop, then start another."

As we observed his other works, I chided myself for imagining sharing an intimate moment with him. No need to worry; I was back in the driver's seat again.

I half-listened as he talked about a large painting sitting in the corner—a depiction of two women on a park bench, one reading and the other knitting. He explained why he'd painted the same scene three times—at morning, midday and afternoon—to study the varying shadows and hues.

Over the next five minutes, more students arrived. "Hello," or "How are you?" Henry said to each one. Guiding them through his studio, he seemed no longer aware of my existence.

Twenty minutes later, when Roger announced he needed to leave for a one o'clock meeting, several others also said their farewells. Finally, only Emily and I remained.

As Henry closed the front door, Emily approached me. "How are you today, dear? You seem quiet."

I felt like I was riding a unicycle and barely maintaining my balance. I was tempted to reach out to her for support, but said, "I was thinking about work. Did I mention I'm in real estate?" I handed her my business card, then wished I hadn't. I'd sworn I wouldn't become one of those agents who took advantage of friends, particularly sweet older women.

"I'll bet you do a wonderful job." She tucked the card into her purse. "Maybe you should give one to Henry, too."

"No, I don't think so." Doing business with him would be excruciating for both of us.

Minutes later I was nearing the University Bridge. I heard its bells tolling, then saw its warning lights flashing, and the arms lowering to stop traffic while a boat motored through the cut. As I waited, I felt irritated and drained. I shouldn't have come. Spending time with Henry Marsh was not what I'd needed today. Why was I speechless around him, like a teenybopper meeting a celebrity? He was just a man, like any other.

∞

Sitting at my desk reviewing the documents I needed to give to the Averys, I glanced at Rob's photo. Even at a young age my son had taken after his father. What happened to my half of the genes? I wondered. Did they lie dormant in Rob's DNA, waiting to surface in the next generation? I remembered what Emily said about grandchildren bringing incredible joy. The thought of a toddler someday crawling into my lap sent a wave of warmth through my chest. But it was way too early to start imagining Rob getting married, and I was too young to be called Grandma Marguerite. What a gruesome thought. Anyway, Rob might never have children. The woman he married could be infertile or already have kids. Those things happened.

Finding the papers, I slipped them into a manila envelope. As I wrote the Averys' name on it, I thought of Phil's and my wedding album, which I'd saved for Rob's sake, although he'd never seen it and might never want to. The photos sat at the bottom of a box, beneath the canceled checks and paperwork I'd saved in case the IRS ever audited me. I hadn't looked through the album since Phil and I split up, but I could remember every detail of the ceremony as it unfolded in my parents' living room. Phil had looked like a movie star in his black suit and pleated tuxedo shirt, which

I never saw him don again. I'd worn a white empire gown with a scooped neckline and a high gathered waist that covered everything. Although Mom begged me to get married in a church with a minister, I'd insisted a justice of the peace guide us through our vows. "A couple needs God on their team, like the third leg of a stool," Mom had said. "Without a commitment to him, I don't know how any marriage makes it."

Had she been right after all? No, it wasn't God I needed, but a better man—one like my father. Growing up, I'd considered Dad to be old-fashioned, like a worn copper penny. But in truth, he was the finest man I'd ever known.

I left the office and pointed my car toward home. Stopping at a crosswalk to let a couple pass, my thoughts returned to Phil. After the misery he'd put me through, our divorce came as a welcome relief. With our final good-bye, a euphoric sense of freedom took root inside me. But within the year, I grew tired of being alone. In spite of the hardships men caused, they filled a void in women's lives nothing else could. In my case, I'd tried inflating myself with food, clothes, work, but nothing satisfied my hunger for intimacy or my sense of inadequacy. Only in a man's arms could I close my eyes and feel whole.

I'd never loved another man besides Phil—not a real one. I'd joked with the Mom's Brigade that all I really wanted was someone to accompany me to the annual company Christmas party. I'd sworn I wouldn't attend the splashy event alone again. I was finished pretending I preferred circulating and meeting new people. Done flitting about like a barn swallow rather than hanging onto one man's arm like a fragile orchid. I envisioned my escort dressed in a suit and tie. He would make witty small talk with my colleagues, but his attention would always be on me.

If I'd stayed with Phil, I thought, he would have refused to attend the party with me, or if he'd gone he would have gotten drunk and acted sloppy. Someone like Henry Marsh would probably consider a bunch of realtors beneath him. Or worse, spend the whole evening talking about himself and trying to sell his paintings. Yikes.

I heard a honk and scanned the crosswalk to see the pedestrians were long gone. As I gunned the engine, I checked the rearview mirror, but could only see the top of the car behind me because I was slouching so much. Elongating my spine, I pulled myself erect to gain several inches. The perfect man for me must exist, I told myself. I remembered Susan saying her husband's friend was a banker, which sounded interesting. Even if he wasn't Mel Gibson, it was time to get real and settle for less than perfection. I was, after all, far from perfect myself.

I pulled to the side of the road and dug out my cell phone. "Hi, Susan, it's Marguerite," I said when she answered. "Do you think Bob's friend still wants to go out with me?"

Her voice sprang to life like a windup toy let loose. "Sure, you bet. I'll call him right now."

"Slow down. How much have you told him?" The way Susan carried on sometimes, this guy probably thought he was going to meet a fashion model.

"I described you as a top-notch realtor, a single mother, and an artist."

"I'm not sure how hot a realtor I am." Some teens cruised by, their stereo bass booming so loud my car windows shimmied. "I don't feel like a mother anymore, now that Rob's gone. And I'm hardly an artist."

"Relax," she said. "It's just a date, not a lifetime commitment."

When I got home, my answering machine was blinking.

"Hi, Marguerite. It's Tim O'Brien. Susan said you'd be expecting my call."

11

When I heard Emily's voice on the other end of the phone, I figured she'd probably gotten my number off my card. But why would she be calling me?

"I hope I'm not disturbing you," she said.

"No, not at all." In truth, Rob's was the only voice I wanted to hear. I'd been working through my frustrations by sweeping, then mopping the kitchen floor, and was considering cleaning the inside of the stove, a chore I hadn't tackled for years. "What can I do for you?"

"Henry asked me to help him out by contacting half of his students to let them know we're meeting outside of class this week to see an art show."

I'd already decided to give myself the week off. "I'm not sure I can make it." I used my free hand to swab the counter with a sponge. The graying linoleum surface wore gashes where Rob had sliced food without using a cutting board and black marks where the former owner had set a hot pan.

"That's a shame," she said. "I've heard realtors put in long hours."

"Yes, I've been buried at work." I was exaggerating, but I had little desire to see an art show. I tossed the sponge in the sink, which also begged for scrubbing. "And Mondays are one of my busiest days."

"Let me tell you where we're going in case you're able to come. All right?"

"Sure." I waited without retrieving paper or pen to write down the address.

"It's at the campus gallery, not too far from the art building."

"Okay, I know where it is." In college, I'd often strolled through its rooms looking for inspiration.

"We'll be looking at a visiting drawing exhibit. According to an article in the newspaper, it's outstanding."

"Yes, I recall seeing it." I hadn't bothered to read further than the headline.

"So far, everyone I've called has jumped at the opportunity to have Henry lead us through it."

"I'll see," I said, then searched for a polite way to change the subject. "How have you and your husband been?" I imagined Emily's spouse sitting close by waiting for her to get off the phone.

"Dear, my husband has been dead for nearly fourteen years. Do I talk as though he were still alive?"

"I'm so sorry." I sat on the nearest chair. "I mean, I didn't realize."

"No need to apologize. Some days it seems as though he is here. There certainly isn't a day I don't miss him. Sometimes I wake up in the middle of the night and feel as though he should be lying next to me. His snoring used to aggravate me no end." She sounded older, tired. "Now I'd do anything to hear it again."

As she spoke, I thought of my mother nudging Dad in the side to get him to stop snoring. Mom was five years younger than he, and would probably outlive him. I knew that, like Emily, someday she would wake up alone and reach out to emptiness.

Mom claimed she'd walked in on Dad and Alice. But I chose to believe she'd taken an innocent moment and blown it up to gigantic proportions after years of festering. I thought of my father engrossed in *Monday Night Football*, his evening paper falling to the floor as he nodded off. He was too old to be fooling around, with his high blood pressure and heart problems.

"Sometimes when I'm folding laundry," Emily continued, "I wish he'd come walking into the room to carry the basket upstairs for me like he always did." She laughed, her voice like a feather, light but textured. "That may sound crazy to a young woman, but I spent most of my life with him."

"What was he like?" I asked, hearing her need to talk.

"Al was my opposite. He was a hard-driving, top-level corporate manager, and I was a stay-at-home mom who didn't wear makeup or curl her hair. His world and mine were so different, I never did understand what he did all day. But he was a kind man and a good father, and we had a lot of fun.

Opposites do attract. Isn't it strange how those things work out so well? We complemented each other beautifully."

"He sounds wonderful. I'm sorry you lost him."

"Oh, we'll see each other again one day in heaven. I'm counting on that. And you, young lady, I hope we see you Monday."

After she hung up, I stood for a moment listening to the furnace sigh, then shut off. The house stood empty, like a birdcage after its tenant had flown away. I lifted the receiver and dialed Tim O'Brien's work number.

⌇

"Okay, so it was a dumb movie." I slipped out of my jacket, draped it over the chair back. "But at least no one got killed, and it had a happy ending." You'd think I'd be done with boy-gets-girl stories, but I still liked them.

Tim chuckled from across the table. "Next time, I get to pick. Okay?"

Next time? "Sure." We'd seen a romantic comedy, the kind some men usually don't tolerate. Yet Tim had gone willingly, saying whatever I liked was fine with him. He'd opened every door—even the car's—bought the biggest tub of popcorn available, and tempted me afterward with a chocolate torte at a nearby cafe.

I had little doubt most women would appreciate his teddy-bear cuteness and rolling laugh. Dressed in a polo shirt and khaki slacks, he was a square-jawed, clean-cut man who could have modeled for an Eddie Bauer catalog. Susan had raved so much about him that I'd prepared myself for the worst.

His black BMW wasn't shabby either. I normally didn't care what a man drove, but a nice car did spell success.

I sliced a ladylike piece of cake. "I shouldn't be eating this." I nibbled into it, allowing the dark-chocolate frosting to melt slowly on my tongue.

"You don't need to worry about your weight." He plunked a wedge of cheesecake in his mouth. "A few extra calories won't hurt a bit."

I patted the corners of my mouth with my napkin, careful not to remove my lipstick. "A few thousand extra, you mean?" I hadn't flirted for ages and was having a good time being charming. I wore a magenta V-necked sweater and the black slacks that made me look thinner than I really was. His lingering gaze told me he found me attractive. He pushed his plate in my direction and offered me a bite.

"Are you trying to be a bad influence on me?" I asked with an exaggerated look of disapproval.

"*Moi?* My mother says I'm an angel."

I hoped upon hope his mother was right. "Hmm." I reached over, cut a sliver of cheesecake, and tasted it.

"Like it?"

"Yes, everything's delicious." I watched his eager eyes sparkle from behind long lashes. There was nothing not to like about him, I decided, even if I didn't feel a tingling spark of chemistry. Perhaps sizzle didn't matter anymore. I knew from experience that red-hot flames burned out quickly, leaving stone-cold ashes behind. Weren't honesty and reliability more important than intense, but short-lived, excitement? I'd heard of people who had known each other for years suddenly discovering passion. Love could ferment and mellow like vintage wine.

"Did you catch the Mariners last night?" Tim asked.

"No." I never paid much attention to sports unless Rob was on the field. "Did you go?"

"Yeah. My dad scored two seats right behind home plate. Things were tied until the bottom of the ninth. Then the Yankees pitcher fell apart, and we hit a homer with bases loaded. It was the coolest thing I've ever seen."

"Sounds like fun."

Minutes later he laughed as he described an interception at a recent Seahawks football game. Apparently he fancied sports as much as my father.

"Then what happened?" I asked, inhaling a yawn.

At the end of the evening, we stood for a moment on my front porch. In an impulsive move, I thanked him with a kiss. Our lips barely touched. Wanting to be held, I almost pulled him nearer. But I wasn't sure I wanted to go out with him again. Did we really have much in common? Tim hadn't asked me about my job or even about my son. Maybe Susan hadn't mentioned Rob, which might be just as well. Finding out a woman has a child whose voice is deeper and shoulders broader than his own might scare a man away.

"I enjoyed your company, pretty lady," he said, hesitating as if he had more to say. Then he took a step back. "I'll give you a call."

"Thank you." Was I thanking him for the movie or his promise to call? It didn't matter. The ball was in his court.

12

I hadn't visited the campus museum once since my college days. But Emily's conversation had touched me with its honesty; I contemplated going just to see her. "Bring your sketchpad," she'd told me. "We'll be using them."

Standing in my kitchen, I had less than forty-eight hours to draw something before class night. With no open house scheduled for the weekend, there was time to sketch right now. I glanced around the room, hoping to find a subject. The small wrought-iron chandelier, with its four arms branching out to hold flame-shaped bulbs, floated above the kitchen table. The wall hutch, crammed with Rob's art projects from grade school and one of his lacrosse team photos, hung next to his framed first-grade self-portrait. Magnets of all shapes and sizes holding pizza coupons, Cathy cartoons, and articles I thought I might need someday littered the face of the refrigerator. My mud-caked walking shoes lay by the back door next to Charlie's basket. Did my house smell like a dog? I wondered. It must, after twelve years of his canine presence.

I picked up my cereal bowl, which still sat on the table from breakfast, and dumped the remnants of uneaten shredded wheat into the garbage can under the sink. Then I set the bowl in the sink on top of several dirty plates and a pan that had been soaking overnight. Dribbling liquid detergent over the stack, I turned on the hot water.

I would draw as soon as I tidied up, I told myself. As I scrubbed the pan, I remembered how, back in college, I could fill a notebook with drawings in one afternoon. In my cramped dorm room, messy chaos hadn't made any difference to me. I'd sat cross-legged on my paisley bedspread with the sketchpad on my lap, outlining my roommate Candy while she drew me. Then I would stare out the window and draw the distant Cascade Mountains or the evergreen trees standing tall outside the dorm.

I rinsed the pan and set it in the drying rack. In my junior year, I recalled, an instructor challenged each student in the class to finish seven oil paintings in a week. I had executed them with gusto, not worrying what else demanded my attention, or whether they were good enough or finished enough. Painting them had been like playing a game: challenging, but fun.

The phone rang. I dried my hands to answer it.

"Hi there," Tim said. "I sure had fun last night."

"Me too." I'd woken up with him on my mind. Tim was as cute as they come, I'd thought as I lay in bed. How many single men of his caliber would swim my way?

"I know this might be rushing things, but I have tickets to the Seahawks game this afternoon. A client gave them to me, and they're great seats. Would you like to go?"

I found football tedious and tried to think of a reasonable excuse not to go, but that was stupid. I wanted to see him again, didn't I?

"Yes, I'd love to." I raced to take a quick shower, then tried styling my hair in a provocative new manner, but ended up parting it the same as always. Dark circles, blotchy skin, and crow's-feet all needed to be artfully concealed. I shuddered to think any man might see me as I really was. In my twenties, even my thirties, I'd blushed with fresh beauty, and thought women who wore tons of makeup were crazy. Not anymore.

As I tucked in my blouse and zipped up my slacks, I heard Charlie growl his warning that a car had stopped in front of the house. He was barking ferociously by the time the doorbell jangled. I dashed down and swung the door open, but Charlie continued yapping up at Tim's face.

"Hi," I said over the dog's throaty blasts. "Go into the kitchen, bad dog." Charlie stood for a defiant moment, then retreated several feet

"Cute," Tim said.

"Sorry. He usually doesn't bark that much." Stupid dog.

"He'll love me once he gets to know me." Tim pulled two tickets from his jacket pocket and fanned his face with them. "I'm glad you could come. These seats are in the one-hundred level at the fifty-yard line. Can you believe it?"

"Sounds great," I said, not remembering how many yard lines there were.

On the drive to the game, I learned that Tim had never been married. I hadn't thought to ask him the night before, assuming a man past age forty must have gone through at least one divorce. Now I admonished myself for my negative attitude.

"Never met the right woman," he explained, speeding up and changing lanes. "I was engaged twice to the same lady. Once I got cold feet, and once she did. We're still good friends, keep in touch." He eased up on the pedal and glanced at me. "But I'm getting to the ripe old age where a man feels like settling down. Being single isn't all it's cracked up to be."

"I know what you mean." I looked out the side window. Below the freeway lay Union Bay and Henry's studio. As I watched a seaplane lug into the sky, I couldn't help wondering if he stood down there painting.

The football game was exciting, and the volume in the stadium deafening. Sitting only a few rows above the players, right in the thick of the action, I found myself yelling and screaming with the other sixty thousand fans, and surprised myself with my own enthusiasm. Later, as we walked back to his car, Tim took my hand. His seemed rather small and even smoother than mine. But he was a banker, not a construction worker, I reminded myself. White collar.

We stopped at a sports bar alive with music and the chatter of jubilant fans. Since I'd nearly lost my voice from cheering, I mostly listened to Tim's stories, all the while wearing a most interested expression on my face. By the time he'd sucked in his last fettuccini noodle, sipped the few remaining drops of his imported beer, and paid the bill, I was tired and ready to go home.

When we reached my front doorstep, I could hear Charlie yapping inside and pawing at the door.

"Can you stand my horrible little dog again?" I asked. "He's usually a good boy."

"No problem, I like dogs."

I led Tim into the living room. We sat on the couch and talked about the great defensive plays that saved the game, then discussed whether the Seahawks held a chance at the Super Bowl. Charlie insisted on lying at our feet, but when Tim tried to give his head a stroke, the dog leaned out of reach and glared, ears tipped back.

I asked about Tim's work at the bank and learned he handled some very prestigious accounts. His voice swelled with pride as he described his job and his lavish office with its roll-top desk and stunning view of Puget Sound.

"I can watch the ferry boats and freighters," he said. "Come by someday. We can have lunch."

I imagined his introducing me to his secretary and coworkers and was flattered. "Sure, I'd enjoy that," I said.

As we stood at my front door saying good-bye, Tim took me in his arms and kissed me. It was a metallic kiss, firm and cool, as he pushed his hard lips against mine. Suffice to say, I felt a surge of disappointment.

After we parted, he said, "Good night. I'll definitely be calling you."

13

Raindrops hit the windshield like bullets of gravel, and oncoming headlights glaring off the slick streets made me squint. My gut told me I should have stayed home, but Laurie had insisted it was my turn to drive to class.

Minutes later, I inched my car into the underground parking garage at the university.

"Tell me, what's going on with you and this golfer guy?" I asked Laurie, my crabby mood urging me to confront her.

"Nothing for you to worry about." Her voice sounded as creamy as ever, yet I detected a false edge.

I imagined her in the arms of some creep. He'd have to

be a jerk to pursue a married woman. "Do you still run into him on Wednesdays? Or has it gone beyond that?"

"I've got the situation under control," she said in staccato. "Case closed." She wrenched open her wallet and handed me a five-dollar bill. "I'll pay for parking tonight. Anything to put you in a better mood."

I took the money and handed it to the attendant, then found an empty stall. As I turned off the engine, Laurie jumped out of the car and shut the door harder than necessary. With her notebook under her arm, she forged ahead to the elevator. I caught up with her as the elevator doors slid open. We got in, standing in opposite corners. As we surfaced to ground level, I leaned against the back wall and stared at her distorted reflection in the metal door.

When we reached the gallery's ticket booth, I spotted several students from class. Laurie paraded over to them, waving hello. A moment later I noticed Henry and Emily entering the lobby together. While Henry spoke to the woman selling tickets, Emily glided over to me.

"I'm so glad you're here," she said. She wore a melon orange silk jacket with a mandarin neck and violet dragons embroidered on the front. Silvery curls of hair, no doubt loosed by the wind, danced above her eyes. She slipped her arm through mine, and we followed Henry, who was leading the group down the carpeted corridor toward the first room.

"Seldom Seen Drawings and Prints by the Masters," Emily read aloud as we paused at the exhibition's sign. She gave my arm a little squeeze against her side, then let it drop. We wandered to the center of the room and stood in silence.

My heart sang with unexpected delight. Each work, elaborately matted and framed, was a tiny masterpiece. When my gaze happened on a Leonardo da Vinci sketch, the highlight of the show, I drank in its beauty, tracing the lyrical lines with my eyes. All sounds of voices and footsteps became muted as I tried to memorize each sepia pen stroke.

Suddenly people were standing next to me, and I experienced the unpleasant sensation of Henry's breath on the back of my neck. I spun around to find myself gawking first into his chest, then up at his face. He was staring over my head at the da Vinci, as if anyone below his height was also beneath him.

"We know this sketch is a preparatory study for the larger painting that followed," he said. "But does the artist's original intent affect its beauty and quality? Is it possible to admire this preliminary sketch as much as the painting that later emerged from it? Anyone have an opinion?"

I examined the drawing further. Its lines seemed spontaneous, alive. I started to raise my hand.

"I want it in my living room," Laurie said with a giggle. "It looks done to me."

Someone else shot back, "But if the artist had been satisfied with the sketch, he might never have made a big painting. That would have been a loss."

"I'd take either one," Laurie said.

Several others voiced their opinions, and by then I was sinking into cowardice. Afraid of sounding like a fool, I kept silent. When the discussion wound to an end, Henry asked us to open our sketchpads, with instructions to scribble notes on technique or to make our own quick sketches, copying the masters. For several minutes, I walked around the room with one hand in my pocket. I drifted up behind Emily, who stood drawing an etching—creating her own marvelous rendition of a British farm scene. The ramshackle barn and cottage and the horse-drawn cart full of hay bustled with life on the page.

"I didn't know committing forgery could be so much fun," she said. Seeing my sketchpad in my hand, she asked, "Why aren't you drawing?"

"I'm much happier watching you."

"Come on, give it a try. No need to be bashful."

"All right." I found a pencil in my purse, then flipped open my pad. "I haven't been in this museum for years," I said as I tried to decide what to do. "It sure looks different." I noticed an etching of a barge navigating a canal that might serve as a good subject.

"Quite a face-lift, isn't it?" Emily's tapered eyebrows rose as she glanced around the room. "I do prefer more traditional architecture, but the lighting and walls are beautifully done." She turned to me. "Didn't you say you were once a student here?"

I was saved the task of reciting my college ambitions by an announcement that the class would gather in the coffee shop on the lower level in fifteen minutes. I completed a hurried sketch, just as Henry said we had run out of time.

Laurie, who'd kept her distance since we arrived, descended the steep staircase with most of the class, and Emily and I followed. By the time I entered the café, the group had dragged tables and chairs together so they could compare drawings. Rhonda, the young redhead, placed her sketchpad on the chair between Henry and Roger, and offered to get Henry coffee. He sent her a wide smile as he handed her money. "Leave the rest as a tip," he said.

Moments later the conversation buzzed. Odd, I thought, how the others had so much to say, even though they had most likely not studied art or art history as I had. And they didn't even seem embarrassed to show their sketches.

Good-hearted laughter erupted as Laurie presented her childlike drawing. "We already know I'm no artist."

"Yes, you are," Toni said. "You're making art, aren't you? At least that's how I look at it." The others agreed.

"I'm with you," Henry said, his face alive. "Remember, some of the drawings we saw tonight weren't recognized in the artists' lifetimes, but that fact doesn't diminish their genius."

"But they're all so good." Laurie turned her palms up. "I could never draw like that."

"Allow yourself to grow at your own pace." Henry scanned the students' faces. "One cannot reach maturity through desire alone. It takes practice and more practice. Use those sketchpads at home every day."

His gaze fixed onto mine. "You'll see results. I promise."

I stared back, feeling relieved he couldn't see through the cover of my almost-empty notebook.

"I need to get home," Roger said, standing. "This has been great. See you all next week."

The others took the last sips of their drinks and gathered up their belongings. I watched Laurie reapply her lipstick, then I followed her up the stairs.

When we reached my car, she said, "Wasn't that fun?" She got in the car and opened her sketchpad to admire her drawing. "Imagine, me an artist. Henry's sure supportive. Not many men would take the time to help a beginner like me."

"That's true." Against all reason, my shoulders drooped as I pictured Henry and Rhonda sitting together. Even if I found him attractive, I couldn't compete with a woman half my age. I worked the key into the ignition and tapped my foot on the gas pedal.

"Did you get together with that guy Susan wanted you to meet?" Laurie asked.

"I've seen him twice." I coaxed the transmission into reverse, then craned my neck to see over my shoulder as I backed up. "He's cute. I mean, handsome." Tim's face loomed fuzzy in my memory. "Not that appearances are everything. During my divorce, Phil's looks meant nothing to me." But how good it would feel to be drawn to a man by that passion we once shared.

I put the car in drive and initiated our climb to street level. "Tim's a banker," I continued, thinking how good he must look in a three-piece suit. "I need a man who works at a normal job, not a flaky artist who's glued to a canvas day and night and can't pay the bills."

"I'd still aim for Henry Marsh. And I'll bet he earns a good income. Roger says he's quite successful."

I jammed my foot on the gas, causing the tires to squeal on the last corner. "He's not interested." I was using my bad-dog voice, the one that sent Charlie to his basket when he misbehaved. "Nor am I. So drop it."

"Gee, you don't have to get so huffy. I'm entitled to my opinion, aren't I?"

I recalled our recent debates about her marriage. I'd been doling out a ration of unasked-for advice; the least I could do was not get defensive. "Yes, of course," I said. "Sorry if I've been a grouch."

I handed the ticket to the attendant and exited the garage. The rain had turned to drizzle, and the streets stretched wide and empty. Through the mist the streetlights glowed like white Chinese lanterns.

"Did I tell you I'm starting tae kwon do?" Laurie asked. "That's why I didn't make it to Henry's studio the other day. We wear these darling black outfits and go barefoot. It's a blast. Maybe you'd like to take it with me?"

"You've got to be kidding. I'm so uncoordinated, I'd hurt myself." I chuckled as I remembered my last attempt at doing the splits. Several years earlier I endured one yoga class and my limbs were so stiff the next day I could barely walk. Now that I thought about it, Laurie had talked me into that, too.

"It's a combination of martial arts and self-defense." She sounded like a flitting sparrow. "Most women can't defend themselves. They're powerless." She rested her elbow on my seat back. "The head instructor is a character. She's tiny, but you sure wouldn't want to mess with her."

I watched the wiper swish lazily across the windshield, then pause. Tiny dots of moisture appeared on the glass, then were swept away as the blade crossed back to the other side.

"Give it a try," she said. "You can be my guest for one free class. Erika and Susan already said no. It seems like only my single friends can ever do anything." Her voice turned cranky. "Dave likes me to do stuff like this. That way he doesn't feel guilty for working all the time. Anyway, I should be able to defend myself. How about it?"

"Think I'll pass on this one. Aren't you continuing with the drawing class next session?"

"Nah. I love it, but I want to try other hobbies. You're the artist. I hope you keep it up."

"I might try a class somewhere else." There was no way I'd walk into Henry Marsh's classroom alone. "I do like Emily though. Wouldn't it be great to be like her when we're her age? She seems so content."

"Unlike me who hates growing old." She fluffed her hair. "You should see my real color under all this frost. There's so much gray it's frightening. Maybe you should visit my colorist too. She can work miracles."

"What for? My hair isn't gray."

"Oh, yeah?" She pointed to a loose lock from my temple.

At the next red light, I flipped down the visor mirror to peer at myself in the dim light and noticed several colorless strands. "When did that happen? Maybe I need glasses, too."

The light flicked green, and I folded up the visor and drove forward. "Better give me her number. I don't want Tim thinking he's dating an old lady." I hadn't mentioned my age to him.

"Henry strikes me as a man who'd find a little silver hair attractive," she said. "He'd probably admire a woman who's at ease with aging." She bubbled with laughter. "Doesn't he strike you that way?"

I gave in and laughed too. It felt good to have the tension between us eased. "Believe me, you'll like Tim better."

When I got home, the light on the answering machine was flashing. I rushed past Charlie to listen to Rob's recorded voice say he was doing fine and would call back in a few days. I replayed the short message, listening for clues to his mood and imagining the tidbits he might have shared with me. Over the years our conversations had shrunk. And after Andrea's arrival, our communications diminished to a quick hello as we passed each other in the morning. Now, a recorded voice was precious.

The corners of my mouth sagged down. "Phooey," I grumbled.

Charlie looked up and tilted his head until his eyes disappeared behind long furry tufts. I bent down, pushed the hair back, then scratched his head. Since Rob left, the dog seemed to sleep more and hadn't demanded a walk in days. Rain and wind had ruled the skies for most of the week, but nasty weather usually didn't keep him inside. I wondered if dogs got depressed like people. Did Charlie miss Rob as much as I did, or was the dog picking up on my frame of mind?

The phone rang, and I answered it to hear Susan's twang. "Hello, there," she said. "Well?"

"Well, what?"

"Tell me all about your dates with Tim, of course. Why didn't you let me know?"

I wound the cord around my finger, something I used to nag at Rob for doing.

"I didn't get much out of my husband," she continued. "So, how did it go?"

"Fine." How much did I want to tell Susan? Most likely she would repeat every word I said to Bob, who would pass it on to Tim.

"You sound like one of my kids. Come on, Marguerite, don't keep me in suspense."

As I unwound my finger, I recounted the movie and football game, including the score and big plays, describing Tim as good-looking and a gentleman. I omitted the questionable good-night kiss and my reservations about our lack of chemistry, on my part anyway.

"Do you like him as much as I said you would? Isn't he a sweetheart?"

"He's very nice."

"I knew you two would hit it off. Isn't it amazing he's still single?"

I tried to think of a diplomatic way to ask why that was. I wasn't sure I swallowed Tim's account of his nervous fiancée. Sure, men got cold feet all the time, but I hadn't heard of many women calling off their weddings.

"Guess he hasn't met the right woman yet," she said. "Men have internal clocks too, and he told Bob he's ready to settle down. I knew it would all work out."

I yawned loudly enough for her to hear.

"Okay, I'll let you go. You can thank me later. Why don't we have lunch this week so you can fill me in?"

"The lunch part sounds good, but there's not much more to tell." The interrogation was over, and I was glad I hadn't revealed too much. Usually, I couldn't keep my blabbering mouth shut and later regretted spouting off too much personal information to my well-meaning friends. They always pounced like cats after a ball of twine, trying to help me or fix me or solve my dilemmas. Susan was probably bragging to Bob right now about her matchmaking skills. Yet I had to admit, Tim was everything she said he was, and more.

On my way to bed, I passed Rob's room and lingered at his doorway. I'd complained for years that I needed space for a home office and this bedroom would work perfectly. But it occurred to me Henry would tell me to convert it into a studio instead, and erect an easel against the far wall to give me plenty of room to step back to view my canvas.

That wouldn't work. I would have to move everything when Rob came home for Christmas, then again in the summer. The room would smell of paint, and I'd probably get it on the rug. What was I thinking? I couldn't even draw for twenty minutes a day, let alone finish a whole painting.

Finally ready for bed, I tugged back the covers, slid between the cold sheets, and rubbed my feet together for warmth. Then I opened *Unearthing Your Childhood Dreams* at the bookmark.

The author suggested recording the answers to various questions in a journal. "List twenty-five things you liked to do as a child. Describe your favorite color, fairy tale, and song at age six. What common thread did they hold?"

The drills seemed like too much work, but I grabbed a small notepad and a pen, and started writing.

14

I lifted the whistling kettle off the burner, then poured boiling water over two tea bags resting at the bottom of my prewarmed Blue Willow pot, the way Mom taught me. I placed it on the tray next to the creamer and a china teacup, usually reserved for company.

I had Laurie to thank for this small act of self-indulgence. As I set the timer for four minutes to steep the tea, I remembered her describing an article in a magazine that stated women should pamper themselves more rather than lavishing all their attention on others, who rarely appreciated the fuss and sometimes even resented it. The article suggested getting a massage and a facial, or spending a week in a spa "because you deserve it."

I envisioned Laurie flitting about town getting pedicures and having her hair styled at the most expensive salons in town. She had asked me to join her, but I rarely allowed myself such extravagancies. A facial and a massage sounded fun, but as a single mother I'd always looked after Rob's needs. I was stingy with myself and would stay that way until he got through college. Or maybe forever.

The tea bags needed two more minutes. I stared at the treasured teapot, which had somehow remained in one piece for more than fifty years of family use. To fill the time, I brought out my sketchpad and with a pencil outlined the pot, cup, and creamer. Next, I drew the pot's intricate design, but something looked wrong. Lifting the pencil from the page, I considered how to best depict a busy pattern on a shiny surface.

I decided color might help. I trotted to the basement and located an old set of pastel crayons. With broken stubs of white and blue, I filled in areas of my drawing and did my best to capture the sparkle of the teapot's surface and its old-fashioned pattern. Still, the picture lacked something, and I wasn't sure what. Then I recalled Henry telling the class, during an exercise, to let our eyes drink in the information. I breathed deeply, relaxed my vision, and noticed the shaded edge of the teapot, which was farthest from the window, now looked hard. The other side appeared so soft and transparent it almost vanished, the way the horizon melds into the sky. The white parts now ranged from buttermilk to light lavender.

I added more color, layer upon layer. A few minutes later, I admired my finished product from across the room. The creamer looked a bit lopsided. I grabbed the white crayon, then dropped it back into the box. Remembering how I'd ruined my cloud drawing, I resisted the tantalizing urge to fix anything. Just to be safe, I wrapped a rubber band around the pastel crayon box to keep the lid tightly shut.

Like a wave folding over on itself, more than an hour had elapsed. The timer must have gone off, but I hadn't heard its beeping. Nor had I poured the tea, which would now be lukewarm and taste bitter because the tea bags had been left in so long.

My mind started plotting the rest of my day; I felt a ripple of guilt for still being home. At eleven o'clock in the morning, I knew Lois would be poised at her desk and impatiently tapping her foot, with an offer for the Henricks' old house in hand. Lois had worked her magic again. How did that woman manage to sell so much?

I left the tea tray on the kitchen counter and hurried to work. As I strode through the front door of the office, I waved hello to Stephanie, the receptionist who'd worked there as long as I, then made a beeline for Lois's desk.

"Have a seat," Lois said, pointing an index finger at the chair across from her. "You're going to love these buyers." Holding reading glasses to her eyes, she looked over the papers for several minutes.

She finally folded her glasses and tossed them into a desk drawer. "Here's the Troutmans' offer, which seems doable." She passed the documents to me. "They might budge a little, but asking for too many concessions might scare them away. You know how old people are."

I nodded. Just like buyer's remorse, sellers sometimes had second thoughts: Was this the ideal time to list their house? Should they have held out for a higher price? Did they really want to move?

While I reviewed the offer, Lois boasted about how she had sold the Troutmans' family home the previous week. "They need a one-level home now because of Mr. Troutman's arthritis, so the Henricks' little house is perfect." She drummed her fingers on the desk, her acrylic nails clicking. "They'll want to remodel the kitchen, of course."

The Henricks' kitchen, with its knotty-pine cupboards, tiled backsplash and gingham curtains, far outshined mine. I hadn't considered it outdated but supposed it paled in comparison to Lois's. I heard she lived in a six-bedroom mansion in exclusive Windermere.

"Isn't it funny?" She glanced at her bejeweled fingers and diamond-studded Rolex. "People are either wanting a bigger home or downscaling. I'm glad they haven't figured out how to make the trade without us, or we'd be out of a job." She paused, her lips pressing flat. "I can't imagine moving into a smaller home even when the kids leave, can you?"

Not wanting to stir up the water, I shook my head in agreement, when in truth the longer I lived alone, the more sense it made.

Lois grabbed the edge of her desk and pulled her chair closer. "Say, that was great the way you took my open house, then sold it. I have so much going on right now, I can barely do my clients justice. Maybe we could go partners on some listings." She nudged one of several framed photographs occupying the corner of her desk closer to me. "Walt and I rarely get away on weekends anymore because I'm always so miserably busy."

"I wish I had your problems." I stared at the picture of Lois and her sun-tanned husband in a Hawaiian shirt posing before a tropical sunset. With Walt slaving away in an operating room removing appendixes and gallstones for several thousand dollars a whack, Lois certainly didn't need to work. She must like it.

"We could try working as a team, co-list a few houses and see how it goes," Lois said, her voice bright again. "You'd be doing me a favor."

"Really? That would be great."

"Fabulous." She shook my hand with a grip so firm it pinched my knuckles. "Let's go close this deal, partner."

I was glad I didn't have to face the Henricks alone. I sank into the cushy leather passenger seat of Lois's Mercedes and enjoyed being chauffeured by a woman who knew her way around town better than any cab driver.

Ten minutes after I followed her into Wayne and Sherry's living room, the couple had agreed to the lower price. Listening to Lois negotiate the deal, I felt as though I were attending the professional sales training class I should have taken years ago. My admiration for the woman grew, and I tried to memorize her polite but firm phrases for future use.

When signatures had dried, and it was time to take the paperwork back to the Troutmans, my stomach began twisting with worry. I dreaded what I called the falling dominos effect. If the Troutmans balked and changed their minds, Wayne and Sherry wouldn't sell their house and couldn't purchase a new one. The whole deal would be off, and all my labor would wash down the drain in a single splash.

"You're really amazing," I told Lois as we strolled out to her car under her Burberry plaid umbrella.

"You're not so bad yourself. I've heard you speaking to clients in the office. You sound very professional." She unlocked the doors with a remote, and we both got in.

"We'll complement each other," she said. She headed us back to the office by making a U-turn, cutting down a side street, then taking a shortcut that knocked several minutes off the trip. "You're more the stay-by-the-phone type, which drives me nuts. I like to be out blazing new trails, putting deals together."

"I guess you're right, I am more comfortable talking on the phone than speaking face-to-face." You see, for me it was easier to hear the word *no* through a piece of plastic. I would be happier manning the office or holding Lois's open houses, where people wandered in by themselves or were escorted by another agent.

Lois pulled up alongside my car. "Tootles," she said.

"Good night, and thanks again."

The moment I was out and had closed the car door, she spun away. Part of me disliked this type of woman: affected and condescending. But so what? Lois was exactly what I needed.

The next morning, as I ambled to the corner for my Moms' walk, dusty clouds lingered high in the sky. It was a welcome respite from the stormy weather that had plagued Seattle, making even the most die-hard Northwesterners cantankerous.

The last to arrive, Susan opened the back of her minivan and her Labrador retriever galumphed out. With much commotion, she fastened on its leash and headed our direction. Charlie marched forward to reacquaint himself with the boisterous dog, causing Susan to trot toward us to avoid being yanked off her feet.

"I just remembered why I usually leave this beast at home," she said, jerking on the leash without results.

After a few moments of sizing each other up, Charlie, in spite of his diminutive stature, claimed the right of top dog with a lift of his leg and a dig into the grass. This done, he lost interest in the Lab and allowed me and the others to start down the street toward the lake.

Erika walked on my left. "How's it going with Tim?" she asked. "You should bring him over for Jonathan and me to inspect."

I'd often appreciated Erika's dinner invitations. Not all married women encouraged single girlfriends to hang around. "Maybe we should wait a few weeks to see if Tim and I are still dating."

"Are you two going out together this weekend?" Susan piped in.

I felt embarrassed for no reason. "He called a couple of days ago to ask me out tomorrow night."

"Sounds serious," Erika said. I could remember her using those words every time I went out on a second or third date. Then again, maybe this time she was right.

"I'm just getting to know him," I said. "But he is nice. And he's cute."

"He's more than cute," Susan said, sounding peeved. Her dog tugged on the leash as a Russian wolfhound paced by, but Susan held her ground. "He's a gorgeous hunk. And he's never been married, so there's no nasty ex-wife lurking in the shadows." Of course I, myself, was an ex-wife, but I took no offense.

"Better grab this one, Marguerite," Erika said. "Sounds like a real catch."

"On the other hand, don't rush into anything," Laurie advised in a big-sisterly tone as she maneuvered her way between Erika and me. "I still picture you with someone extraordinary. A man of mystery."

"I've had enough uncertainty to last me a lifetime." I picked up the speed. "A boring old banker sounds pretty good right now."

"One more piece of advice." Susan's hand landed on my forearm to slow me down. "Remember, no man is perfect."

"You can say that again," Laurie said, and we all laughed.

Determined to get out of the spotlight, I asked Susan how her son Brandon was doing with his classes. For the next forty minutes, we shared stories and bragged about our college students.

I knew it was ridiculous, but I almost choked with loneliness each time I spoke Rob's name. How I missed him. Just any young man to the rest of the world, he would always be my boy, the one out of millions who filled me with delight.

15

$\mathcal{I}$ pulled my mail out of the slot next to the front door to find an invitation to Candy Hooper's opening night for her newest show of paintings. On the bottom of the postcard, Candy had written, "Marguerite, please come," in bold script. There was no way for me to squirm out of going.

One of Candy's abstract paintings adorned the front of the card. I rotated it several times trying to figure out which end was the top, but couldn't tell. She'd veered away from the traditional into a world of what looked to be unrecognizable garishly tinted shapes and blobs. But her large-scale paintings were attractive enough to end up in attorneys' offices and hotel lobbies. Nice enough to land her one-artist shows at the top galleries.

For the most part, she and I had gotten along like sisters. There had been only a few tense moments during our long friendship. The worst was in our freshman year of college when I set my eyes on Phil, with whom Candy had a non-reciprocal crush. In the end she agreed Phil and I were a better match and insisted girlfriends were more important than men. "I've prayed about it," Candy had said. "Now it's time to let it go." I often wished I had lost that battle and seen those two get hitched instead. But then I wouldn't have had Rob. I couldn't win.

As I brought the postcard and other pieces of mail into the kitchen, I remembered the time spent with her at our church high-school youth group, something we rarely spoke of anymore. Candy had quit asking me about my faith and about my painting years ago, but she still seemed interested in my work life and always asked about Rob. We got together every other month or so, usually at her invitation. She had a husband and three kids, but had barely skipped a beat in her career as an artist. Her home was often in disarray, with piles of unfolded laundry on the couch and dirty dishes in the sink that seemed to go unnoticed by the happy household. I usually insisted we meet somewhere else, away from the mess. Away from the painting.

When I promised at our last luncheon to attend Candy's opening, she'd mentioned she was experimenting with a new technique and wanted my opinion. What for? I had no clue what was hot in the art world anymore or what the public might fancy.

As I affixed the postcard to the refrigerator with a magnet, I decided I would pop into the gallery and cruise around the room at light speed. Then, blaming my departure on an early morning meeting, I would come right home.

∞

I'd forgotten how Pioneer Square percolated with activity on Thursday nights. I drove past the gallery and around the block twice looking for a parking space. I finally paid too much money to park at a crowded lot and walked several blocks. Inside the gallery intense lights bounced off high white walls and a frenzied jazz tape played in the background. I scanned the long room and saw only a few people gazing at the paintings.

Then I heard my name being called and saw Candy clapping across the room atop sandals with two-inch soles. She hugged me and kissed the air next to my cheek.

"You made it. I'm glad you're early," she said. Long-legged Candy looked as skinny as ever, and her midback-length hair lay parted down the middle exactly as it had twenty years ago. Only cobwebs of fine lines around her eyes divulged her age.

"Come tell me what you think of this new one before too many people come in. Then all I'll want is unrealistic praise."

She led me to the middle of the nearest wall and spun around so the tails of her tunic swung out. "It's quite different from the landscapes I've been doing. See, I added more texture and scrubbed some of the color out." She watched my eyes for a reaction.

"I like it," I said, stepping back a few feet to see the large painting more clearly. I wanted to give her a definitive opinion, but couldn't muster up a creative answer. "Very nice," I said. Wondering what the turquoise blue and chartreuse rectangular shapes represented, I read the title card on the wall. *Savage Land and Still Water.* Next to the title a red dot indicated it had been purchased. "Wow, sold already. How wonderful." I was always startled anyone could afford to spend five thousand dollars for a painting. "Who bought it?"

"Some woman came in this afternoon saying she didn't know much about art, but the colors matched her living room." Candy's sweet giggle reminded me of the girl I knew in high school.

Assessing her piece again, she chewed her thumbnail. "I'm pretty happy with the result."

"So am I." I wanted to give her positive feedback. "Beautiful colors." Which was true.

"I know it's not your cup of tea. You always stuck to realism."

"Yeah, realism in art, but unrealistic in every other part of my life."

She giggled again. Then her gaze darted across the room. "Don't look now, but your ex-husband just walked in."

I was afraid I might see him; this was his territory. "Thanks for the warning." Maybe if I was lucky, he wouldn't notice me.

"I'd better start circulating," Candy said. "I'll check back in a few minutes, okay?"

"Sure, go mingle. I'll look at your paintings."

A moment later I heard Phil say, "Hey, Margo." I looked over my shoulder to find him and Henry standing close by.

"Hello," I said, then glanced back at the painting as though I were enrapt with its magnificence.

"Hank and I were out for a bite to eat," Phil said, stepping between me and the painting. "I talked him into coming down to check out the Thursday night scene. Darla's meeting me here. Have you run into her?"

I put on a syrupy smile. "No, not yet."

Henry, at my side, asked, "What brings you here?" He sounded like a teacher addressing his student.

"The artist," I said. "Candy Hooper and I have been friends since high school. Her paintings are great, don't you think?"

He eyeballed the room, then moved closer and spoke in my ear. "Not a thing wrong with them, but I'll bet you could do as well, if not better."

Those were the last words I expected to hear. "I doubt that very much." I scrutinized the painting again. He might be right about Candy's work. Maybe she didn't produce masterpieces—the kind future generations would acclaim. But was he right about my potential? No way. Then it occurred to me he was reciting catch-phrases of encouragement, as he did with all his students.

I heard Phil say, "Hi, sugar," then noticed Darla slinking our way. She sidled up next to him and slipped her arm under his.

"Hi, sweetie." She snuggled against him like a cat marking its territory. Then she whispered something into his ear that caused a snuffle of laughter and a shake of his head.

Looking for an engagement ring, I tried to see her left hand, but it was tucked under Phil's arm and not visible. I said hello, but she didn't answer. I was sure she heard me, but decided to let it go. I had nothing to say to her and didn't feel like being the brunt of her snide remarks.

Dipping her chin, Darla gazed up at Henry. "Hello, there," she said. "We still need to get you together with you-know-who."

Henry gave her a strained look, one I couldn't decipher. "Hello, Darla."

When Phil introduced Candy to Darla, her glossy smile widened. "I'm delighted to meet you," she said, her voice gushing. "Your paintings are fantastic."

"Thank you," Candy said. "I can never hear that too often."

"I want to be just like Candy when I grow up," Phil said. His arm curved around Darla's petite waist, and he pulled her close. "Ms. Hooper's getting to be the big fish in the little pond around here. I hear she sells every canvas as soon as the paint's dry."

Candy beamed with pleasure as she discounted Phil's praise. "Phil, you're making my head swell." Then she and Darla fell together in rapid conversation, as if knowing Phil automatically made them old friends.

"I absolutely adore this one," Darla said of the painting nearest us. She blinked up at Phil. "Sweetie, don't you think I need something like this in the shop?" Darla turned to Candy to describe her boutique, located several blocks away.

"Darla's Choice is your store?" Candy's voice trembled as if she were asking the Queen of England if she really lived in Buckingham Palace. "I love that place. You have the most beautiful clothes in town. Tell me what days you work, and I'll be sure to come in when you're there."

I watched Darla in her body-hugging sweater and knit pants that draped her rear and legs seductively. No wonder Phil couldn't resist her. Yet when her left hand finally came into view, I could see she wasn't wearing a ring.

"I just got in a fabulous new line that would look stunning on you," Darla told Candy. "They're a little pricey, but you won't run into yourself every time you turn around."

"I'd love to see it," Candy said. "I'll come in tomorrow."

"Good, I'll look forward to seeing you. Maybe we can grab a cup of coffee too."

"Okay."

"Hank, old man." Phil's voice drowned out the women. "Darla needs me to help her move some display cases at the shop. I'd better run over there right now. Hey, Margo." He tapped my shoulder like a little kid trying to get his mother's attention. "Could you give this professor of yours a ride home? You two live pretty close to each other. You don't mind, do you?" He waited for my response, an expectant smile on his face.

"I guess I could," I said.

"Perfect. I'd better get this over with." He slid his arm back around Darla's waist and planted his hand on her hip. "Sugar, let's get out of here."

Darla suddenly gaped at me, as if discovering my presence for the first time. A look of disdain soured her face. She muttered several words under her breath, then turned away.

Phil saluted Henry. "See ya, buddy."

In less than a minute, Phil and Darla said their farewells and left me staring at the door.

I wandered to the next painting, which was so similar to the last that I had to glance back to make sure I'd moved.

My temples began to pound, drowning out the recorded trumpet that was galloping up and down the scales. Seeing Darla and Phil shouldn't hurt, but it did. I hated them both. I hoped Lois hadn't told Darla to include me in her quest for a condominium. I would rather starve than earn a commission from her. And now I was stuck driving Henry home. Normally I was pretty quick with a comeback, but what would I say to him in the car?

I inched around the gallery, which was filling with more people. I heard complimentary remarks about the show, people using words like *avant-garde* and *sophisticated*. The red dots, the words of praise, the respect Candy had earned: Everything rattled me.

From midway across the room, Henry strolled over and stood next to me. I traveled at a snail's speed, hoping he would get impatient and leave. But he stayed close by until I'd finished inspecting the last painting.

"What did you think?" he asked.

"I love her stuff." I wondered if he could tell I was stretching the truth. "Did you know we roomed together in college? I'm so proud of Candy." That was a fact. I admired my friend even if I didn't understand her art. As I read the painting's title my mind whizzed back to the figure drawing class she and I had taken together. I remembered glancing at Candy's work and seeing a drawing that looked like it had been executed by a child—stiff and out of proportion.

"Back then, I thought I had all the talent," I said. "But she never gave up, the way I did. Now look at her."

"Your life's not over yet. I saw real ability in the drawings you did in class. Have you been sketching?"

"I did one the other day I liked."

"Bring it to class on Monday, and we'll talk about it."

"Okay." He would probably forget all about this conversation by then, I thought. And why would it be a big deal? I told myself to relax as I reexamined the last painting. Henry may be my teacher, but that didn't make his opinion the final word.

"Look, about the ride," he said. "If it's too much of an inconvenience, I'll hop in a cab."

"No, it's all right, I don't have to be anywhere." I felt foolish for not being more cordial. "Phil said you live near me."

"Well, you know Phil and his imagination."

"Yes, I do." All too well, I thought. He made up the plot as he went along.

"He mentioned you live over by Green Lake, and I'm way up on Capitol Hill."

It would add fifteen minutes to my drive, but I said, "It's fine, I'm glad to help." It wasn't as if I was needed elsewhere.

Out on the sidewalk the evening breeze crept up the sleeves of my jacket. I rubbed my forearms, then shoved my hands in my pockets. Henry and I waited for the light to change, then crossed the street. Three people approaching from the other direction forced me to walk close to him. My arm bumped against his in an awkward way. I only wanted to get this chore over with.

I led him to my car and crawled into the passenger side to remove the clutter off the seat. "There you go," I said, tossing the last paper into the back. When I reached my own door, he'd already gotten in and unlocked it. The instant I started the engine, oldies music blared out of the radio speakers, making us both jump, then laugh. I switched off the radio as quickly as I could.

"Sorry," I said. No need for the heater. Warmth was radiating up my neck to my cheeks.

I headed east, passing under the freeway, then driving north on a quiet avenue. For several minutes neither of us spoke. I considered asking Henry questions about my drawings and whether he really thought I had talent. I figured now was the ideal opportunity, but I was too nervous. What if he didn't give me the answers I was seeking?

"You and Phil seem to get along pretty well," he said.

I slapped the turn indicator as I thought of all the times I wanted to strangle Phil. And tonight would be added to the long list.

"We've found a way to coexist, for our child's sake. When we fought, it only hurt Rob." I glanced over to see Henry looking at me.

"I've met Rob several times. A fine young man. And he's off at college?"

"Yes." My fingers began to throb, and I realized I was gripping the steering wheel. I loosened my hold. "The truth is, things haven't been going well for me since he left," I said with staggered words. "I've been bumping around aimlessly." Now, why had I told him that?

"I'm sorry."

I fiddled with a button on the dashboard. "I shouldn't have bothered you with this."

"It's all right, I've been there myself. There was a time when I didn't think I'd ever laugh again. Here, take a left at the light."

A hollow gap of silence followed. I glanced over to see his head pushed back against the headrest, his eyes closed.

He cleared his throat. "One day I was the happiest man alive. I had a loving wife and two beautiful daughters." His

words sliced the air like a blade. "The next day, I was sitting in an oncologist's office looking at my wife's
mammogram and biopsy results, talking about radiation
and chemotherapy."

I took the corner slowly, as if an injured person were on
board. No one in my immediate family or close circle of
friends had been diagnosed with breast cancer, for which I
was grateful. Of the three women I knew who'd had it—a
coworker, one of my mother's friends, and a neighbor—
only my neighbor was still living. A woman about my age,
she and I'd sometimes stopped to chat as we walked our
dogs or when she was out front gardening, and she'd
appeared to be in excellent health. Five years ago, I recalled,
I didn't see her for weeks. When she reappeared, she was
wearing a turbanlike hat, which I imagined was covering a
bald skull. "I have breast cancer. I found it myself," she'd
said proudly. "It was only the size of a pea under my
armpit, but it felt different. I could tell it didn't belong
there." Every time after, when I saw her and asked how she
felt, I wondered if her ticking bomb had spread to the rest
of her body.

Henry spoke again, snagging my thoughts back to the
present. "Six months later, my wife died, and I was a single
parent." He rubbed his eyes, then dragged one hand through
his hair. "At first, I was so consumed with the pain I couldn't
function. But I had to keep going. I had two young girls
depending on me." He pointed at the stop sign. "Take a
right."

He inhaled, holding his breath for several seconds before
expelling it. "I didn't pick up a paintbrush for over a year.
Slow down, it's that house with the porch light on."

My front tire scuffed the curb as I rolled to a stop. I left the engine running and set the transmission in park. I didn't know what to say. If we were good friends, I would have cried for him, consoled him, told him how much I ached for his unfair loss. But I hardly knew the man. And he'd given me the keep-away signal since we met. He might as well have been wearing barbed wire.

"Say, do you want to come in?" he asked, catching me off guard.

"I'd better let you get some sleep," I said, unable to see his shadowed face clearly. "It's pretty late."

He opened his door a few inches. "Please, I can't send you off into the night on that depressing note. Come on."

"Okay, just for a minute." I followed him up cement steps, then wooden ones, to a porch. He opened the door, then flicked on the inside lights with one sweep of his hand.

Slipping into the kitchen, he said, "Want something to drink? I'm going to make some herbal tea, but there's pop and apple cider too."

"No, thanks, I'm fine." For several minutes I surveyed the light-taupe walls and sleek, modern furniture in textured eggshell whites and beiges. On the walls hung a collection of paintings and drawings, none done by Henry's hand. Native American and Asian sculptures stood on pedestals and custom-built shelves. It was nothing like my home or any other I'd seen before.

I situated myself on an armchair. "Is it always this neat?" I said. It sure didn't look like the typical man's home.

He sputtered into laughter as he entered the room carrying a tray with two earthenware mugs and a rustic handmade teapot. "One person doesn't make much of a mess." He set the tray on the coffee table. "I made a full pot of tea in case you change your mind."

He relaxed onto the couch and stretched out one arm. He looked at ease, the master of his domain. "Sorry I got going on that morbid subject in the car," he said. "My point is that I did go on with my life. My two girls needed a sane, functioning father. For a while I drowned in my own self-pity. But eventually, in spite of myself, I began to experience small glimpses of joy. Finally, I started painting again. This time, though, I had something important to say."

He poured tea and handed me a mug. "Candy's work is pleasant enough, but when I look at a piece of art I want to learn something new—either about its creator or about life." He paused to sip his steamy drink. Then, looking into my eyes, he said, "You strike me as a person who has a story to share."

"Me? I've barely said two words to you since we've met."

"Sometimes those who speak the least have the most to say."

Despite his transparency while describing his wife's death, I had no intention of revealing my idiosyncrasies to him. I'd already said too much. I swigged a quick mouthful of tea, tasting a blend of orange and cinnamon.

"I'd better get home," I said, standing.

He got to his feet and made it to the door ahead of me. His hand resting on the doorknob, he turned to speak. "If you're free Saturday evening, come by my studio anytime after seven. I'm having a get-together. I mentioned it before class the other night, but I don't remember if you were there."

"I must not have been. But I can't come, I have a date that night." In truth, Tim and I had plans for Friday, not Saturday.

"You're both welcome."

I couldn't see Tim shooting the breeze with a bunch of artist types. I was glad he wasn't part of that frivolous world; that was one of the reasons I liked him.

"I'm not sure he's interested in art," I said. "He's a banker."

"Plenty of people will be there who aren't artists. I invited several gallery owners and those sorts, but I also know businessmen." The corners of his mouth quirked up as he opened the door. "A banker or two would round things out."

16

Tim arrived exactly on time. My attempts to switch our date to Saturday hadn't worked. "I'm going over to help my folks," he'd said on the phone earlier. "You're welcome to join us for dinner." I wasn't ready to meet his parents, although I felt flattered by the invitation. I couldn't remember the last time a man had welcomed me into his inner sanctum.

As Tim spread open the entertainment section of the paper, then recited the list of movies playing, my mind drifted. I'd slept restlessly the night before, shredded images of Henry burrowing through my mind. Losing his wife had devastated him. And his poor children must have been heartsick growing up without a mother. I'd envisioned

Henry helpless, watching the person he loved the most in the world slowly wither to nothing. Had he held her at the last moment? Did he still stretch out his hand in the middle of the night longing to feel her warm skin?

"Here's a good one," Tim said. "But we need to boogie to make it on time." He stood, tromping on Charlie's foot. The dog growled and moved out of his way. "Sorry, pooch. You're so little I didn't see you."

"He does get underfoot sometimes."

"You can teach him not to. My parents' beagle behaves perfectly. I'll get you the name of the obedience school."

"That's okay." I leaned down to pat Charlie's whiskered face. "He's too old to change his ways."

"No, it's never too late. You just have to be consistent with the discipline."

I couldn't help wondering if a man who'd never reared children knew what consistent discipline meant. Anyway, I liked Charlie the way he was. But I decided to play it safe and keep my thoughts to myself.

Twenty minutes later Tim sped us into the parking lot of the Oak Tree Cinemas. He circled around looking for a place where his car doors wouldn't get dinged and finally parked in a corner spot at the far end of the lot.

"You're going to love this show," he said, then hopped out and jogged around the car to open my door. "Let's hurry. We don't want to miss the previews."

The fast-paced action film was the kind I usually avoided. Even as I watched hair-raising car chases and hand-to-hand combat, I found my thoughts reverting to Henry. His melancholy face appeared in the flashing darkness. I asked myself why I'd fled his house so quickly. I should have stayed longer, taken time to examine each work of art. I could have explored the smooth stone surface of the greenish black carved bird displayed on a tall pedestal, and asked about the beaded moccasins sitting on a windowsill.

Well, I missed my chance. I would never go back there again. I gave my teacher a ride home, and he'd shared a personal story only to illustrate a point, to teach his fledgling student a lesson. It made no sense why I even cared.

Glancing at my watch several times only seemed to make the movie drag by more slowly. When the hero finally saved the world, Tim's arm wrapped around my shoulder. Minutes later, after the credits rolled, he suggested we go out for dessert.

"I'm pretty tired tonight," I said.

"Then we'll just get something to drink. It won't take long." He placed both hands on my waist as he followed me up the sloping aisle. "You're not getting away from me yet, pretty lady."

We walked hand in hand across the parking lot to a Starbucks. "Save us that table by the window, and I'll get something," he said, pulling out his billfold. Sitting where he'd suggested, I watched him hand the woman at the counter a twenty, then carefully count his change without leaving a tip. He returned with two vanilla lattes, even though I'd requested a plain one.

"You'll like this better," he said. "I've never met anyone who hasn't."

I tasted my latte, but found it too sweet, causing the inside of my mouth to pucker.

"Like it?" he asked, and I smiled back. Looking across the table at the dimple on his chin and his long eyelashes any woman would envy, I knew I should find him appealing. He was sweet and considerate, unlike some of the self-centered men I'd dated. And Tim apparently found me attractive judging from the way he was looking at me with hungry eyes. Between sips his hand reached across the table and lifted my fingers to his lips for a kiss, then a nibble.

Later, when we got to my front porch, I said, "Thank you, that was fun."

"This is more fun." He drew me into an embrace, his mouth covering mine. Again his lips felt cool and hard.

Why didn't I feel the flame of physical attraction? I wanted to enjoy the kiss, but felt numb inside. Maybe it wasn't him. Maybe there was something wrong with me. Was my resistance to him some psychological hang-up?

"I'm sorry I'm so tired tonight," I said. "I hope you don't mind if I say good night."

"I understand, pretty lady. This is only our third date. There's no need to rush things."

He gave me another extended kiss, then nuzzled my earlobe. "I want to see you again soon," he murmured. "I'm going to enjoy getting to know you better."

"Me, too." Then why was a tug-o-war battling inside mind? I gently extricated myself from his grasp and stepped inside.

17

"Don't you worry about a thing, I'll handle it," I heard Lois say to someone on the phone as I approached her desk the next morning.

Lois dropped the receiver in its cradle and grinned to herself. She finally noticed me. "Don't sneak up on me like that," she said. "But since you're here, that was Sherry Henrick on the phone. Things are sailing right along."

In spite of Lois's somewhat patronizing tone, I liked having her at the helm. Using phrases like "piece of cake" and "no problem," she sounded confident the sale of Wayne and Sherry's home would close soon. After we finished some paperwork, Lois and I discussed co-listing a small bungalow that would come on the market in a couple of months.

"I'm glad you're up for this," she said. "We'll see how this one comes together, then the sky's the limit. This is great. I need an assistant." She paused to regroup her thoughts, no doubt. "I don't mean you'll be my second-in-command." Her exuberance returned. "You'll be my partner on these transactions. It'll work out perfectly."

"I agree," I said, hoping with all my might she was right.

After Lois raced off to play nine holes of golf, my time at my desk crawled by. Henry's invitation nagged at me like an itchy mosquito bite that I swore I wouldn't scratch.

Of course I won't go, I told myself. But five minutes later, I found myself contemplating what I might wear if I changed my mind.

Around three, my phone line lit up. I picked up the receiver to hear Tim tell me how much he'd enjoyed spending the evening with "such an incredible lady."

"Have you changed your mind about coming over to my folks' for dinner?" he asked. He was still helping his father clean out the garage while they listened to the game on the radio, but when they finished I could drive over for some of his mother's fried chicken. The invitation sounded awfully dear. Another example of what a nice guy he was. But I wasn't ready to be scrutinized under a parental magnifying glass.

"My art teacher's throwing a party," I said. "I think I'd better put in an appearance."

"Then you'll have to come over another time. They really want to meet you."

"You told them about me?"

"Sure."

After I hung up, I called Laurie to ask if she was going to Henry Marsh's party.

"No can do," she said. "Dave and I are off to a black-tie fund-raising auction. I wish you were here to tell me if my favorite little dress still looks good after all the food I've been devouring the past few weeks."

"I could come over." I enjoyed looking through Laurie's wardrobe. She owned more clothes than any woman I knew, and the figure to show them off.

"That's sweet of you, but no. Spend the time getting yourself prettied up and go to the party."

"What if Phil and Darla are there?" Of course, they would be. My stomach clenched at the thought of seeing Darla. "I couldn't face them again without a date."

"Isn't he your ex? Don't let that guy have so much influence over you. Go."

If I didn't run into someone I knew from class, I could always leave, I promised myself while driving to Henry's studio. Once more, I was obliged to park my car a block away. As I neared the studio on foot, I could hear music and voices. Recalling my last visit there, I froze for a moment. No, this would be different. And mingling was a great way to meet new clients.

I figured no one would hear my knocking. I pulled the front door open and a billow of warm air smelling of sweet-and-sour sauce and shrimp floated out. Ahead loomed a crowd of strangers. Nobody seemed to notice my entrance. Forgetting my pep talk, I felt small and alone—like an outsider who had no business being there. I backed out and slowly shut the door. Descending the first step, I saw Phil coming up the walkway.

"Hey, this is great," he said. "I've been wanting to talk to you. You're not leaving already, are you?" He wore a day's worth of stubble on his chin, giving him the carefree look of a man on vacation. He reached past me, opened the door wide, and made a gesture for me to enter.

There was little free space for us to wade in. Most of Henry's paintings were stacked out of the way to accommo- date the gathering of fifty or so people. An old wooden door set on two sawhorses served as a table and lay heaped with trays of hors d'oeuvres and drinks.

Phil, walking ahead of me, exchanged hellos with several people. Across the room I spied Henry, who stood chatting with several young women, among them Rhonda from class. Besides them, I recognized no one. My first impulse to leave had been a good one.

Phil slowed his pace to speak to me. "Margo, I'm wor- ried about Rob," he said, but he appeared too happy to be worried.

"A few days ago, he told me everything was going fine." That was a slight exaggeration. Rob rarely spoke in superla- tives, and our most recent conversation lasted two minutes. "He said he'd just taken a math exam. He could be worried about his grades."

"Maybe. But the guy seems mighty homesick."

I tried to recall Rob's tone of voice. "He didn't sound that way to me." My son had yet to tell me he missed me, or home.

"I think he's more Andrea-sick than anything. He misses that girl terribly." In other words, Rob opened up to Phil and not me.

"He'll find a new girlfriend," I said. "Eighteen is too young to be in a serious relationship."

A woman wearing black-rimmed glasses swooped by carrying a plate piled high with goodies. "I love your new work," she told Phil. "Give me a call or stop by the gallery so we can talk."

"Thanks, I'll do it." He turned back to me, but his attention seemed to be elsewhere. He was probably anticipating his honey's arrival.

"Where's Darla?" I asked.

"She had something to do tonight." He waved at a man just walking in. "Sorry, there's someone over there I need to talk to. I'll see you later."

He took off, leaving me standing alone. I searched for an opening in a conversation, but all the tight circles of people appeared impenetrable. Working my way between groups, I came to the food table. I selected two shrimp puffs and an egg roll and arranged them on a plate like a happy face. I clunked several ice cubes into a tall glass and filled it with diet Pepsi until the bubbles threatened to topple over the side. Hands full, I wandered to the window and stared at the darkening bay. After several minutes of forced appreciation, I allowed my eyes to casually find my host.

Henry now stood with his arm around the shoulder of a pretty blonde. Out of nowhere, a strange sadness engulfed me. The room was sweltering, and my forehead felt damp. I set down my plate of uneaten food and my glass, and wove my way toward the door and freedom.

"Marguerite, you made it." Henry appeared next to me. He'd caught me trying to vamoose without saying hello first. "How long have you been here?"

"Not long." It would be impolite for me to leave now. "This is quite a party. It's a little warm in here though."

"I was just coming to open the door." He pushed the door open, and a glorious burst of cool air gushed in. He helped remove my jacket and hung it in the closet. "Did you get something to eat?"

"Not yet."

He guided me back to the hors d'oeuvres. I stood at his side while he said "Good evening" and "How are you?" to several acquaintances.

The young blonde appeared, and without hesitation he kissed her lightly freckled cheek.

"See ya, Daddy," she said, then kissed him back.

"Marguerite, this is my daughter Terry." Terry's complexion was fairer than her father's, but I detected a strong similarity around the expressive eyes and the bridge of her regal nose. I shook her hand and said, "Nice to meet you."

Rhonda strode over, her hips swinging. "And you know Rhonda, from class," he said, putting his other arm around her shoulder.

Rhonda looked even more attractive than she did on class nights. Her emerald green dress, cut low enough to reveal a hint of cleavage, mirrored her vivacious eyes. And she looked awfully alluring when directing her gaze in Henry's direction.

"Rhonda's Terry's best friend," he said. "She's practically another daughter." He mussed her strawberry blonde hair, and she stepped out of his reach and patted it back in place.

Moments later, after the two young women had departed, Henry said, "Marguerite, I'd like you to meet some good friends."

I shook hands with a stylish couple, the Tangs, who'd recently purchased one of Henry's pieces. They seemed to assume I was either an artist or a collector. Rather than describe me as his student, Henry simply gave my name and nothing more.

The Tangs started talking about celebrities and events in the art world I'd never heard of. When Henry joined in, he played the devil's advocate, asking if society should feed the arts while people were starving. This question sparked a round of lively debate. With my girlfriends, I never had to verbally tread water to keep from sinking like an uneducated rock. But it was fun to at least appear to be a part of this conversation. I nodded knowingly, as if fully aware of everything being discussed.

When the Tangs said they must get their babysitter home, they told me they hoped we would meet again. "I'd enjoy that," I said, although I knew it was unlikely.

The room thinned out, and the upbeat jazz changed to a leisurely saxophone solo, which sounded soothing and peaceful.

"Want to dance?" Phil said, and I noticed him swaying next to me.

I folded my arms across my chest like a coat of armor. "No, thank you, I don't."

"Come on, you used to love to dance. And you were always the prettiest girl on the floor." He moved closer, and I backed away, into Henry, who I didn't realize was standing on the other side of me.

"What's going on over here?" he asked.

"I was just reminiscing with Margo," Phil said. "She's still as pretty as she was twenty years ago. Hank, you should do a painting of her." He stared into my eyes with far too much familiarity. "Hank does portraits, when he finds a face he can't resist."

"I'm sure he has plenty of models to choose from," I said, shooting Phil the evil eye and wishing that for once it would drop him to his knees.

"I've already considered painting her," Henry said, sounding somewhat sincere.

Before I could respond, we were interrupted by a woman's deep vibrato. "Henry, my dear man, we haven't talked all evening." A tall, large-framed woman with shiny dark hair slicked back into a bun steered Henry toward a corner.

"That's Mrs. Mitchell R. Lamont," Phil told me. "Seattle's favorite patroness of the arts. She puts her husband's timber money to good use. I'd love to get to know her better myself."

I knew Phil wasn't the type to grovel at anyone's feet. "Once she sees your sculptures, she'll be calling you."

"Thanks. Say, I'm heading out. You staying?"

I glanced at Henry. Mrs. Lamont, her red lips fluttering only inches from his face, looked like a vampire ready to draw blood.

"No, I was about to go myself," I said. At that moment Henry glanced our way, and I waved at him. He made a move in our direction, but Mrs. Lamont latched onto his arm and kept talking.

Phil insisted on escorting me to my car. "I'll be fine," I said, heading briskly down the stairs to the sidewalk.

He caught up with me. "Come on, let me be a gentleman for once."

The sky was black, the street deserted. The smell of damp pavement blended with diesel exhaust and trace smoke from someone's chimney. Neither of us said another word. I listened to the scuffling sound of our shoes, heard a distant siren, a dog barking. When we reached my car, I unlocked the door, then turned to say good-bye.

Phil stood right behind me. "Good to see you, Margo," he said, bringing his face closer and gazing into my eyes. "I'm glad we can be friends."

Then, without warning, he hugged me.

18

After the party I went straight to bed, but I couldn't find rest. In my mind's eye, I could see Phil's face. No doubt about it, he'd grown better looking with age. Had his newfound success or his recent sobriety made him more attractive? Or was it the fact that a knockout like Darla found him delectable? I hated to think I'd let her influence me.

My focus shifted to Henry. In the stillness I remembered his saying he'd considered painting my portrait. Was he serious or just having fun with Phil, who loved a joke? Disappointment, followed by anger, jumbled through my head, causing a pinging in my ears. Phil and Henry were kidding me—and it wasn't funny.

At noon the next day, Tim called to invite me to brunch. "I woke up hungry for a kiss," he said. "How about if I swing by in thirty minutes?"

I dressed in jeans and a striped knit top, then searched the hall closet for my black jacket, without success. I glanced out the window and saw Tim's BMW cruising to a stop in front of the house. Charlie growled, then barked. Deciding I couldn't deal with the dog today, I grabbed a sweater and hustled outside.

Tim was opening his car door when he noticed me. I hopped into the passenger seat.

"You look nice, as always," he said, then gave me a quick kiss. "Is there a good place to eat near here?"

"Several."

We chose a casual restaurant located one block from Green Lake and only a few minutes' drive from my house. An hour later, as I nibbled the remains of my coffee cake, I felt Tim's leg resting against mine under the table. I watched him swallow the last bite of his omelet, leaving his plate spotless.

He asked for the bill—and I've got to say it was nice dating a man who didn't expect me to foot half of it—then he suggested we walk around the lake. "I'd better work off those calories." He patted his tummy. "All I've done is eat all weekend, and tomorrow it's back to my size thirty-four slacks."

I agreed I could use the exercise too. My parents were expecting me for an early dinner later and I needed to show up with an appetite.

He grasped my hand as we made our way toward the water and stepped onto the busy path. I'd say there were twice as many people at the lake's perimeter than on weekday mornings. When my girlfriends and I walked, we prided ourselves on making the loop in fifty minutes or less. But Tim strolled leisurely, even stopping a few times as he explained a transaction at work that might further his career. I took a deep breath and tried to follow his lead.

Almost around the lake a woman from work jogged by, gave Tim the once-over, and called hello to me. Knowing how people loved to gossip, I figured the whole office would soon know I was dating someone cute, which pleased me. I imagined Tim would look smashing at the company party. It couldn't hurt to plan ahead.

When we got back to my house, we went into the kitchen for a glass of ice water. As I ran the tap, Tim came up behind me, his arms lassoing my waist.

I snapped off the water. "I thought you were thirsty."

"That can wait." His lips found mine. His kiss didn't seem as foreign anymore. Not what I would have wished for, certainly not like I'd seen at the movies, but not bad. I tried to relax and return his affection.

The telephone rang, but Tim trapped me against the counter and said, "Leave it. You're busy."

"But it might be Rob." I wriggled free and reached for the receiver. "Hello."

"Marguerite? It's Henry Marsh. You left your jacket last night. Luckily a receipt in the pocket had your name on it."

Of course, I thought, that's where it was. "Shall I come by the studio to get it?"

"No, I brought it home with me. You could stop by my house. I'm not planning to go anywhere today."

"All right, thanks." I stood for a moment after the line went dead, wishing I'd asked him to lay it outside his door.

"Now, where were we?" Tim asked. He snaked his arms around my waist, then kissed me. But his lips had lost any potential magic, and his hands felt groping.

I gave him a little shove and glanced at my watch. "I hate to kick you out, but I'm having dinner at my parents' tonight and need to run an errand first." I contemplated taking Tim along. He was the kind of guy Dad would like: a businessman and a sports enthusiast. And Mom would like his outgoing personality. Tim used excellent table manners and was well spoken, but I couldn't bring myself to ask him to dinner. It was too soon—or something.

"Sorry, I'd better get going." Tim offered to come with me, but I said family matters needed to be discussed. Although I almost dreaded another tête-à-tête with my mother, I wanted to be available for her, as she'd always been for me.

With a forlorn expression on his face, Tim said, "You and I need to spend more time together, pretty lady. I can come back later, when you get home."

As I neared Henry's house, I eased up on the accelerator.

I didn't really need my jacket today, even if it was one of my favorites. I should have asked him to bring it to class. But I was already here, and retrieving it would take only a couple of minutes. I mounted the stairs and tried the bell twice. Finally, Henry opened the door. His mussed hair and sleepy eyes told me he'd been napping.

"Hello, come in," he said through a yawn.

"I apologize if I woke you."

"That's okay. I needed to get up anyway. I don't want to sleep the whole afternoon away." He smoothed back his hair and stretched. "Your jacket's around here someplace. Have a seat." He yawned again. "You want something to drink?"

"No, I'm in a hurry to get to my parents' for dinner." I scanned the room, but didn't see the jacket. "Mom's preparing her famous pot roast. She's an excellent cook, always makes enough to feed an army."

"Sounds delicious. Do you think there'd be enough to feed another hungry soul?"

"Uh, what do you mean?"

His words came out deliberately. "May I join you?"

"Go to my parents? Right now?" I must have heard him wrong.

"If you don't mind. My fridge is empty, and I'm starving. And it'll give us a chance to talk about your work. Unless of course, I'd be intruding."

I knew my parents wouldn't care, and I guessed I didn't. "All right." As soon as I uttered the words, I regretted them. What was I thinking?

He stepped into the kitchen and came back carrying my jacket. Ten minutes later we were turning onto my parents' street. This neighborhood, where I grew up, usually beckoned me in like a warm hearth. But not today. I almost kept driving as a wave of uncertainty made me ease up on the gas. I didn't have to go through with this, I told myself. Henry wasn't holding me hostage. And it wasn't against the law for a woman to change her mind.

But my parents' suppers were informal affairs, I reasoned as I stopped in front of their two-story home. And Mom had often suggested I bring a friend.

My mother wore a surprised smile when she opened the front door. I'd described Tim to her, so perhaps she was trying to understand her daughter's dubious portrayal. Henry, relaxed and confident, reached out his hand to shake hers and said, "I'm Henry Marsh."

With a quizzical look on her face, Mom said, "And I'm Dorothy Marsden."

"Henry's my art teacher," I said. "I should have called first. I hope it's okay that I brought him."

"Certainly, the more the merrier. Please, come in." Dad descended the stairs, and Mom said, "I'd like you to meet my husband, Vern." Dad shook Henry's hand, then invited him into the living room where a football game was concluding.

I set the table while Mom rinsed and dried the lettuce. The aroma of freshly baked biscuits and buttery mashed potatoes, which usually made my stomach groan with hunger, smelled flat. All appetite gone, I felt my forehead with the back of my hand. Maybe I was coming down with something.

"This is a nice treat," Mom said. She carried the salad, tossed in a wooden bowl, to the table. "Henry seems pleasant. Make sure you set enough places."

"As I said, he's my art teacher, nothing more. I stopped by his house to get the jacket I left at his party last night." I could see Mom's eyes widen. "It wasn't a date. He invited the whole class." She gave me one of her I-can-see-through-you expressions, but I kept rambling. "He said he didn't have any food in his house, and I felt sorry for him."

"Of course, dear."

During dinner my parents, oblivious to my embarrassment, shared several childhood anecdotes. I picked at my food while the others enjoyed seconds. My stomach had shrunk to the size of a walnut. If I spent much more time with Henry, I'd lose those extra pounds.

Mom drizzled gravy over Henry's potatoes. "Marguerite was such a talented child," she said. "We couldn't keep a crayon or paintbrush out of her hands. See that?" She pointed to my still life of peonies in an aqua-colored glass vase, which hung above the sideboard. "She did that her last year in college."

A queasy feeling passed through me as I watched Henry rise to inspect the acrylic painting more closely. When he sat down again, he agreed it was well done. "Very nice composition, and I like your use of colors. It reminds me of an early Manet."

What a generous compliment, I thought, or was it? I tried to remember the paintings Manet produced in the beginning of his career, but I could only recall his later works as an Impressionist. Was Henry trying to tell me I could have matured into a proficient artist if I'd kept working at it? Or was this praise to buoy up two parents?

Forty-five minutes later, my parents and Henry finished their blackberry pie a la mode, which I didn't even try. In the last two hours, he'd learned most of my history, at least what my parents knew, including the fact I sold real estate.

"Delicious dinner, Mom," I said, when the conversation lulled. I stood and pushed back my chair. "You want me to help you clean up before we leave?" I emphasized the word *leave*.

"Are you sure you don't want more coffee?" Mom asked. "I could brew another pot in a jiffy."

"Not tonight, Mother."

Henry patted his mouth with his napkin. "Thank you, Mrs. Marsden, for a meal I will long remember."

"You're welcome, and please call me Dorothy."

I carried a load of dishes to the kitchen sink while Henry got to his feet, then strolled to the front door with my parents.

"Glad to have met you, Henry," Dad said, giving his hand a shake.

"Come back anytime," Mom said.

I squeezed past them. "Thanks, Mom, see you, Dad," I called over my shoulder as I darted to my car.

On the drive back to Henry's place, I wanted to ask him if he really liked my painting. Not that I could paint another one like it now. A person can never go back in time. A child athlete wouldn't be able to score the winning goal at a soccer game or a dancer perform a pirouette after years of inactivity.

Instead, we chatted about my parents. Gracious and genuine was how he described them. "I hope I'll get to see them again sometime," he said.

Highly unlikely, I thought as I shoved my foot on the gas pedal. Yet the dinner was not a complete bust. It had been reassuring to see my parents getting along so well, just like old times. I supposed Mom's anger had been alleviated by a dozen yellow roses, Dad's usual offering after a tiff.

I pulled up to Henry's house. "Good night," I said.

He sat silently for a moment, then turned to me and slowly moved closer. As I watched his features blur, I realized he was going to kiss me. And I was going to let him.

Tim's face suddenly flashed through my mind like a wagging finger chastising me. Was I being unfaithful to him? He and I hadn't agreed to date each other exclusively, but was this wrong? Before I could answer myself, Henry's lips brushed mine. Then I felt my mouth melt into his. The kiss, lasting only a moment, left me limp. When it ended, I sat back to drink in its luxury. I couldn't believe he'd kissed me. And what a kiss.

He was still only inches away. "I shouldn't have done that." He expelled a hard, quick breath. "I'm sorry."

Before I could speak, he got out of the car and mumbled a hurried good-bye. I felt stunned, like a bird that had flown into a windowpane. Was that all he could say? That he shouldn't have kissed me? I watched him disappear up his stairs. Part of me wanted to follow him and rush into his arms, but I could only sit in dumb amazement.

19

As I entered my kitchen, the phone was ringing. No one called me this late. It must be Henry explaining his bizarre behavior. I'd rehashed the kiss over and over on the ride home. Never in my life had a man kissed me, then immediately apologized and practically run away as if his life were in danger. What was his problem? We were both single adults, even if I was Phil's ex-wife. Did Henry have an aversion to divorced women? If so, why had he kissed me?

I answered the phone and heard Tim say, "How about if I come over? I could be there in fifteen minutes."

"I'm about to go to bed," I said. "It's been an exhausting evening."

"Poor baby. Why don't you let Dr. O'Brien come over and make you feel better? We got stopped in the middle of something special today, and you've been on my mind ever since."

I tried to decide whether I wanted to go out with Tim again. I had just kissed another man, and enjoyed it. I wasn't a two-timing type of woman who could juggle men like bean-bags. But I didn't trust my emotions. How many times had I thought I was making the right choice, only to discover I was living in a fantasy world?

I thought about Tim's good points and reminded myself the list stretched long. And he seemed genuine, uncompli-cated. With Tim what you saw is what you got.

"Not tonight," I said. "But we'll see each other again soon."

At one the next afternoon, Lois and I met for lunch at Azteca Restaurant. Feeling little interest in the Henricks' deal or any real-estate business, I sat as a foggy spectator while Lois's elastic mouth emphasized the words *closing* and *co-list*. I hadn't slept well the night before, and the three cups of cof-fee and two doughnuts I consumed during the office meeting had drained me.

Trying to impress me with her most recent sale, Lois heaped guacamole and sour cream on her taco salad, then dug in.

"You must have the metabolism of an eight-year-old," I said. I'd never heard her complain about her weight. The woman seemed to shine twenty-four hours a day. "How do you manage to stay so slim?" I asked.

"I drink more than I eat." She must have noticed confusion on my face, because she added, "Water. I chug at least eight glasses every day, and I walk on my treadmill in the morning while I watch the news."

"Your routine must work, because you look great."

"So my hubby tells me." She swallowed another mouthful. "Say, you could help me out. In thirty minutes I have an appointment to show Darla Bennett a condo, and it may cut my golf game short. Maybe you could fill in for me."

I dropped the tortilla chip I was about to plunge into the salsa on the edge of my plate. "Darla is my ex-husband's girlfriend." I felt like I'd just unloaded my top bureau drawer, where I hid my private effects, on the table, but she deserved an explanation.

"So? You've been single ever since we met. You must have gotten divorced ages ago."

I grabbed the chip again and dragged it through the chunky red sauce. "Real life's not like the movies, where everyone can be best friends after they break up."

Lois stared back without understanding. "Then wouldn't it be an outstanding revenge to earn a fat commission check from her?"

"No, I think I'd better keep out of it."

"Have it your way."

After she left to meet up with Darla, I stashed my half-eaten enchilada in a doggie bag and drove home. I made a stab at straightening the house, threw a load of laundry in the washing machine, even took Charlie for a walk around the block, then tumbled onto the couch for a quick nap.

The neighbor's leaf blower woke me up. I tried to move my head, but my neck felt locked in place, as though rigor mortis had set in. Swinging my feet around to the floor, I pushed my torso to a sitting position with my arms, which started my head pounding. I checked my watch and realized I'd slept two hours. Laurie would be around to pick me up in twenty minutes.

Feeling woozy, I splashed cold water on my face, then checked myself in the mirror. Nothing I tried alleviated the puffy half-moons under my eyes and the sleep creases on my cheek. My hair lay matted flat on one side, but fiddling with it made it look worse.

Laurie's horn tooted out front. I finished changing out of my work clothes into jeans and a turtleneck sweater.

"Tell me all about the party," she said as I piled into her car.

"Not much to tell. There were tons of people there, but the only one I recognized from class was Rhonda. Phil was there, but at least Darla wasn't hanging on his arm."

"What did you and Henry talk about?"

I glanced down at my loafers, and noticed I was wearing one black sock and one blue sock. "He was surrounded by admirers and rich patrons most of the time. We didn't talk much."

"That's strange. I'd swear he's been watching you in class."

"He probably thinks I'm a still life." I tried sounding nonchalant. I was tempted to divulge the dinner at my parents' house and the kiss, but I ran my tongue over the inside of my teeth to keep myself from jabbering. I wasn't ready to talk about it—whatever *it* was.

"Enough about me," I said, pivoting in my seat to read Laurie's reaction to my question. "How's your golf swing?"

Her face remained unchanged. "That's all over. I might even switch golf lesson days. That man means nothing to me." She took a hard left, forcing my shoulder against the car door.

"I'm glad to hear that," I said, not completely buying her explanation. Laurie often acted giddy, but she seemed different tonight. Her voice sounded tinny, and her speech scattered.

"You can quit worrying, okay? You're worse than my mother. I moved two thousand miles to get away from her meddling." She glanced at me as she slowed for a red light. "That guy still might come in handy. He's an investment counselor who could give me free advice. It's time I started my own stock portfolio." The light turned green, and she zoomed forward, almost grazing the pedestrian who was leaving the crosswalk. "Our broker acts like I don't even exist. If I answer the phone when he calls, he automatically asks for Dave without even saying hello to me first."

I watched her lips move as she muttered under her breath at the driver in front of us, a tiny woman whose head barely cleared the steering wheel. A moment later, Laurie passed the woman by crossing a double-yellow centerline.

I clung to the armrest. "There are lots of investment brokers out there. You should find someone else."

She sailed through the tail end of an amber light. "Thank you, Mother." When had she become such an aggressive driver?

Arriving at class, I spied Henry standing at the far side of the room talking to several students. In spite of my determination to remain indifferent toward him until I made sense of things, I found being in the same room with him maddening, yet delicious. I looked away and tried to concentrate on opening my sketchpad and checking my pencil tip.

Minutes later I watched him arrange fruit in a flattish wicker basket, then demonstrate a drawing technique, but I heard little of what he said. He really did have a beautiful face, its expressive lines carved out of experience, heartbreak, and intelligence. I wondered if he'd noticed me yet. When he glanced around the room, his gaze drifted by me without stopping.

I heard the movement of paper and realized everyone else was starting a drawing assignment.

"What did he want us to do?" I asked Laurie.

She tilted her head toward the arrangement. "We're supposed to use gradational shading to make the basket look solid."

I positioned my pencil on the page, but worked with only half my concentration on my drawing. The other half kept Henry in sight so I wouldn't be startled if he approached.

He never wandered over.

He left the room at the beginning of the break. Waiting for his return, I lingered by the coffee thermos and spoke to every person who poured a cup. When Henry did show up, he avoided looking at me.

By the end of class, it finally hit me. My esteemed professor was snubbing me again. This was worse than high school.

As the class broke up, and students started packing their materials, I dallied. While rearranging my pencils, I chatted with Emily until I saw Henry standing alone gathering up the basket.

Refusing to be treated like a nonentity, I boldly walked over wearing a phony expression of confidence. "Good evening," I said, forcing buoyancy into my voice.

His eyes looked worried, almost frightened. "I'd like to speak to you, but not here. May I call you at home?"

"Sure." A lemon rolled out of the basket and landed near my foot. I bent down to grab it, then dropped it back in. "Give me a ring."

When I returned to my desk, Laurie wiggled her eyebrows like Groucho Marx. "What were you two talking about?" she said.

I was so flustered I could barely get the words out. "I asked him which kind of eraser he recommends."

If only I could find something to erase all memory of him from my mind.

I'm too old for this, I told myself in the seclusion of my kitchen. Kicking off my shoes and tossing my purse on a chair, I wanted to scream. I refused to let Henry dictate my mood. I must be in the grasp of PMS or premenopausal craziness. Or maybe I was suffering from depression again. I hoped not. I couldn't face seeing a shrink—rehashing my divorce and how I messed up as a parent.

Telling myself I would be perfectly fine, I started up the stairs. But by the time I reached the bedroom, I felt myself slipping into a dark pit. Desperate to divert my thoughts, I spent extra time brushing and flossing my teeth. I considered getting them bleached. That might knock a few years off my looks. If I looked better, I would feel better.

I arranged my pillows, got into bed, opened my book, and pretended there was nowhere else I would rather be. I began the next chapter, entitled "Building Your Dream

House." The writer described the foundation blocks on which exciting new lives were erected: childhood dreams, the things one had always wanted to try but hadn't because of fear of failure. The author started from the basement up and suggested tools one needed to proceed, such as finding mentors and enrolling in appropriate education.

At around age thirteen, I thought, men became my foundation blocks. First, I was Daddy's good girl—the oldest child. Then I tried to be what Phil wanted. After the divorce, as a single woman, I was temporarily relieved of the burden of trying to please a man. But loneliness took hold of me and I started searching for another mate. In the dating scene, I'd molded myself to be whatever I deemed each new guy wanted, until I felt suffocated.

I slapped the book shut. It was time to find new bricks and mortar, and construct my world on something other than the opposite sex.

I glanced up to the cracking ceiling. God, I thought. Are you just another man who let me down?

Of course not, because he didn't even exist. Or did he? Closing my eyes and bowing my head, I whispered, "Okay, I'll give you one more chance to show yourself."

My eyes snapped open as the room echoed with emptiness.

20

*T*he doorbell chimed, and Charlie scrambled to the front hall. I noticed the clock read 7:00, exactly the time Tim said he would arrive. He'd phoned me once a day for almost a week asking to see me. Feeling drained of all stamina, as though I were coming down with a virus that never materialized, I'd put him off. All I'd craved was solitude.

Henry hadn't called, and I'd convinced myself I didn't care. I could kick myself for wasting one moment thinking about him. How dim-witted it would be to get involved with another deadbeat artist when someone as nice as Tim liked me.

"I'm coming," I called, then swept the door open and flashed Tim a smile. Wearing a sports jacket and slacks, he stood for a moment eyeing me as though we barely knew each other. I could see I'd hurt his feelings. How could I have been so thoughtless?

"Come in," I said, reaching out to take his arm. He stepped inside, but instead of kissing me, he said hello to Charlie, whose ears tipped back.

"It's good to see you," I said, and led Tim into the living room. He parked himself on the far end of the couch and crossed his arms. Scooting close enough so our knees almost met, I asked about his last few days. His stony features slowly relaxed, and one arm slid to the back of the couch as he described a recent bank transaction. But when he finally suggested we grab a bite to eat, he made no attempt to help me with my jacket or even open the door for me.

We headed to Ray's Boathouse Restaurant, and in thirty minutes sat at a table overlooking Shilshole Bay. Below us boats, their white hulls vivid, motored by in the jet-black water as they departed the Ballard Locks on their way into Puget Sound.

With my encouragement, Tim described in detail an important bank transaction with a wealthy Seattle family I knew by name and reputation. As we ate, I conjured up enough questions to supply him with two hours of explanations. By the time we finished our dinners and the check arrived, my eyelids were drooping. He quickly paid the bill so he could take "my sleepy lady home."

In his car he invited me to his condominium for a cup of coffee. "I've been wanting to show you my place. Then I'll run you right home, I promise."

"Okay." I'd wondered where he lived, but I hadn't wanted to give him the wrong idea by asking to see it.

We crossed town, then cruised over the expansive floating bridge to the East Side. I watched the lights of Kirkland and Bellevue grow brighter and soon saw waterfront homes taking shape. Tim said something, and I glanced over at him. The greenish white beams from the towering lights lining the bridge cast ghostly shadows across his face. He suddenly looked like a stranger.

I clamped my eyes shut for a moment. Now was no time to turn back, I told myself. He'd be furious and never ask me out again. I wouldn't blame him. We rolled down the exit ramp, then traveled north along the banks of Lake Washington. He deposited the car in his reserved spot, and we rode the elevator up to the third floor.

"Welcome to my hideaway," he said in a Dracula-like voice. He led me through the spacious living room to the deck, which stretched out over the water. In one corner of the deck stood two chairs and a table with an umbrella. A potted Boston fern in need of a thorough soaking and a dose of fertilizer hunkered in the other corner.

Listening to the rhythmic waves lapping below us, I rested my elbows on the railing and inflated my lungs with moist air. Tim stood behind me, his cheek resting against mine.

"Do you like it?" he asked.

"Yes, it's beautiful. You must come out here a lot."

"Not really, I'm not home much. I'd spend more time here if I had someone like you to keep me company."

From behind he enveloped me in his arms. I shivered from the chilly breeze seeping through my jacket, and he tightened his hold. Hoping to move indoors, I turned around to find his eager lips waiting for a kiss. I shuddered again, and he rubbed my back.

"Let's get you warmed up," he said and reached for my hand. We moved inside; I sank down on the couch as he went into the kitchen. He returned carrying two brandy snifters and a crystal decanter containing tea-colored liquid, then sat next to me.

"May I?" he asked, removing the decanter's stopper.

"None for me." I wondered what had happened to his offer of coffee.

He filled his glass, took a sip, then licked his upper lip. Then, sliding his arms around me, he pushed my weight back into the couch's thick cushions. He kissed me, and I tried to share his affection in a way that would replicate the moment I'd shared with Henry. Those lips had rendered me helpless, but with Tim I felt like a wooden doll.

He pulled back a few inches. "You and I belong together," he said in my ear. "You're different from the other women I've met. Beautiful but also intelligent and independent." I could hear his breath becoming staggered. "You could stay here tonight," he said, his hand moving to my hip.

I stopped him from exploring further. "I think I'd better go," I said.

"All right, pretty lady." He wrapped a strand of my hair around his finger. "If you're not ready, I'll respect that."

Staring into the nubbly carpet, I searched for a witty answer to placate his hunger, but found none.

"We'll do it your way," he said with a sigh. "Good things are worth waiting for." He massaged the back of my neck, then my shoulder. "But first I want to show you the rest of

191

my abode." He guided me through to the kitchen, then his bedroom. With its brocade quilt, accent pillows, and matching Roman shades, it looked as though a decorator had picked out every item in one fell swoop, giving the rooms a sterile feel.

"Someday you could watch the sunset from my waterbed," he said, then gave the bed a push, sending an undulating wave across its surface.

I didn't enter beyond a step or two.

At eleven thirty, we said our final good nights at my front door. When he left, I wandered into my kitchen to check for phone messages.

"This is Henry Marsh," I heard. "It's seven o'clock. I'll call back tomorrow."

As I listened to my morning coffee spatter in the coffee-maker, I contemplated not walking with the Mom's Brigade. I might just stay at home, but what would I do? Wait for Henry's call? No, I refused to sit by the phone like a high-school sophomore hoping the senior jock would ask her to the prom.

I found my walking shoes, snapped on Charlie's leash, and headed out the door. The silver clouds looked tissue-paper thin and would probably burn off into a sunny afternoon, but a cool wind tickled my face, making my ears tingle. I spotted Laurie at the corner wearing a fleece jacket I hadn't seen since last winter.

"It's freezing out here," she said, and rubbed her hands together. "I hope those other two get here soon so we can get moving."

At that moment Erika, her hair tucked under a knit cap, rounded the corner. Five minutes later Susan drove up in her minivan and jumped out, panting. "I'm sorry, but the telephone rang as I was going out the door." The others rolled their eyes.

It was too chilly for dawdling; I noticed the group was moving faster than our summer speed. Even Charlie acted friskier, standing on his back feet and straining at the leash.

"I can't believe how fat I'm getting," Susan said once she'd regained her breath. "That's one reason I was late. I couldn't find anything to wear. I was five pounds lighter when I weighed myself last week. Where did it come from?"

With the greatest diplomacy, and without mentioning that Susan's sweatpants had been fitting snugly for months, we each recounted our various diets and exercise routines.

"I tried that already, and it didn't work for me," was Susan's answer to every suggestion.

"Hey, everyone, did I tell you about our trip to Kauai in December?" Erika asked, slowing down and giving her hips a hula swish. "Picture me and Jonathan strolling barefoot on the beach after a day of snorkeling. Doesn't that sound perfect?"

"Don't get near me when you come home," Susan shot back with a laugh. "I avoid suntanned people all winter."

"Hey, I deserve it."

"Dave's been promising me a vacation for a year," Laurie said, sounding like a pouting child about to throw a tantrum. "But I've given up. Unless work's involved, he's not interested."

"He's a hardworking man," I said. I remembered our discussion about Christian men at Barnes and Noble and added, "There are worse things. He could get his nose pierced and dye his hair orange."

"Not Dave," she said. "He's too uptight. He wears the exact same thing every day. Boring."

I was growing weary of Laurie's bellyaching. "Boring beats unpredictable or reckless."

"I agree," Erika said.

"Ooh. Look at that guy," Laurie said, as a lanky runner sprinted by.

I glared at her and arched an eyebrow.

"I'm only looking," she said.

⚭

The phone was ringing as I opened my door. Charging in, my limbs seemed to move in slow motion. I nabbed the receiver and brought it to my ear. "Hello?"

"Marguerite?" I recognized Henry's voice.

My tongue felt too large for my mouth, but I managed to say, "Henry, how's it going?" in an offhand manner.

"The truth is, not well." His voice sounded mechanical, like a computer-generated message. "I've acted very badly. Please, forgive me."

"For what?"

"Teachers should never get involved with their students on a personal level. This is the first time I've crossed that line."

"I'm hardly a schoolgirl." I didn't know whether I was annoyed or hurt.

"I realize that, and some might find me old-fashioned, but I believe it's for the best."

"You didn't come on to me. I invited you to my parents' house."

"As I recall, I invited myself."

"I didn't mind." I remembered how happy I'd been when he admired my painting. "And my parents liked you."

"I liked them, too. Very much. The problem's not with you." He paused long enough for me to wonder if we'd been disconnected. Then he said, "Truth is, I'm choosing not to date anyone."

Not dating anyone, or not dating me? "Don't worry, it was no big deal," I said. "If you like, we can pretend the whole thing never happened." Although I couldn't imagine how I would accomplish that feat.

"Thank you." He sounded more at ease. "I would like to talk to you about your work sometime. How long since you last painted?"

With an affected laugh I said, "I can't remember," which wasn't true. I could well recall my final unfinished painting, a self-portrait. I'd depicted myself sitting in the window seat of the apartment Phil and I shared. I wore a peasant blouse, its soft neckline shirred by a ribbon that tied in the front. My long hair, which hung almost to my waist, had been braided on top of my head and was intertwined with daisies. With most of the larger areas of the painting finished, I'd one day lost interest and never completed it. I'd left the work sitting on my easel for several months. Then, to make room for a new piece of furniture—was it the bassinet?—I folded up the easel and stuck the painting behind the couch. When I moved, I took my art materials and canvases to my parents' house, so the painting could still be stored somewhere in their basement.

"I encourage you to start again," Henry said. When I didn't answer, he added, "Maybe I can help. Why not stop by my studio so we can discuss it further. I assure you, I'll be a perfect gentleman."

I wondered what his idea of gentlemanly behavior was. I had a rough time believing he'd act any differently than he had in the past, which was positively rude. And as for my painting, how could I trust a man like him to be straight with me?

22

I "I'm glad you're here," Lois said as I approached her desk. She opened the desk drawer a few inches, dropped in a nail file, then closed the drawer with her knee, checking afterward to make sure she hadn't snagged her panty hose. "Not to worry, but there's a glitch in the Henrick deal."

My left eye twitched when I heard the word *glitch*. "What's happened?"

"Old Mr. Troutman fell yesterday and broke a hip. It may be serious."

I hate to confess this, but the first person I thought of was myself. My clients, my sale, my commission. But then

I envisioned an older man stumbling off a curb and not getting up again. "The poor man."

"Now his wife's contemplating moving into a retirement center instead of another house."

"A broken hip can be disastrous at his age." I thought of my own parents: Mom balancing atop a step stool to change a light bulb, and Dad wandering about the house reading his paper, not watching where he's going. If either fractured a bone, even twisted an ankle, who would care for them? Mom was used to catering to Dad, but she wouldn't be strong enough to lift him, let alone get him to the bathroom. And Dad? He would have no clue about how to take care of Mom. He could flip burgers on the gas barbecue on the Fourth of July, but I wasn't sure he even knew how to scramble an egg.

Lois lay one hand on her desk and glanced down at her plum-colored nails. "Oh well, in our business, if it's not one thing, it's another, right?"

I didn't know how she could act so jolly. Even Lois Grimbaldi couldn't mend a broken hip in time to complete the deal by closing.

"I'm running over to the hospital right now to check it out," Lois said. She pushed her chair away from her desk and stood. "If Mr. Basetti calls, would you talk to him? We've been playing telephone tag for days."

When she returned several hours later, I'd given Mr. Basetti the price and other details on a home his wife had driven by. No sweat. With him, I had nothing to lose, so I didn't get rattled.

"Great," Lois said. "We can work on this together if you like."

"All right."

She noticed my serious expression. "It's still too early to assess Jim Troutman's condition. What a trooper. He was in good spirits, so let's keep our fingers crossed." She wrapped her middle finger around her index finger, then gave her hand a small shake. "It'll all work out somehow."

When I got home, I found a message from Phil waiting for me. "Give me a jingle, okay?" I phoned him back, and Darla answered in her purring voice.

"Hi, this is Marguerite."

Silence.

"I'm returning Phil's call."

"Just a moment, I'll get him," she said with hostility.

I waited several minutes for Phil to come to the phone, making me wonder if she'd even told him I was on the line.

He finally picked up the receiver. "Have you talked to Rob yet?" he said. "I can tell there's something wrong, but I can't pry it out of him."

Clamping the phone against my ear with my raised shoulder, I began sorting through the mail while I listened. I ripped open my gas bill, which I imagined would soon sky-rocket now that the weather was cooling. I couldn't bring myself to think about Rob struggling with his classes, or about his following in his father's footsteps. Phil came close to graduating, but dropped out during his senior year. I remembered his lame-brained dispute with a professor. The man was trying to encourage Phil to produce some decent work, no doubt, but Phil had been too pigheaded to accept his help. He'd snatched up his canvases, huffed out of class, and never returned.

Following Lois's strategy, I told Phil it would "all work out." It had to.

After checking in at the office the next day, I stopped by my parents' house. Mom, dust rag in hand, came to the door wearing an unflattering tan-colored blouse and a beige skirt. Looking into her pale face, I noticed she wasn't wearing makeup. I still considered my mother to be a beautiful woman, but I'd never seen her look more dowdy.

"You and I should go shopping together and buy you some new clothes," I said.

"I've already got a closet full of things I never wear."

"Then keep me company. We could have lunch afterward, like we did when I was a girl." I would take her by the cosmetic counter too. "Where's Dad?"

"Out somewhere."

My hand reached for the banister, and I took the first step up the staircase. "I'm going to run upstairs and weed out some of my old books." My father had asked Nicole and me to empty the floor-to-ceiling bookcase in our old room so he could store his ever-expanding collection of *National Geographic* magazines there.

"That should make Dad happy," I added. When Mom didn't answer, I turned to see her shuffling into the living room. She'd always been on my case to stand up straight, but her shoulders rounded like an old lady's. She was even developing a hump on the back of her neck.

I continued to the second floor and headed into the bedroom Nicole and I had shared as kids. The same ruffled bedspreads and frilly pillows still covered our twin beds.

Mom said she used our room for guests, although she and Dad never seemed to have overnight visitors.

The bookcase stood jam-packed. Listening to the vacuum cleaner whirring in the living room below, I scanned the titles: *Rebecca, Wuthering Heights, Emma.* I remembered in high school and college practically inhaling those stories as the words transported me to a different time and place. But it was unlikely I would read them again. I could imagine Nicole and her fifteen-year-old daughter sorting through the books, and decided to let those two take what they wanted. Then I might donate the rest to a charitable organization.

On the bottom shelf lay my high-school annuals. I folded my legs and sat on the Chinese hook rug, a backdrop for many childhood games, and spent several minutes browsing through my senior yearbook, something I hadn't done for decades. I glanced at my photo and was glad to see I wasn't the only girl with a less-than-perfect complexion or a hairdo once known as dorky. I turned the page and noticed that next to her photo a girl named Carol had written, *You're the best artist in the school. I'm jealous.* A few pages further a boy with long sideburns had written, *Remember me when you're famous. Okay?* I hadn't seen either of those people since the ten-year class reunion. On that evening, both had asked about my career in the arts, and they'd seemed disappointed to learn I was just a mom and a realtor. "I love real estate," I'd said, handing them each a card. Then I'd escaped to the other side of the room.

I'd elected to skip the twenty-year reunion. I told myself the only person I cared to see was Candy, whom I got together with often enough. I'd dated a few guys in high school, but nothing serious. When I met Phil I was grateful I'd saved myself for the one true love of my life. What a laugh, I thought, slapping the album shut and shoving it back into the bookcase. I didn't feel like carting the yearbooks home, that was for sure. Where would I store them? Anyway, I wanted to forget the past and only think about the future. I considered discarding them in my parents' garbage can, but I couldn't bring myself to do it, just like I clung on to everything. Maybe if I ignored them long enough, Dad would get fed up and toss them out for me.

The vacuum cleaner noise came to a halt. As I descended to the first floor, I heard Mom open the kitchen door, then walk outside onto the back porch. Quietly, I continued down to the basement. In the back of the storage closet, jammed in with Dad's old hip waders and other fishing gear, I found the familiar wooden box. My fingertips stroked the dusty surface, once lacquered and smooth, now scarred from years of use. I remembered standing by the ocean in fragrant salty air and listening to the steady roaring and crashing of the surf, my paint box spread open like an unfurling flower.

I unlatched the metal hook. Partially used tubes of acrylic paints and half a dozen weathered brushes lay inside, as if frozen in time. Both hands exploring, I gave several tubes a gentle squeeze. Some felt rock hard, but most were still pliable. As I closed the lid, I noticed a smallish, unused eighteen-by-twenty-four-inch canvas on the bottom shelf.

Hoping to take the box and canvas to my car unnoticed, I mounted the stairs with them in my arms. In the kitchen I found Mom removing two cups from the shelf. I felt shy, like a child caught playing with dolls after she is too old for such games.

"I'm taking some of my old garbage out of the basement," I said, trying to carry my booty inconspicuously.

"Great. But don't run off." She insisted I sit down for a cup of tea, which was steeping in a pot on the kitchen table. "We certainly enjoyed your friend the other night," she said, pouring the mahogany-colored liquid into our cups. The smell of lavender hung above the table, a sure sign she'd prepared Earl Grey.

"He's just my drawing teacher. I told you that. A friend of Phil's." I gulped my tea too quickly, burning the tip of my tongue. "I am dating a man named Tim. I'll have to bring him over."

"That would be fine, Marguerite. But do invite Henry back."

"I don't think that's going to happen." I could guarantee it. "On another subject, I'm glad to see you're doing better now. I guess all your worries about Dad were for nothing."

She raised her cup to her lips and blew across the brim. "We haven't spoken about it."

"Maybe that's for the best."

She returned her cup to the saucer without drinking. Her lips pursed, whitening from the pressure.

"Everything is on an even keel again, isn't it?" I said.

"Not exactly. I told your father I'd leave him if he ever sees Alice again." Her eyes were melting behind a film of moisture, but she blinked the tears away. "I should have put my foot down years ago, but I was afraid of being left alone." Her head fell into her hands; her shoulders began to tremble. "Last night he confessed everything, how for years he snuck off to see her, and even brought her to dental conferences with him." She pulled herself erect. "I told him to go ahead and marry the woman if he liked her so much. 'I won't stand in your way,' I said."

I tried to envision Dad kissing another woman, and my stomach twisted with revulsion, as if I'd tripped over decomposing garbage.

Mom let out a sob, then blotted her eyes with a paper napkin. "I'm sorry."

"Mother, you have nothing to be sorry for." I reached over and grasped her hand. "But don't rush off and do anything you might regret later." At least Dad didn't drink, and he provided for the family. "Sometimes I think I would have been better off if I'd stuck it out with Phil. Besides, what would Jesus say?" It felt ludicrous bringing up his name, but I was desperate.

"You're right, honey." She sounded like a wounded animal with its leg caught in a snare. "Forgiveness is what the Lord is all about. But I don't know if I'm strong enough to do that, or if your father even wants it."

On the way home I lowered my car window and listened to an oldies station playing artists like Diana Ross and The Supremes, Stevie Wonder, and Tina Turner. As I sang along, the brisk air lifting my hair off my scalp helped clear my mind. I didn't want to think about my parents or work or Rob.

I carried my paint supplies into the kitchen. Setting the box on the table, I held the canvas at arm's length. I'd probably assembled it myself by stretching linen across a wooden frame, then preparing it with white gesso. I tapped the canvas's surface, and it resounded like a far-off drum, vibrating in my chest.

I headed into the living room and hauled the stack of magazines out from under the coffee table. Leafing through them page by page, I saw photographs of supermodels and landscapes, remodeled bathrooms and cheese soufflés. Nothing I wanted to paint. Just as I was about to give up, I noticed a photo of a woman with a toddler in her lap. The boy, his inquisitive eyes gazing up at his mother, reminded me of Rob at that age. Ripping the photo out of the magazine, I took it into the kitchen. In pencil I sketched a likeness onto the canvas. I opened the paint box, chose a brush, and tested the bristles, which were stiff but still pliable. I picked up one tube of paint and read the name cobalt blue. It didn't sound familiar, and I tried to remember if I had liked the color or if it was left over because I didn't like it. Unscrewing the cap, I squeezed an inch-long snake onto a plastic dish and was pleased with the blue's brilliance. Then I did the same with other colors: phthalo green, cadmium yellow, alizarine crimson, and raw umber. I filled a jar with water and dipped the brush in to moisten it.

Four hours later I stepped back and looked at my creation. Where had this painting come from? I was surprised to find tears filling my eyes. Why was I crying? Nothing in life made sense anymore.

With great care I signed my first name at the bottom in deep amethyst. In college I'd used my last name, but that didn't seem right now.

Viewing the work from another angle, I saw areas needing more definition. With a parent's tender care, I worked briefly on the child's face and arms. I wondered about the skin tone and whether the pattern on his shirt was legible. Finally, I accepted the colors and left the brushstrokes visible and loose.

I placed my plate of colors in the sink, where the tap water carried them in ribbons down the drain. Before allowing myself to inspect my work again, I also scrubbed my brush. Imagine using one old brush and such a small palette of colors, I thought. Back in school I would be cleaning a half-dozen paintbrushes and re-screwing the caps on twice as many tubes.

The cleanup complete, I stood on the other side of the kitchen and let my eyes rest on my piece.

"Dear God, it's actually good."

My shoulders felt taut, and the small of my back ached. Stretching my arms, I glanced out the window. The sun, now low in the sky, flooded the room with coral-colored light. The afternoon had flown by like a pebble snapped from a slingshot.

I felt restless; I didn't want to be alone. Finishing a painting was like scaling Mount Everest; I was filled with a desire to share my news. My first thought was to tell Mom, but I didn't want to be drawn into her sadness—not now. I would wait, talk to her later when I could listen patiently.

I called Tim at work, and his secretary put me through to him. We chatted for a few minutes before I said, "I've been painting most of the afternoon."

"That's a man's job. Wouldn't it be better to hire a professional?"

I realized he thought I'd been working on the interior of my house. "Not the living room, a painting-painting," I said.

"Oh." I could hear a clicking sound that must be his fingers working a computer keyboard. "I could come by after work to see it," he offered.

Judging from his tone of voice, I wasn't sure he understood what I meant. Unless he was an artist, himself, how could he? "My painting's not ready for viewing yet," I said, suddenly protective of my new creation. Then I said a hurried good-bye and hung up.

I got into my car and drove off without any destination in mind, yet ended up approaching Henry's studio. From down the street, I could see him coming out the front door. By the time I reached the studio, he was walking around the hood of an old blue Ford pickup. I slowed, and he spotted me, giving me a wave. Rolling to a halt, I was tempted to fabricate an excuse for being there, but there was no reason in the world I would be in that neighborhood except to speak to him. I put down my window and said hello.

"What brings you by?" he asked.

"I was in the area. Just wanted to talk."

"I'm glad you came when you did, you almost missed me. I was headed out for a bite to eat."

"It can wait until Monday."

"No, if you're hungry, come join me. We can talk over dinner."

I realized I hadn't eaten since breakfast. But sitting across the table from him for a whole meal would be like Charlie sharing his food dish with the snooty Pekingese next door.

"It's a five-minute drive," he said, as if reading my thoughts. "You could follow me there, and then leave when you want."

A moment later I was trailing him up the hill. He put on his blinker, and at the red light he came to a stop. From my car I could see the back of his head high above the headrest and his eyes glancing at me in his rearview mirror. When the light changed green, I hesitated, wondering if I should turn the other direction and go home. But Henry was the logical person to talk to. Who else was there?

I pushed my foot on the gas pedal and caught up with him. Stop worrying, I told myself. Henry didn't date; he still loved his wife. He was a bit of an odd duck, but he seemed safe enough, the kind of man who would make a decent friend. Weren't friends what I needed most?

Minutes later he turned into the parking lot of a restaurant on South Lake Union, and I pulled up next to him. Soon we were seated at a table and receiving our dinner. We passed time in polite conversation, then discussed Leonardo da Vinci, his mathematical abilities, his love of music—how he could sing and improvise on the lyre.

"And I heard he loved animals," I said, recalling what I'd learned in an art history class. "He would buy birds from vendors, open the cage doors, and let them fly away."

"An amazing man." Henry said. "It's hard to imagine a person with more talents. Aren't we fortunate he loved painting the most?"

"Yes, indeed." As I finished the last bites of my salmon, I still hadn't mentioned my painting. Soon the waitress removed our plates and brought us coffee.

I finally blurted out, "I painted something today."

"Really." He looked like a parent hearing his child had aced a test. "That's marvelous. Tell me about it."

I avoided his gaze as I recounted my afternoon.

"It's crazy, but I barely remember painting it," I said, my eyes finally meeting his. "I got so involved, I felt transported, as if sucked into a time warp where nothing else mattered."

"Yes, I've had days like that where it felt like someone was painting through me. I was the vehicle, not the driver, off on someone else's joyride. The next thing I knew it was dark outside."

"And afterward, I cried," I said, then wished I'd omitted that detail. "Isn't that weird?"

"No, not really. For me, painting opens a floodgate of emotion."

The waitress delivered our check. Henry took it from her, then pulled out his billfold and left money on the table.

"Shouldn't I pay?" My hand reached for my purse. "I invited myself."

"No, I told you I'm old-fashioned. And anyway, your parents fed me like a king."

We strolled out to the parking lot. "Maybe you and I should take a look at your painting," he said, following me to my car. It crossed my mind he was kidding, but he stared back at me in earnest.

I found my keys in the bottom of my purse and wrapped my fingers around them. "Right now?"

"Unless you'd rather bring it to class on Monday?"

"No, I wouldn't want to do that. But it probably needs more work." I felt my cheeks redden and hoped it was too dark for him to notice. "You're such an accomplished painter. I'm afraid you'll be disappointed."

"I doubt that. Come on, there's no time like the present."

My palms stuck to the steering wheel as I directed my car toward home. My fingers felt like icicles, but my torso sweltered under my jacket. I could see Henry's headlights in my rearview mirror, and I hoped he would get stuck behind another car and lose sight of me. I flicked on the radio, surfed through the dial, then turned it off again. I listened to a new rattle somewhere under the rear of the car; the drive home had never taken so long.

Charlie, his tail whipping back and forth, leapt up on Henry's legs as he came into the house.

"Henry, meet Charlie," I said, wishing, for once, the dog would raise a racket. Things were moving too quickly. When I caught a glimpse of my painting, I knew it was a mistake to let him see it. Propped on the counter and leaning against the microwave, it looked insignificant. I should have defined the background better, I told myself. And one of the woman's arms seemed out of proportion, and her skin tone wasn't right. The more I looked at the composition, the more I hated it.

"There it is," I said. As I watched Henry examine my work, I almost started to point out its flaws. I wouldn't blame him if he didn't like it, but I knew his words would sting worse than stepping into hornet's nest, which I'd done as a child.

Finally, he said, "This is very good."

"Thank you." But what did *good* mean? I'd often said "Good dog" to Charlie for nothing more than finishing his kibble. And I said "good morning" even when I was in a foul mood. "Really? You mean it?"

"Yes, it's better than good. " he said with conviction. "In fact, it's excellent."

I felt like dancing a jig or letting out a whoop. I couldn't remember the last time I'd felt this kind of satisfaction.

At that moment the telephone blared. I decided to ignore it. There was no one else I wanted to talk to—not even Rob. But when Henry's gaze shifted to the phone, I answered it.

"Are you sitting down?" Phil asked, his voice charged with electricity.

I knew Phil liked to make a big deal out of things. "No, I'm standing up, and I'm busy. Can't this wait?"

"No, it's too important."

What could be so monumental? Then I realized he was probably calling to announce his engagement to Darla. I felt like hanging up, but doing that would only delay the inevitable. Better to swallow the bitter poison all at once.

"What is it?" I said.

"There's no easy way of breaking this to you. Andrea's pregnant."

My legs giving way, I leaned against the counter. Had I heard correctly? No, it must be a mistake, some mix-up.

"Margo? You still there?"

"Yes." My voice came out barely a whisper.

"They're getting married in a couple of months, so it's going to be okay. Hey, we're going to be grandparents!"

I dropped onto a chair. "Are you sure?"

"It's still early in the pregnancy, but yeah. She's been tested by a doctor."

My hand wrapped around my throat.

"Andrea's parents had a fit, as you can imagine," he said. "But they're grateful she didn't get an abortion."

I let the knowledge pour over me, but my every fiber rebelled against it. "How will they live? They're just kids themselves. They can't take care of a baby."

"I'll help them. Rob's going to stay with me until we figure out what to do. Next quarter, maybe he can enroll in junior college and work part-time."

"You know the chance of their marriage working out. Even my folks are ready to split."

"I'm sorry to hear that. I like your parents, even if your dad thought I was a bum." Phil chuckled. "Hey, he was right. You were way too good for me." He sounded happy, which made the conversation even more absurd. Had he lost his mind?

I hung up and sat with my forehead in my hands.

"Are you all right?" Henry asked.

I'd almost forgotten he was in the room with me. I looked up and said, "It's Rob's girlfriend. She's pregnant." There was no point in trying to cover up what Phil would eventually tell him.

"I'm sorry."

"I know Phil's your friend, but I could kill that man." It might be worth facing the death penalty.

"I'm sure you're upset, any parent would be. But how is this Phil's fault?"

"Of course it's not. It's just that he's acting like Andrea's pregnancy is the greatest thing on earth."

"I doubt Phil thinks that. He's probably trying to make the best of a difficult situation." He laid a hand on my shoulder for a quiet moment. "Let me know if there's any way I can help."

Too exhausted to answer, I nodded.

"Your son will be in my prayers," he said as he prepared to leave. "The Lord can change your darkness into light."

Yeah, right, I thought. How could anything but heartache come from this?

23

Rain splattering against my bedroom window woke me. It was already seven in the morning. In spite of everything, I'd rested soundly for almost nine hours.

Entering the kitchen, the first thing I saw was my painting. I stood staring at it as if a stranger had moved into the house while I was sleeping. With its flowing brush strokes and areas of dappled color, it looked unlike anything I'd ever done. In college, I would have considered using a magazine shot for a subject the cheap trick of a lazy artist. And a little boy and his mother would have seemed too sentimental for a proper subject. But as a grown woman, this scene filled my heart with gladness. On closer scrutiny the boy looked remarkably like Rob as a toddler. Without setting out to do so, I had painted my son.

As Rob was growing up, I'd tried extra hard to be a good mother. I'd read all the recommended parenting books, was home after school to assist him with his homework, attended all his games. I'd hovered over my son, but apparently it hadn't been enough. I'd always assumed that he was an exceptional child—not the type to be a college dropout with a teenage wife and an unplanned baby. What about his aspirations to become a dentist like his Grandpa Vern? Or were those only my dreams?

There had to be something I could do to make things better. Should I call Andrea's mother? I remembered meeting the girl's parents, Joe and Lucille Walker, at Rob's high-school graduation in June. Four months later, I knew little more about the couple than I had known then, except that Joe was a big-time attorney with the reputation of being a bulldog in the courtroom, and Lucille was a homemaker. Over the summer I'd chatted on the phone with Lucille several times while trying to track down Rob, and the woman seemed pleasant enough, but distant. Our calls usually ended quickly, with Lucille saying she needed to get back to her housework or run to the store.

As I walked toward the phone, a wave of dread grabbed my stomach. Lucille would be furious and probably blame the pregnancy on Rob. If Andrea were my daughter, I might do the same thing. Not that Andrea hadn't been a willing participant, I reminded myself. The girl could have said no.

I moved to the sink and filled the coffeemaker with water. A moment later, as I measured grounds into a filter, my hand shook, strewing dirt-colored particles across the counter. I felt like screaming or breaking something. Wasn't there any way out of this nightmare? The thought of Rob and Andrea in bed together sickened me. If only Rob had never met the girl. If only he had controlled his lust.

I grabbed the sponge and began wiping the coffee grains into the sink. My thoughts orbited to Phil; our conversation from the night before droned in my ears. How could he be happy about this catastrophe? If only his call had been a prank, some sick joke. In the old days it would have been just like Phil to manufacture the whole story to drive me nuts. Maybe he was hitting the bottle again. Since when did I believe anything he told me? He was the most unreliable person I knew. No, in spite of his almost intoxicated elation, Phil had been deadly serious.

I strode over to the phone and punched in Rob's number. When he answered, I said, "It's your mother," sounding like a middle-school principal.

"Hey, Mom," Rob said in a garbled voice. "What time is it?"

Containing a tidal wave of anger, I gnawed the inside of my cheek for a moment. Finally I said, "Do you have something to tell me?"

I heard the rustle of fabric; he was probably in bed and pulling himself up to a sitting position. "Dad called you?"

"Then it's true?"

His voice grew childlike. "Mom, I'm sorry."

Trembling inside, I felt like a coiled snake, ready to spew out venom. I wanted to say, "How could you be such a fool?" but I curbed my tongue. Lambasting him wasn't going to help anything. And those cutting words could never be retracted.

Finally I said, "How do you know you're the father?"

"Andrea's not that kind of a girl."

"I'd say she is." I could kick myself for not warning him about feminine guiles, and about women like me.

⌘

Later that morning I found Lois in the back room of the office leaning over the copy machine. Clad in a Chanel-style suit emphasizing a trim waist, she removed a printed page from the copier and looked it over.

"Hello," I said, and she noticed me.

"My quarterly newsletter," she said, her face awash with pride. "I like to keep in touch with my clients. Don't want them forgetting me." She pressed a button, and the machine began to stir, then spit out more copies. "By the way, the Troutman-Henrick sale is dead."

I attempted to hide my shock, but frantic words tumbled out. "That's impossible. What happened?"

"The couple buying the Troutmans' home had their inspection yesterday and found out the electricity and plumbing needs to be updated. They bailed out, don't want to buy the Troutmans' house anymore—which is just as well since there's no way the Troutmans can move right now."

"But the Troutmans made a deal with the Henricks." My words sounded like mush, like my mouth was clogged with oatmeal. "They can't change their minds now. The Henricks are buying their new home on the contingency that they sell their old."

"Yes, I know." Her face remained composed, her voice like velvet. "The Troutmans are willing to let the Henricks keep their earnest money and just bag the whole thing." She eyed her newsletter again; the corners of her mouth turned up. She glanced back to me. "Win some, lose some. Right?"

I couldn't stand on the sidelines and do nothing, not after all the hours and work I'd poured into this sale. I inched toward the door. "I've got to call the Henricks."

"Don't bother. I just spoke to Sherry a few minutes ago. She said it would be bad karma to force an elderly couple to buy their house, and wasn't it cool she and Wayne made all that money?"

"Isn't there anything we can do?"

"I'm afraid not. The sale just isn't going to fly."

All I could think about was how much I needed the commission money. I felt like running out the door and never returning. Tears were threatening the backs of my eyes, but I willed them away. Lois was the last person I would want to see me fall apart.

"Are you okay?" she said.

"Sure." I tried in vain keep my bottom lip from quivering. I sucked it in and held my breath. I couldn't admit that I barely had enough cash in the bank to cover my mortgage payment. What was I going to do for food and gas?

"Come on." Her eyes probed mine. "You should be used to this sort of thing by now. It's all part of the real-estate game."

In an effort to save face, I said, "I'm having some other difficulties in my life."

"I know how that goes. In a few minutes I'm making my mandatory daily visit to see my mother." The copier crunched to a halt, and a light started blinking, indicating the machine was out of paper. Lois yanked out the paper tray.

"Father and I put her in an Alzheimer's unit a few weeks ago." She stuffed in more paper and rammed the tray back into the copier. "She's never been a very nice person to be around." She stabbed the start button. "Now she's impossible, tells me she hates me."

"I'll bet she doesn't mean it."

"If you only knew my mother."

It was the first time I'd seen anything but self-confidence radiate from Lois's symmetrical face. "I'm sorry." I stepped closer, into a zone I'd never before entered. "Is there anything I can do?"

"Not unless you know a way to keep me from growing old and losing my mind. My grandmother had Alzheimer's too. How's that for crummy genes?" Her eyes became glassy. "I don't want my Walt getting stuck with a loony wife." She spun around, as if to check the copy machine, but I could see her dabbing the corners of her eyes with her fingertips. I reached out to touch her shoulder and felt rocklike hardness.

She jerked away as if I'd hurt her. "I'm all right. I must be coming down with something."

I thought of my own parents, how important they were to me. "I'd like to help," I said. "I could fill in for you if you want to take that vacation you were talking about."

"Thanks, but I can't leave my father alone right now."

How unfair, I thought. I remembered Henry's futile attempt to comfort me. If his God could change darkness to light, why would he let Lois's mother's brain decay?

24

Through the driving rain I could see my mother's aged station wagon sitting in their carport. Since Mom loved Rob almost as much as I did, I figured she would be the best person to offer support and advice.

Opening the car door, I squinted as blobs of water dampened my face. I zipped my jacket to my chin, then strode up the walkway. Ahead, by the front door, three large crows darkened the branches of the rhododendron. The birds cawed as I approached. In an effort to frighten them away I waved my arms, but they stared back with shiny black eyes. I clapped my hands, and they finally flapped their wings and hopped to the neighbor's yard.

I pushed the bell and heard the familiar ring, but no one came to the door. I used the knocker and still got no response.

Thinking my mother might be out back, I trotted around the side of the house. I scanned the small yard and noticed the grass needed mowing. Mom's prized rose bushes growing under the kitchen window needed pruning, and weeds had assaulted the perennial beds beneath them. Mom had always prided herself on her gardening ability, but maybe this neglect was all part of growing old.

I took care not to slip on the wet boards as I climbed the porch steps. Peering through the backdoor window, I could make out the silhouette of my mother slumped at the kitchen table. Weird.

"Mom," I called, rapping on the glass. I watched her slowly pull herself to her feet, move across the room, and open the door. Clad in her bathrobe, she looked terrible. Her eyelids were swollen, and her greasy hair lay flat on one side.

She was an early bird; she never slept in. "Did you just get up?" I asked, checking my watch and reading eleven thirty. I entered the room and inhaled a bitter cloud of burnt coffee.

Mom said nothing. She went to the sink, trickled water into the kettle, and placed it on a burner.

I took off my wet jacket and draped it over the back of a chair. "I'm glad you're home." I reached around her hip to turn on the burner.

She fell back onto her chair and propped her chin in her hands. I sat across from her.

"Are you coming down with the flu?" I leaned over and felt her cool forehead.

"No." She shook her head in slow motion. "Nothing like that."

I listened for the sound of the TV in the living room or my father's footsteps, but the house stood silent. I hushed my voice. "I need to talk to you in private." I wasn't ready to tell Dad about Rob and Andrea yet. I couldn't face my father's criticism. "Where's Dad?" Now that I thought about it, I hadn't seen his car on the street.

"He moved out."

The image of him literally moving out refused to gel in my mind. "If that's a joke, it isn't funny."

She shook her head again. I hadn't witnessed such sorrow on her face since her sister died.

"When?"

"Last night."

"You two had a fight?" Dad probably went to cool off someplace. "Don't worry, he'll be back."

"He packed two suitcases."

"You watched him leave and didn't try to stop him?"

A tear leaked from her eye and slithered down her cheek. "Why should I?"

"Because he's your husband. Because you love him." I sprang to my feet. "I'll call Dad and get him to come home. Where is he?"

"I have no idea. Probably at Alice's house."

"No way. He'd never go there." Would he?

The kettle spewed several blasts of steam, then began wailing. I got up and lifted it off the burner. I stared at the kettle's chrome surface. Mom had used this kettle to boil water for as long as I could remember. This kitchen had always been the hub of the house, an oasis of safety and love where the real family conversations took place. Until recently, I realized, my siblings and I had done most of the talking—sharing our problems or triumphs—and Mom listened, throwing bits of advice our way when we were done.

She pulled a crumpled mass of Kleenex out of her bathrobe pocket and blew her nose. Between snuffles she said, "You came over here with something important on your mind, and I've been doing all the talking."

"It's nothing. We'll discuss it later."

Minutes later I plodded out to my car. Again, the crows cawed. In the mood I was in, I might have opened fire on them if I'd owned a shotgun. I dumped myself in the driver's seat and nosed the car away from the curb.

I'd left Mom cocooned under a blanket on the couch. Her eyes shut and her lips moving, she was praying. A lifetime of her prayers had fallen on deaf ears, I thought. Either there was no God, or Mom wasn't good enough to get his attention. That thought made my skin itch, feeling like prickly sun rash. If Mom wasn't good enough, no one was.

Steadying the steering wheel with my knee, I whipped out my cell phone, called the office, and asked the receptionist to look up Alice Foster's address. I scribbled the numbers on a scrap of paper, then headed south toward Madison Park not knowing what I would do if I found my father.

I tailgated the compact car in front of me until it turned onto a side street, then I flew through the next intersection just as the amber light shifted to red. A motorist off to the right honked, but I didn't bother to look, not caring if someone was mad at me. Whoever it was had better keep out of my way.

Several blocks shy of Lake Washington, I took a left, entered a neighborhood of smaller homes, and found Alice's address affixed to the porch of a pink-colored bungalow. Yuck, I thought. What kind of a woman would paint her house that color? I didn't see Dad's car, but a late-model beige-metallic Cadillac Deville sat out front. Next to the house stood a garage with its door closed; anything could be hidden in there.

As I came up behind the Cadillac and jammed on the parking brake, I tried to recall what little I knew about Alice, only remembering she was single—not whether she was widowed or divorced.

I got out and marched across the edge of the lawn. The grass, I noticed, was clipped short enough to be a putting green. I tromped up the front steps. On either side, window boxes filled with fading geraniums sat under lace-curtained windows. In the mail slot next to the door, I saw outgoing stamped envelopes waiting for the mailman's arrival. Macy's, Nordstrom. Who was paying for all this? I wondered. Was Dad supporting his mistress? Had he bought her a nicer car than his own wife?

I jabbed the bell several times.

Alice, wearing the same platinum blond, crimped hairstyle and simpering facade she'd always sported, opened the door right away. At first she didn't seem to recognize me, but then said, "Marguerite? What are you doing here?" Her lips pressed into a tight smile that didn't mask her discomfort.

I inhaled a dense cloud of gardenia-scented perfume. "Is my father here?"

"No. Why would he be?"

I brushed past her and stalked into a small living room that sparkled with neatness. I felt like a detective snooping through a crime scene. Plush furniture lined the walls. A collection of ceramic figurines sat on the fireplace mantel, before an ornate gilded mirror. A low Florentine coffee table stood on the flowery carpet. I saw no evidence of my father—not his reading glasses, wallet, or the extra change he sometimes left by his easy chair.

"I haven't spoken to Vern for over a week." Alice said, remaining by the front door, one hand on her hip. "Is he missing? Maybe I can help."

I hurled my words like daggers. "You're the last person on earth I'd trust. I know all about you, how you've been throwing yourself at my father." As I neared the fireplace, I was tempted to sweep my arm across the mantel and crash the expensive statuettes to the floor. Let Alice experience what it was like to have an intruder destroy her home the way she wrecked Mom's.

Alice must have picked up my thoughts, because she lunged over, shaking her hands. She squeezed between me and the fireplace. "There are two sides to every story," she said.

"Shut up, you tramp."

Her pupils shrank to pinpricks. "Listen, I don't care whose daughter you are. This is my home. I don't have to put up with this."

"Who pays for this house anyway?"

"I don't have to answer your questions. If you don't get out, I'll call the police."

I had no doubt she would do just that. I flung her a look of disgust, then bolted out the door. It slapped shut behind me, then I heard the clunk of a deadbolt locking. Out on the

225

sidewalk, I rifled through my purse in search of my keys. Something sharp—maybe a pen—poked into the palm of my hand. I was so frustrated I felt like overturning my purse and strewing its contents on the sidewalk. But I figured Alice was watching me out the window. The last thing I wanted to do was give her something to laugh about.

I dug into my purse again, found the key, and rammed it into the lock. Listening to the motor sputter to life, I glanced over my shoulder at Alice's house and wondered what kind of a life this woman led. If she loved Dad, her world had to be a pathetically lonely one. Before my father retired, he was usually home for dinner, on the weekends, and during holidays. And now he rarely left the house. He always carved the turkey on Thanksgiving Day and handed out presents on Christmas morning. Had Alice waited for him to show up when he felt like it, like Charlie under the dinner table begging for scraps?

Then I envisioned Mom curled on the couch in a fetal position, and my momentary pity for Alice flipped back to animosity. The woman deserved to suffer.

I pictured my father arriving here, perhaps with a bouquet of flowers in his hand. Would he buy her roses, too? He'd always seemed like such a good husband and father. Growing up, I'd practically worshipped him. But the truth was, he was a rat. Even worse than Phil.

I released my foot from the brake pedal, and the car puttered down the street. Something flickering on the dashboard signaled a problem. The idiot light? What did that mean? I checked the gas gauge and noticed the needle resting on empty. I'd meant to fill up the tank the day before, but was so preoccupied I forgot.

By the time I'd reached the nearest gas station, the light blazed red. I pulled in behind a Suburban and waited for the driver to pay before I could coast forward into position. A gust of soggy air billowed into the car as I stepped out. The sky opened up, whipping raindrops under the gas pump over-hang. I selected the cheapest grade, pulled up the lever, and dragged the hose over to my car only to remember that the gas tank was located on the other side. Muttering words that hadn't entered my mind since my teens, I stretched the hose over the top of the trunk and rammed the nozzle into the gas tank.

It would be nice to have a man with me right now, I thought. Dad always pumped Mom's gas, but maybe never again. Was it possible my parents would get a divorce? That seemed ridiculous. Yet, if I were in Mom's shoes, I might do the same thing she'd done: kick the good-for-nothing out. Were there no decent men? Even my son had turned out to be a louse.

The nozzle handle lurched in my hand, indicating the tank was full. As I pulled the nozzle out, an elongated dribble of gasoline spurted across my pant leg. I read the dollar amount, opened my wallet, and found just enough cash to cover it.

Finally at home, I felt like I'd run a marathon. Charlie demanded my attention; the dog sat on his haunches, his paws crossed. I scooped him up and cuddled him, and his wiry body trembled with ecstasy.

"You're my best buddy, aren't you?" I remembered the Scottish tale of a small terrier that slept on his master's grave after the old gentleman died. The compassionate townspeople fed the dog, who refused to leave the graveside. Now that was devotion, I thought, the kind rarely found among humans.

"You'll never leave me, will you?" I asked him.

His moist tongue flicked out, and I offered my cheek, then gave him another hug.

My thoughts turned to Rob, and an encore of disappointment and sadness saturated my chest. But I couldn't deal with Rob's situation yet. Not while my mother sat alone, brokenhearted.

My life had been built upon the fact that Dad was an honest man. He'd been one of the stone pillars supporting my world. I now knew he was a fake, a fraud, and my bones ached as I tried to accept the truth. He was a liar, I told myself. If he'd been dishonest with Mom, what else had he covered up? Was he living a double life? I felt lopsided, as if one leg were suddenly shorter than the other.

I carried Charlie into the living room and sat on the couch. The weight of the dog's warm body in my lap comforted me. I stroked his ears and felt my pulse slow down a notch. With my free hand I lifted the phone. I wanted to talk to Mom, but she'd promised to call if she heard from Dad. Had the scumbag still not bothered to call home?

I dialed Laurie's number and Dave answered on the second ring. When I asked for Laurie, he said, "I thought she was with you."

"Uh, no." I stopped patting Charlie and sorted through my memory bank. I was sure Laurie and I hadn't made plans for today. "Maybe she's with Susan or Erika."

"No, she said you two girls were going shopping together." He sounded perturbed. "Some big sale."

"Maybe we got our wires crossed. I've been at work, then at my parents'." But Laurie knew my work number, and she would have tried to call me on my cell phone if I hadn't shown up for a date.

"If you see my wife, tell her to come home right away."

"Is everything okay?"

"No, I have an important meeting today and can't find a pressed shirt. Laurie was supposed to go to the dry cleaner, and is probably driving around town with my laundry in her trunk. In the meantime I'm looking like a bozo wearing the same shirt I wore yesterday."

"Okay, I'll tell her." I heard the line go dead as Dave hung up. I scratched Charlie between the ears, then my fingers stiffened as I contemplated if Laurie was lying to Dave and using me for an alibi. If so, where was she? I considered calling Dave back to warn him now was the time to work on his marriage, not worry about wrinkled shirts.

Charlie whined softly as he waited for me to continue. I tickled him under the chin. "Sorry, boy." I closed my eyes and envisioned Laurie sifting through a rack of clothes at Chico's, her favorite shop, spending a bundle. But was Chico's or any other store holding a sale this week? I hadn't received a notice in the mail or seen any ads in the newspaper.

The phone chirped, and I stuck the receiver to my ear, expecting to hear Laurie's voice.

"Marguerite?" a woman's wire-thin voice said. "It's Lucille Walker, Andrea's mother."

26

When I spied Alice sitting across the restaurant table from Dad, I was furious enough to walk out of my father's life forever.

Alice, her lime green satin dress barely covering her knees, leaned toward him and spoke with intensity. Her hand reached to take his as though they were two lovebirds. Mom sat at home crying, I thought, while Dad was out on a date with his girlfriend.

Finding him had been no easy chore. I'd spent an hour phoning every major hotel in town and finally located him at the Washington Athletic Club, with its fitness rooms, spa, restaurant, and overnight accommodations. Was this why he'd held onto his membership there? So he could use the club facilities for his rendezvous with Alice?

The hostess approached me. "Would you like a table?" she asked.

"No, I won't be staying." I took a step toward the door. But leaving would make things too easy for them. I should stay and confront the two lowlifes, never mind the other people in the restaurant. I would march over to Dad and Alice's table and overturn their luncheon plates in their laps, then toss ice water in their sorry faces.

Thinking how good that would feel, I noticed Alice shoot to her feet, then pitch her napkin down on the table. With squared shoulders and arms swinging like a soldier, she charged toward the door, almost colliding with me. We stood face-to-face for a moment. Hatred spewed out of her eyes, and I glowered right back at her, almost hoping she would give me an excuse to pop her in the nose. Her mouth flapped open, but she flounced past me without speaking.

Dad, clad in his favorite tweed sports jacket, still sat at the table. He didn't seem to notice me when I stalked over with my arms folded across my chest. A roast beef sandwich, looking as if it had just come out of the kitchen, sat on a plate in front of him.

I cleared my throat, forcing my voice to sound like his when he demanded someone's attention.

He finally glanced up, and a half smile formed on his thin lips. "Hello, honey."

A whirlwind of condemnations danced on the tip of my tongue, but all I could say was, "Shut up."

He shot me his patriarchal look, which used to make me melt into a puddle. But not anymore. All respect for him gone, I glared down at the reprobate with disgust. He looked older: His face bore a cobweb of craggy lines, and the top of his head shined through a thinning mat of hair.

A waitress appeared at the table, cleared Alice's empty plate, and asked me if I wanted a menu.

"No thanks, I've lost my appetite."

"Please sit down," Dad said, gesturing to Alice's seat.

I lowered myself gingerly, leaving my chair several feet from the table.

Dad played with his spoon, flipping it over and back several times. "I take it you've spoken to your mother."

"I talked to her, all right."

He rotated the spoon between his thumb and forefinger. "It wasn't my idea to leave. I told your mother I'd never speak to Alice again and begged for forgiveness, but she tossed me out."

"What did you expect her to do?" I said it with such ferocity that several heads turned.

He placed the spoon parallel to his knife. "You're right. She's right. I deserve everything I get."

My mind struggled for equilibrium. I realized the best scenario was Dad's going home and reconciling with Mom, even if he wasn't good enough for her. That was the only conclusion that would make Mom happy.

I tugged my chair closer to the table. "Was Alice the only one, or were there more?"

He shook his head glumly. "No, just Alice." His cheeks blanched gray, like worn cement. "I told Alice it's over between us, forever."

I scowled. Years ago, when I'd lied about doing my homework, Dad had spouted, "A man's only as good as his word." How gullible I'd been to buy into his self-righteousness.

Looking at him now after all those years, I saw an insignificant little man with shoulders bent forward like a vulture and a face shriveled like a prune.

"I've tried to break it off with Alice before," he said. "Many times. But I was weak. I couldn't keep away from her."

I screwed up my face. "You couldn't keep away from Alice? She's ugly."

The waitress arrived at the table with the check. She glanced down at Dad's sandwich and asked, "May I wrap that up for you, sir?" Then she carted his plate into the kitchen.

Dad charged the meal to his room by signing his name at the bottom of the check. "I was a lot younger when I got myself into this mess," he said. "And your mother wasn't an easy woman to live with."

I recoiled, my weight lifting off the chair. I couldn't believe he had the gall to place any guilt on Mom. "That's your excuse?" I said. "No one's easy to live with all the time. Don't expect any sympathy from me."

His voice faltered. "I don't blame you for being angry." His features twisted down, as if he were going to cry, something I'd never seen him do. "I'm trying to make things right. I called your mother a couple of hours ago and said I'd like to come home and patch things up." His mouth hardened when he added, "But she told me not to bother, that she hadn't slept so well for years. She informed me she's changing the locks today in case I get any ideas about coming back to the house."

He sat straighter, arms crossing. "Did she mention anything about hiring an attorney? She'd better not plan to use mine."

234

Was retaining his lawyer and protecting his finances all he could think of? His callous remark sent me to my feet and out the door.

⌒

I reached into my cubby and picked up my telephone messages as I entered the office. I sorted through the slips of paper and read the words *Bill Avery, please call ASAP*.

I turned to the receptionist, Stephanie, who was sitting behind her L-shaped desk, and asked, "Has Lois been in yet?"

Stephanie's exaggerated smile revealed displeasure. "She went to Palm Springs for a month. I assumed you knew. She told me you'd handle all her calls."

"Are you sure?"

"Yes." Stephanie, a slim blonde in her early thirties, wore dark-rimmed glasses that gave her a determined look. "In fact, she told me it was your idea."

"I offered to help out if she needed a vacation, but she said she couldn't leave town."

Another agent strolled through the door, and Stephanie waited for the man to pass by before she said, "Welcome to the club." She checked to make sure no one else was within earshot. "Lois is always unloading surprises like this on me." She stood to hand me a weighty stack of manila folders, each bulging with paperwork. "Here, she said to give you these."

With the phone messages stashed in my pocket, I balanced the folders in my arms and just made it to my workspace before they started slipping. The papers landed with a thud on my desk, sounding like the foundations of a building giving way. I plopped down on my chair and stared at them. This scene reminded me of my recurring nightmare in which I arrived at a strange classroom to find I needed to take a final exam without preparation. I thought of Lois. That woman could probably bulldoze her way through the test and come out with an A. She was a shrewd businesswoman, one of the most organized and goal-oriented people I'd ever met—not the type to throw her house sales away on a whim. Her mother must have died.

My hand flew for the phone, and I called Lois's home number.

Her husband, Walt, answered. "She's visiting an old friend," he said, his words hesitant. When I asked to leave a message, he stated, "She can't be reached."

"Would you please ask her to call me? We're working on some transactions together."

"I said, she can't be reached."

I remembered talking to Walt on a number of occasions. He'd always seemed a jovial fellow and quite chatty. "Is everything all right?" I asked. When he didn't answer, I added, "Lois told me about her mother."

I heard a muffled sound, then a sniff. "It's not her mother who's having the problem," he said. "It's Lois. But you've got to promise not to tell anyone. Not that keeping this a secret has helped either one of us."

Maybe Lois was in the hospital being treated for heart disease or cancer, I thought. I could imagine a woman like her wouldn't want the whole office knowing she was incapacitated. "Of course," I said. "I won't tell a soul."

"It's her drinking. She'd been keeping it under control— only one glass of wine with dinner, maybe a couple on the weekends. But when I got home last night, she was talking crazy, making no sense. When I tried to smell her breath, she came unglued and said she was going to divorce me if I didn't quit hounding her." He sucked in a raspy breath, then his exhale hissed through the receiver. "In the bottom of the trash can under the kitchen sink I found an empty vodka bottle."

I swallowed an astonished gulp. I'd hardly ever seen Lois ingest alcohol—a few times at company parties, but in moderation. The woman was forever cool and collected, always in control.

"Where is she?" I asked.

"Residence Twelve, a rehab for women. It's not her first visit there."

I massaged my throbbing temple with my free hand. "I'm sorry. I had no idea."

"Few people did."

After I hung up, I glanced down at the top folder and saw the name Basetti scrawled across the top. Had Lois found the man a home and neglected to inform me? This thought made my head spin. I was sure we had agreed to work on that sale together. I tipped opened the folder and found Mr. Basetti's check and an earnest money agreement dated three days earlier. I recognized the seller's name and the house I'd discussed with Mr. Basetti on the phone. The seller had yet to sign the papers, I noticed. Had Lois even presented the offer to him?

I sorted through the stack of folders and found several unfinished house deals with missing documents. One sale was supposed to close in a week, but I couldn't find the inspection report required by the lender. Another file contained a request from a bank for verification of a buyer's income. A third held phone messages from a seller saying he couldn't vacate his home until January, while the buyers stated they needed to move in by the first of December.

It occurred to me the needed documents probably lay somewhere in Lois's private office. I had no choice but to search for them. I gathered up the folders, moved to Lois's desk, and sat on her ergonomically correct leather chair that made mine feel like a park bench. Pulling open the top drawer, I was surprised to find a confusion of pill bottles, nail files, and makeup. The middle drawer contained a hodge-podge of papers and files, some dating back three years. I tugged open the bottom drawer and heard something roll, hitting the back of the drawer with a clank. Digging behind a stack of *Golf Digest* magazines, I spied several miniature bottles of liquor, the size served by airlines.

Shutting the drawer, I recalled how the office gang sometimes headed to the restaurant down the block after work. The same waiter always took our drink orders. He would ask Lois if she wanted "the usual," and Lois would send him a winning look and say, "Sounds good, Harry." While I drank diet Pepsi and some of the others drank white wine, Lois sipped her iced tea, no sugar. She never acted sloppy, never laughed uncontrollably, and always left a generous tip.

What was really in that tea? I considered running down the street to ask the bartender if he'd doctored Lois's drinks, but he might lie. And what good would it do? Lois obviously had a problem, or she wouldn't be in a treatment center.

Pacing back to my desk, I remembered the phone message from Bill Avery. At least that deal was sailing along. I relaxed into my chair and dialed Bill's office number in Pittsburgh.

"Bev's pregnant," Bill said after a brief hello.

"That's wonderful." I envisioned the home they were purchasing. The small bedroom beside the master suite could be used as a nursery. "Congratulations."

"Thanks, but now Bev's decided she doesn't want to move."

"What?" I must have misunderstood. Bev, a friendly young woman, had been ecstatic the day the couple wandered into the open house. "Are you sure? She loved the house. Remember how she raved about the fireplace in the family room and the fenced backyard?"

"Not anymore. She told me if I move to Seattle, I'm going by myself."

My pulse pounded in my ears, sounding like a semi careening down a gravel road. "But your job. I thought you had a great promotion." My words slurred; I sounded like a woman teetering on the edge of a ravine. "Maybe I should call Bev. Seattle's a beautiful city. I'd be glad to help her get settled here."

"It's her folks. She doesn't want to leave them now."

"Oh." I recalled the dreary afternoon Mom had invited me over on the pretense of lunch. Eight months pregnant with Rob and hauling around thirty extra pounds, I'd waddled into my parents' home and started complaining about how miserable I was. Phil had stayed out past closing time again, we only had two hundred dollars in the bank, and my morning sickness was back with a vengeance.

"Surprise," Mom had said with a mischievous grin, and presented me with a white wicker bassinet with an eyelet skirt. A moment later my sister, Candy, and several other girl-friends, each carrying an elaborately wrapped baby gift, materialized from the kitchen where they'd been hiding. Of course Bev wanted to stay near her parents, I thought. And I admired Bill for supporting her decision.

"I understand," I said to Bill. "You're doing the right thing."

27

Andrea's parents lived in a three-story brick mansion standing partially hidden behind a six-foot fence and tall evergreens. I steered my car into the circular stone-paved drive and coasted up to the front door.

Rob had never mentioned Andrea came from a wealthy household. Our home was miniscule compared to this one—about the size of the Walkers' four-car garage. No wonder Rob liked hanging out at Andrea's.

Leaving the safety of my car, I dreaded facing Lucille, and wished I'd insisted we meet in a public place so she couldn't cause a scene. Not that I was responsible for what had happened. It was Lucille's daughter who'd called Rob in the first place. Andrea had chased after him the way girls do these days. She wore revealing clothes, a slit of seductive bare midriff often flirting out between her T-shirt and low-riding jeans. Even her ponytail swished across her back in a provocative manner.

Of course Rob had tried things. Any boy would. It was up to the girl to put on the brakes. Not that I'd resisted Phil with much effort.

I rang the doorbell and a gonging arpeggio chimed throughout the house. As I waited, I tried to peer through one of the tall rectangular windows flanking the door. Maybe Lucille wasn't home, which would be a relief. After several minutes, I started back toward my car just as Lucille opened the door.

Her face was devoid of expression, as if I'd roused her from sleep. I remembered her as tall, blonde, and robust—like one of the Nordic athletic beauties I'd seen on the ski slopes. But the woman who stood before me looked as though she were suffering from chronic fatigue syndrome. Her pale cheeks were gaunt; her frumpy hair drooped.

"Come in," she said, barely moving her lips.

I tried to appear at ease as I stepped onto the black marble floor. I scanned the front hall with its graceful staircase curving up to the second floor. A crystal chandelier almost big enough to illuminate an auditorium sparkled overhead, casting a kaleidoscope of light across a floral arrangement sitting on a round table in the center of the room.

"This way," Lucille said, pointing me toward the living room. My eyes took in the spacious area with its baby grand piano poised in one corner. An original Andy Warhol hung above the couch, and on another wall a painting by Joan Miro. Out the window stretched an Olympic-sized swimming pool with a diving board at one end, and behind that lay Lake Washington. I felt like a kid watching *Lifestyles of the Rich and Famous* on TV.

"Please, have a seat," Lucille said, wringing her hands. "May I get you something?"

I sat on the far end of the couch. "No, thanks. I'm fine." Which wasn't the least bit true.

Lucille perched on an armchair next to the couch. She chewed the cuticle around her thumb for a moment. "I assume you know why I asked you to come."

"Yes, Rob told me." Not that he'd said much. I'd been in a daze when we spoke, and I hadn't thought to ask some pertinent questions.

"It's a tragedy. My daughter's life is ruined."

"I'm sorry," I automatically said, then realized it sounded like an apology. "It's terrible for both kids. Their lives will never be the same."

"But it's a hundred times worse for the girl."

I agreed with her, but I said nothing. On the way over, I'd decided to let Lucille do most of the talking.

"And what will our friends and neighbors think?" she said. "I'll never be able to look them in the eye again."

I heard elephant-sized footsteps on the staircase. A moment later, Joe, clad in a black suit and red silk tie, swaggered into the room. Not much taller than Lucille, he had a wrestler's wide shoulders and a broad belly, dark wiry hair, and a brushy moustache.

"Do you remember my husband?" Lucille asked, her gaze lowered.

I said, "Yes, hello." Joe's cold eyes stared back without a show of recognition. I offered him my right hand, but he folded his arms across his chest.

"Joe came home early today. Unexpectedly." She motioned for him to sit, but he remained standing with knees locked and feet spread wide.

"Is this the boy's mother?" He directed his words to Lucille, as though I weren't there.

"Yes."

He spewed a blast of air in my direction. "You've got your nerve coming here."

"Please, Joe," she said. "I invited her over. We need a plan."

"What we need is to put that juvenile delinquent son of hers in jail."

Could that happen? No, Rob hadn't done anything wrong. I shot to my feet. "My son has never been in trouble in his life." That was a slight exaggeration, but I returned Joe's ugly stare as if I were on the witness stand and my life depended on it.

"He raped my daughter." He spit out his words like rotten meat. "I'll prosecute, stick him behind bars where he won't hurt anyone else."

I was horrified. I felt like standing up to the bully and tossing the blame where half of it belonged—on Andrea. But I was unable to speak one word to a man who looked ready to punch me.

Lucille jumped to Joe's side. "Please, darling," she said, touching his wrist, then retreating. "Let's not argue."

He paid no attention. His face flushed purple; blood vessels coiled around his thick neck like serpents. He spun around and stomped across the floor, causing a glass-faced cabinet to shake.

Lucille and I stood listening to him pound up the staircase, cross the landing, then slam a door. I turned to Lucille and saw fear masking her face. What a horrible brute she'd married. I felt sorry for her, but that didn't change things. The man had threatened to press charges, and he was an attorney, used to battling it out in the courtroom. Could he do that? Rob and Andrea were the same age, but what if Andrea claimed Rob had forced himself on her?

"I'm sorry," Lucille said. She gnawed at her fingernail. "Joe gets a little excited sometimes, but his heart's in the right place."

A key rattled in the front door, and she went to open it. Not wishing to be caught alone if Joe returned, I followed her.

"Mom." Andrea, one hand holding her abdomen, moved across the threshold like a woman five times her age. She looked as if she'd lost weight. Her jeans hung loosely on her hips, and her eyes were sunken.

"Baby, are you all right?" Lucille asked.

"Biology class." Andrea's voice shuddered. "We had to dissect a dead frog. The smell made me throw up."

Her head jerked when she saw me. "Oh, hi," she said.

I was unable to take my eyes off of her. Inside this young woman lay a fetus, I thought. If Andrea was telling the truth, it was my grandchild. I started calculating when the baby would be born. By next summer anyway. Would it be a boy or a girl? Which parent would it favor? What would they name it? I imagined cradling the newborn infant in my arms, and a wellspring of tender emotions almost like love swept through my heart.

"I invited Marguerite over." Lucille tipped her head toward the ceiling. "And your father's upstairs."

Andrea's wince told me she was accustomed to her father's outbursts. She trudged into the living room, her hand still pressing on her abdomen.

"Why are you walking that way?" Lucille asked. I trailed behind them like a shadow.

Andrea kicked off her shoes and tumbled onto the couch. "I don't feel good." She rubbed a circle on her belly to show where it hurt.

Was she having a miscarriage? An ectopic pregnancy? I hurried to her side, knelt on the carpet, and took her hand. I felt warm, moist skin, but didn't know if that was a good sign or a bad sign.

"What does it feel like?" I asked.

"A dull ache."

"Get in the car," Lucille said. "I'm taking you to the emergency room."

"No," I said, maintaining a hold on the girl's hand. "Call the doctor, but in the meantime Andrea should stay where she is and keep her feet elevated."

I'd heard that a quarter of all pregnancies ended in spontaneous miscarriages. But I wouldn't allow myself to envision the fetus washing down a toilet.

"Joe!" Lucille called, her voice shrill. In a flash Joe was roaring down the stairs and lumbering into the living room.

"Andrea's in pain," Lucille said.

He glanced at Andrea, then turned on me like a junkyard dog finding an intruder. "Get away from my daughter," he yelled, stabbing his finger at me. As he advanced toward me, I shrank away, falling back on one hip.

His voice turned savage. "Get out of my house and never come back."

I choked back a gasp. Using a hand to push myself up, I struggled to my feet. Joe's face—distorted like a grotesque Halloween mask—hovered a foot away. I turned and ran to the front door, hearing his menacing footsteps behind me as I raced across the threshold.

I was barely outside when a fist of air whisked by me as the door slammed.

28

The rain pelted against my bedroom window. "Storm warnings, with gusts of wind up to forty miles an hour," the weatherman had predicted on the eleven o'clock news the night before. "And more rain is headed our way tomorrow."

Squalls had pummeled the southwest corner of the house all night. With Joe Walker's voice bellowing in my ears, I'd tossed in my sleep like a swimmer caught in an undertow. Memories of fleeing the Walkers' home like a thief escaping with his plunder kept my adrenaline pumping, and I woke to find my legs tangled in the covers and my pillow off to the side.

Getting up and wrapping myself in my bathrobe, I pattered down to the kitchen to find Charlie standing by the door waiting for me.

"Are you sure you want to go out there?" I asked, knowing he had no choice. When I opened the door, a gust of chilly air funneled in, lifting the hem of my robe. I shivered as I watched him meander over to his water dish. Then I shut the door.

My thoughts turned to Andrea, and I wondered what happened after I left. I imagined the girl lying in a hospital bed—the tiny life inside her womb forever snuffed. I was surprised at the intensity of my feelings. A miscarriage would solve everyone's problems, but I felt numb with sadness.

I decided to call Lucille. If Joe answered the phone, I could always hang up—before he hung up on me. I dialed the Walkers' number, and Lucille answered on the first ring.

"It's Marguerite," I said. "Is it safe to talk?"

"No."

"Please tell me, how's Andrea—and the baby?"

She hushed her voice. "Better. Andrea's cramping has subsided, but she's staying home from school today. You were right, the doctor said the best thing for her is to stay off her feet." Then she hung up without saying good-bye.

"Thank God," I said into the mouthpiece. In one way the crisis was over. But Andrea was still pregnant, and my son was still about to take a giant step into manhood long before he reached emotional maturity. The situation was far from settled.

Replacing the receiver, I considered what it would be like if Rob and Andrea got married, and the Walkers became Rob's parents-in-law. I couldn't imagine conversing civilly

with Joe after the way he'd treated me, and he would probably be equally abusive to Rob. It would be a blessing if he
never spoke to either one of us again.

As I climbed the stairs to my bedroom, my thoughts pro-
gressed to my parents. I'd reached Mom on the phone the
previous night and was disappointed to learn Dad hadn't
moved home. Mom had announced she was perfectly content
living alone. "I think I'll take a trip," she'd said in a chipper
voice, sounding nothing like the woman I'd spoken to the day
before. "I've always wanted to take one of those European
tours, where they do all the driving and pamper you. Travel
through Italy, track down my cousins. Your father would
never go anywhere unless there was a golf course."

I didn't ask Mom if she'd changed the door locks for fear
of reminding her. "Maybe you should call Dad," I suggested.

"No, I'm done being his doormat." I heard a man's voice
talking in the background. "I need to hang up and get back
to Rick Steves on PBS. He's doing a segment on Rome."

I needed to get ready for work, but I felt like crawling
back into bed, pulling the covers over my head, and hiding
for the rest of my life. But I had bills to pay and needed to
spend the day trying to locate the Henricks another house.
With my luck, Sherry and Wayne would decide not to
move after all. I also needed to contact Mr. Basetti and
Lois's other clients to see if I could make those deals fly, as
Lois would say.

In the bathroom I threw off my robe and stepped into
the shower stall before the water had thoroughly warmed.
The icy droplets pricked at my skin. As I lathered myself
with soap, I tried not to think about Andrea or Rob, but it
didn't work. I'd never left them in the house alone and

wondered where their romantic tryst occurred. It must have been at the Walkers' or in Rob's car. Either way the thought revolted me.

The water finally heated up enough to bring my body temperature back to normal just as I was ready to get out. I blotted myself with the towel. Glancing in the mirror, I saw a leathery face that had aged in the past week.

The cordless telephone by my bed squealed. It must be Mom, I thought. Or was it Rob? I wrapped the towel around my torso and ran to answer.

"Hello?"

"It's me," Laurie said.

"I'm glad you called." I needed a friend to talk to.

"I've really had it this time," she said in a scratchy growl.

"What happened?"

Her voice swelled with indignation. "Dave accused me of having an affair."

"Are you?"

"No. Is that what you told him?"

"Of course not, but when he said he was looking for you, I didn't lie." Out the window, I could see the treetops bend and shake as the wind picked up. "Where were you?"

The line fell silent. "Okay, I was having lunch with someone—a man—in a public place."

"Laurie, are you crazy? Why?"

"Because I'm lonely. Because Dave loves his work more than he loves me. If he came home to find the house had been ransacked, he'd check to see if his computer was missing before he'd worry about his wife and kids."

"I wouldn't go that far. And even if he did, that doesn't justify your seeing another man." I wished we were speaking face-to-face so she could see the full force of my disapproval. "Did Dave find out about your date?"

"Sort of. When I got home, he was on the warpath. Where had I been? Why hadn't I left my cell phone on? If I was shopping, where were my packages? Acting like some private detective."

Goose bumps erupted on my arms as a draft wafted across my damp skin. With my ear clamping the receiver against my shoulder, I dropped the towel to the floor and struggled into my bathrobe.

"I never should have married him," she said. "If I had it to do over again, I would have stayed single—except for having the kids, of course."

"Dave may mess up sometimes, but he adores you. Look at how he treats you."

"You mean all the presents? He loves buying things because he has a spending addiction. That's why we never have any money in our savings account. What I need is a man who's really there for me, emotionally and physically. Someone who appreciates me for more than raising kids and serving dinner at six o'clock, assuming he happens to show up. You wouldn't believe how many times Dave's called at seven to say he's tied up at the office."

What could I say? For years I'd envied Laurie's lifestyle. I loved my friend, but her complaints sounded like teeth biting into Styrofoam.

"Anyway, I'm thinking about getting a legal separation," she said. "I've already started looking in the classifieds for an apartment, in case he refuses to move out."

"You can't be serious. You're making a huge mistake."

"No, I'm not. You did it. You got divorced, and you've been telling me for years it's the best move you ever made."

If only I could take those words back. "But Phil was an alcoholic and a womanizer. Dave's sober and supports you like a queen. What will you do for money?"

"I've been thinking about getting a job anyway. It's boring having nothing to do all day."

I tried to envision Laurie showing up for work every morning, even when her hair wasn't frosted or her nails polished. "Okay, if you want to work, try something part-time," I said. "But boredom's not grounds for ending a marriage. Please, promise me you'll wait a day or two before you say anything to Dave."

When she didn't answer, I knew it was time to get real— no more pretending. "You don't know how lonely I've been, how many times I've wished I'd stuck it out with Phil." I watched raindrops rolling down the windowpanes like tears sliding down a woman's face. "How would you like to see Dave with another woman the way I have to watch Phil and Darla? And think of the kids. Growing up in a single-parent family hasn't helped Rob one bit."

Laurie began to weep. "I thought you'd support me. Now I don't know what to do."

I knew what Mom would say, that Laurie should turn to God for guidance. "Maybe this is a good time to pray," I said for lack of anything wiser.

Hanging up, I fell onto the bed and closed my eyes. It had been almost eighteen years since I came home to find my apartment in shambles and Phil gone. I'd yanked open the top drawer of his bureau, where he kept his socks and underwear. Emptiness had gaped back like a crater. I'd spun around and eyed the room. No dirty laundry piled in the corner. No toothbrush and comb by the sink. He was gone.

A torrent of sorrow took over my heart that night. I'd looked up to heaven and asked, "God, how could you let this happen?" Bitterness had tightened my throat; the sob erupting from my gut solidified in my chest.

I had once believed that all the shattered fragments of my life would be repaired miraculously if I loved God. But that was a bunch of religious malarkey. How many times had I lain awake praying, wondering when Phil would stumble in reeking of cigarettes and alcohol? When he finally did show up, I'd tried sniffing through the tavern stench to detect perfume and searched his collar for lipstick or stray hairs. He'd always promised he would get straight and never do it again. But he lied.

Back then Rob was an infant. "You can depend on me, little one," I'd whispered into his tiny pink ear. Rocking him with tight arms and kissing his salty eyes, I realized I was the only one I could depend on too. Phil and God had both deserted me.

A blast of air shook my bedroom window. I opened my eyes and sat up. It was way past time to let poor Charlie in. I tugged on some sweats and trotted downstairs. When I pushed open the door a crack and called his name, he didn't come.

"Charlie," I said again, shoving the door further. "Charlie, come here this minute."

Then I noticed the opened gate. I usually latched it carefully. Had the storm forced it open?

Stepping into my walking shoes, I reached for my hooded jacket, grabbed Charlie's leash, and headed out to the street. The wind was driving the rain down in heavy sheets. I looked in both directions but didn't see him. A car swished by, its windshield wipers working feverishly. In the gutter newly formed rivers gathered leaves.

I made the choice to turn left, toward the lake, at first trying to avoid the bigger puddles, then ignoring them. Visions of my dog disappearing under a car tire kept me running. I tried to remember if he was wearing his collar. Sometimes it slipped off. Not that anyone would bother with a wet dog.

I heard a volley of thunder in the distance. "Charlie, come!"

As I sloshed through the side streets, scanning every yard and alley, the wind knifed through my pants. My thoughts vacillated between the dog's disappearance and Rob. Were both my fault? I'd willfully screwed up my own life by getting pregnant and marrying the wrong man. Before I met Phil, my future had showed such promise, like a rose that never bloomed. My parents had advised me to wait until I graduated from college, to get myself firmly anchored before committing to marriage. I couldn't tell them the real reason I wanted to get married so quickly.

After a futile hour of searching, my voice was hoarse, my legs stiff, and my feet floated in my shoes. Then a pleasing thought hit me. Charlie had probably circled the block and ducked down the alley to sniff garbage cans, and was now moping by the front door.

255

Making my way home, I turned the last corner. He wasn't there.

29

I spied Henry's pickup pulling away from the curb in front of my house. He must have spotted me in his rearview mirror, because I saw the brake lights flash on. I jogged over to the truck as he cranked down his window.

"My dog ran away," I said, almost squawking.

"Get in, I'll help you look for him."

I climbed onto the wide bench seat, and we headed down the street. "How long has he been gone?" he asked.

"Over an hour, maybe two." Shivering, I realized I was drenched. I pulled back my jacket hood and tried to peel off the strands of wet hair plastered to the sides of my face. I must have looked like a bag lady, but it didn't matter.

"We'd better hunt along Highway 99," he said, taking us in that direction. Moments later we were traveling at forty miles an hour on the six-lane road. In spite of the standing water on the highway, cars were moving only slightly slower than they did on sunny days.

"Charlie would never make it across here alive," I said. Seeing piles of wet debris stopped my heart several times, and I thanked God under my breath each time I realized it was only a wad of crumpled newspaper or cardboard.

After half a mile we got off the highway and zigzagged through the side streets. Finally Henry patted my knee. "We'd better get you home and into some dry clothes."

I kept my eyes turned to the street. "Charlie had an ID tag attached to his collar," I said. "Someone might have called. One of us should have stayed home to answer the phone."

The rain eased to a drizzle, as if the sky had run out of moisture. Leaves from the corner oak tree lay in wet mounds around the storm drain. An old gentleman in a trench coat stood kicking them away.

Henry's truck stopped at my front door. I dashed inside to check the answering machine. No one had called.

I could hear Henry coming up the front steps. "I'm in the kitchen," I said, tugging off my jacket and hanging it on the doorknob.

As he entered the room, he asked, "Anything?"

"No." I was sapped of all energy and hope. "You must think I'm a hysterical female." I wiped under my eyes. "Until recently, my life was normal—positively dull. But over the past few weeks, things have started flying apart." I gave a little laugh as I pictured a meteor catapulting through space and colliding with a planet. "Maybe I'm going crazy."

"Why don't you take a hot shower and put on some warm clothes. I'll wait by the phone."

I returned to find that he'd made toast and a pot of tea. I sat down, feeling like a guest in my own kitchen. He poured me a cup of tea, and I took a sip, the hot liquid soothing my throat. I didn't need to ask if anyone had called.

I talked to fill the silence. I told Henry about my life as a single parent, first portraying myself as a capable young woman, then becoming more honest. I shared things I'd never told anyone, not even my parents or my girlfriends. Like what a tough time Rob had in school, a fact I never wanted anyone to know for fear they would think I was doing a second-rate job raising him.

"I used to cringe when I heard the teacher's voice on the phone. 'Your son's not paying attention. He hasn't turned in his homework. He forgot his book again.'" I'd tried to emulate my mother and father. Being the only parent in the house, I'd attempted to listen with two pairs of ears and see with two sets of eyes. Each time Rob floundered, I'd pushed harder. "I probably should have hired a tutor or sent him to private school or held him back a year." Or maybe I'd just been a lousy mother. "Now Rob's about to become a teenage parent. Why didn't he tell me about the pregnancy himself? After all I've done for him, why was Phil the one he turned to?"

"I wouldn't take it personally," he said with empathy. "No matter how tough they act, all kids hate disappointing their parents. I'm sure Rob loves you very much. In fact, you may be the one he wants to please the most."

"Then why does he want to live with his father instead of me?"

"Maybe so he can feel more independent. Phil's pretty loose, and you'd be across town if Rob needed you." He reached over the table to take my hand. "Don't give up hope. I married young and went to junior college for two years, then finished my education at a university."

I could feel calluses on his hands. But they were gentle. My shoulders relaxed as I felt his warmth move up my arm.

"Marguerite, no matter how much we try, we can't guarantee our children's futures."

"That's true. I had model parents, and I sure didn't fulfill their expectations."

He withdrew his hand. "Your parents seemed proud of you at dinner the other night."

I was like an uncorked bottle, the way I spilled out my thoughts. "I'm the least successful of their three children. The one who took all the wrong turns."

"There are many kinds of success, and many paths to reach them," he said. "Sometimes those dumb mistakes still lead us to where we want to go. God gave us free will, but he's still in charge."

The phone rang so abruptly it made us both start. I leapt up to answer it.

"I have your dog here," said a Mrs. Binder in a voice sounding like my grandmother before she died. "He's been visiting my little Georgette. She's a miniature poodle. Charlie's been sampling her food while he dries off. Your dog certainly was wet when he arrived, but he's just fine and dandy now."

Mrs. Binder described her house and how her husband had passed away two years before. Finally she disclosed her address, only two blocks away, and I flew out the door, leaving

Henry at the table. In ten minutes I returned with Charlie in my arms. On the walk home I'd contemplated how to repay Mrs. Binder. A plate of cookies or a coffee cake wouldn't work for a granny type, who was probably far more proficient in the kitchen than I was. I decided to buy her some flowers and deliver them in person, with Charlie at my side. If the woman wanted a long chat, as she'd seemed to today, we would stay for a visit.

Charlie was fluffy dry, having had a thorough brushing, something he didn't tolerate at home. Once in the kitchen he tottered to his basket, folded his legs, and dropped onto his mat.

I sat down. "What a relief. That little guy and I have been friends for a long time. I'd be heartbroken if anything happened to him." There would never be another Charlie. Long ago I'd decided not to attempt to replace him when he died of old age.

"I understand," Henry said. "I like dogs too."

I'd seen no evidence of one at his house. If it were true that dogs reflected their owners' personalities, I wondered what kind he'd chose.

"Have you ever owned one?" I asked.

"Yes, just one."

"What kind?"

He poured both of us fresh tea, then watched the steam rise from his cup. "Some sort of collie mix. My folks gave him to me when I was six."

"How long did he live?"

"Less than a year." Pausing for a moment, he expelled a long hard breath through his mouth. "I arrived home from school one day, and Laddie wasn't waiting for me on the front porch, as he always did. I went into the house, calling his name, but he didn't come. My mother told me he'd been hit by a car."

"How awful. How did it happen?"

"My parents let him run free. I begged them to build a fence, but they wouldn't. I guess they didn't know any better. I haven't thought about Laddie for years. Crazy, but it still makes me want to cry."

"Some things take a lifetime to recover from."

He nodded. "Whenever I see a woman with a scarf on her head, it reminds me of Barbara, and I have to look away." The color drained from his face, as if all blood had sunk to his feet. "She and I didn't know how to talk about her illness, as if she'd get better if we ignored it. I watched her fade away, like a melting patch of snow."

I sat motionless. I wanted to hear his story, but could I bear his tears without breaking down myself?

"The chemo devastated her," he said, his gaze journeying past me to another place and time. "Her long hair fell out in chunks and collected in the shower drain. Her graying skin became looser each day as she shrank from lack of nourishment. Even as she lay in a coma, I prayed she'd live on. Unable to speak. Unable to eat. But at least alive." His eyes hollowed, like two caves. "That's how selfish I was. I should have prayed she'd be released from her pain."

I didn't know what to say. I wanted to hold him, rock him as I'd done with Rob when he was little, but I sat like a spectator watching a play unfold.

"That's why I've built this barrier around myself," he said. "A deep moat and a wall too high for anyone to scale. Except you, apparently."

Me? What did he mean? I searched his face looking for clues, but found none.

Before I could respond, he stood and said, "I almost forgot." His voice returned to its usual timbre. "I brought something for you. Let me run out to my truck."

He left and came back with a large plastic bag from which he pulled three stretched canvases about the size of the one I found at my parents' and a dozen tubes of paint, then spread them out on the table like a picnic.

"I can't accept these," I said, picking up one of the tubes and reading *ivory black.*

"Of course you can. I've got paint coming out my ears, and I can certainly spare a few canvases. I don't use this size much anyway."

"But I may not have any more paintings in me." I set down the tube and turned over a larger one to read *titanium white.* "Really, it was thoughtful, but I won't put them to good use."

"I think you will. Go ahead and start something else."

"But—"

He cut me off. "No more excuses, young lady. Just dive in. And go easy on yourself. Give yourself permission to paint badly. If you don't like what you've done, you can always cover it with gesso and start again. Just dare to paint."

He looked around the room. "You need a more permanent spot though. A kitchen will do, but if you have a room where you can leave your supplies and easel set up all the time, it will make a big difference."

I led him up the stairs, guided him into Rob's room, and opened the curtains.

"Great lighting," he said, his eyes perusing the room without seeming to notice its need of new paint. "This will be perfect. Do you still have an easel? If not, I could lend you one."

"I can't remember what I did with mine." That felt ridiculous to admit, but it was true. I hadn't seen the easel at my folks' house. For all I knew, it had been used as kindling. "I'll let you know."

As we descended the stairs, he said, "Say, I forgot to tell you, someone named Tim called while you were in the shower. He said he'd call back."

In the front hall I opened the door. "Thank you, for everything." I was touched by his willingness to help me. I couldn't remember the last time someone other than my mother had dropped everything to come to my aid. Even though I doubted I'd use the paints, I might write him a thank-you note.

"It was my pleasure. I'm glad Charlie made it home in one piece."

"Thanks. I notice he's too tired to come say good-bye. That's a first. I'll bet he sleeps through till tomorrow."

Henry stepped toward the door, but as he passed me he slowed. Before I knew what was happening, he cupped my face in his hands. We stood staring into each other's eyes for several moments. I felt like one of Phil's statues: frozen, suspended in time.

His face moved closer to mine. Was he going to kiss me? I knew it was a bad idea. I should turn my head, tell him not to. But here he was—so handsome, so caring. I felt myself being drawn toward him like a shaving of steel to a magnet.

Suddenly, he straightened up and leaned away. "I'm sorry, I can't," he said, and a barren wasteland opened up between us. His arms dropped to his sides like useless appendages. "Please, forgive me." He walked out the door and got in his truck. Without buckling his seatbelt, he gunned the engine and sped away.

"That's it," I said. "I can't take it anymore." Finally I got the message: Men caused nothing but disappointment. My definition of insanity was repeating the same thing again and again and expecting different results. So why did this Cinderella keep expecting a Prince Charming to rescue her? From now on, if I needed someone to talk to, I would call one of my girlfriends or my mother. If I wanted to go to a show, I would venture out by myself. No more sitting by the phone like a ninny, no more jittery stomachs, no more broken hearts. I longed for serenity, and I was going to concentrate on getting my life straightened out. If that meant being a spinster for the rest of my life, so be it.

As I finished my vow, the rain stopped, which I took as a sign I was doing the right thing. I sat down on the front steps, my elbows resting on my knees. I heard a car approaching, and a few seconds later, Tim's BMW sped around the corner and skidded to a stop. I closed my eyes for a moment. I'd just sworn off the male half of the human race, and here I was, already being confronted with one of them. What should I do? How should I react? My mind was spinning like a penny flipping through the air, not knowing whether it was landing heads or tails.

Tim bopped out of his car. "Hi, there, pretty lady. I know I'm a little early, but I couldn't wait. Hey, who answered the phone when I called?"

"A friend." I gave him the abridged version of my traumatic morning.

Tim took my hand and pulled me to my feet. "Poor baby, come here." His hands grasped my waist, and his lips puckered for a kiss.

I drew back. "Tim, this isn't working."

"What do you mean?"

I hated conflict, hated having people mad at me, hated hurting others' feelings. "I don't think we should date anymore." The words slid out before I could think them through, which was just as well.

His cheery expression wilted. "But we're so good together." When I didn't agree, he said, "Why are you doing this?"

"You're a wonderful guy, but I'm going through a crazy time right now." A pang of self-doubt shot from my legs up to my shoulders, almost forcing me to recant my words. Was I making a dreadful error? No. "I'm sorry."

He snorted a chuckle, his upper lip curling up to expose his square front teeth. "Let me get this straight. You're dumping me? That's a laugh." He stomped back to his car, then yelled across the hood, "You're lucky I ever took you out."

At eight o'clock the next morning, my doorbell rang several times in rapid succession, sounding like a smoke alarm. Charlie barked from the kitchen, but remained in his basket, his legs sore from his foray into the neighborhood. He must have pulled a muscle somehow.

Still in my bathrobe, I squinted through the peephole to see Darla's face reduced to the size of a Cheerio. What was she doing here? Phil must be out there too. I decided not to open the door. I was in no mood for entertaining those two, and I knew I looked terrible. As I tiptoed into the living room, someone's knuckles rapped urgently on the door, and then the bell rang again. I turned back and cracked the door a couple of inches.

Darla stood alone. "May I?" she said. With her shoulders thrown back, she shoved the door open and barged across the threshold. A mass of cold air flooded the hallway. I peered past her at the Porsche 911 Carrera sitting out front, a sign her boutique was flourishing.

"What do you want?" I assumed she was looking for Phil. What else could it be?

"Henry called Philip last night to tell him the good news. Apparently you two have something going."

If she only knew how wrong she was. "No, we don't, not that it's any of your business."

"I wish I were wrong." She sounded like she was announcing a death in the family. "Henry said he's falling for you."

"Don't believe it." I relived the awkward moment he and I shared in this same spot less than twenty-four hours earlier. "Now, please leave."

"Philip thinks it's great," she continued as if she hadn't heard me. "He said we can all hang out together, double date, be friends. He thinks you've changed into a perfect little princess, but you don't fool me for a minute." Spittle flew from her mouth and landed on my shoulder. "We both know you wanted to kill his unborn son. And you would have if he hadn't stopped you."

The lump in my throat made speaking difficult. "But I didn't go through with it."

"Your intention was there. Any woman who'd want to kill her own child is evil."

"But I was so young back then." I felt a place deep inside my abdomen cramping, sending an ache across my belly. "And I was scared to death."

"You weren't too scared to get yourself pregnant, were you? Philip thinks it was an accident, but you and I know better."

I said nothing. It would be futile to argue with her.

"When he refused to marry you, you threatened to have an abortion, out of revenge." Her tirade rebounded off the walls. "It's the oldest trick in the book."

"That was nineteen years ago. And I live with that guilt every day. Don't you think that's enough punishment?"

"You don't look like you're suffering to me. But you will someday. God will have the last word."

Her words pierced my eardrums like shards of glass. I had to get her out of my house. I inched toward the door, grasped hold of the knob.

"We heard through Rob that you were over at Andrea's parents', probably pushing for Andrea to have an abortion," she said. "Your solution to everything."

"I wouldn't do that."

She moved halfway through the doorway, then she swung around, bringing with her a fresh round of contempt. "You stay out of my life. Unless you find a way to do that, I'll tell Rob everything. And how about Henry? Wouldn't he be surprised to find out what you're really like? Not to mention Lois Grimbaldi."

"Please." My hand reached out, but I was afraid to touch her arm. "Why are you doing this? What do you want?" I was ready to pay whatever it took.

"I want you to disappear, to vanish from the face of the earth." Her nostrils flared. "Steer clear of Philip and Henry. It wouldn't work out with him anyway. He loves his wife. He still has her picture in his bedroom. You must have seen it. Or haven't you wormed your way into his bed yet?"

I ignored the slam.

"You're not his type. Henry's a godly man who deserves someone better. I happen to know the perfect woman for him. My friend Vicki has had a crush on him for years. She's just like Barbara—virtuous. Unlike you, she's been saving herself for the right man. Once you butt out, she'll have a chance."

She shot me one more look of scorn. "Women like you make me sick." She whirled around and strode down the front steps.

Listening to her car rumble down the street, I shut the door and leaned against it. At first, I thought I was fine, but then I felt my features contorting, and a moment later tears rushed out of my eyes. I covered my face with my hands and cried.

Everything Darla said about me was true. When I fell into bed with Phil, I made no effort to protect myself, as they say. I assumed he would marry me if I got pregnant. Sure, he would be upset at first, but he would get over it in a few days, and we would live happily ever after. When I missed my period, I experienced a short-lived time of euphoria, followed by debilitating morning sickness and regret.

I remembered breaking the news to Phil. He took on the look of a man who was being sentenced to a lifetime imprisonment in Siberia. "How could you let this happen?" he yelled. "I'm too young to be a father, and I'm sure not ready to get married." His words almost bowled me over.

During the next few weeks, I felt like an alien had invaded my body. One day, after a miserable hour of vomiting, I called a woman's clinic. That afternoon, I went in, and the nurse assured me these predicaments happen all the time. "You don't want to bring an unwanted child into the world, do you?" she asked. No, I didn't want the baby. I'd been stupid, I was losing Phil, but I could set things right again. I made an appointment to go in the next day to eradicate my horrible mistake.

The next day as I dressed to go to the clinic, I listened to my clock ticking, and it occurred to me that the unborn fetus's heart was also beating. I stood paralyzed by indecision. Was I doing the right thing? Was there another way out of the nightmare? Then I felt nausea churning through my gut like the onset of food poisoning. I raced to the bathroom. Leaning over the toilet, I lost the only meal I'd eaten in twenty-four hours.

As I was getting in my car, Phil raced up in his old Volkswagen van. "Stop," he said. "Don't do it. It's my child too." He wept, tears streaming from his eyes. "Okay, you win. We'll get married."

Seven months later, Rob was born, yellowed with jaundice. He remained a sickly baby who suffered from eczema and colic. I remembered his legs kicking frantically as he screamed through the night. I tried to breast-feed him, but I developed one breast infection after another. Feeding time was a painful ordeal for both of us. Several months into Rob's life, I felt depleted and resented my infant son. Days passed when my staggering depression drove me to consider giving him up for adoption. Wouldn't Rob be better off in a real family with a mother who didn't cry all the time and a father who wasn't a drunk? I reasoned.

Now Rob and Andrea stood in the same boat. Maybe it would be better if Andrea ... "No."

I clutched my chest and imagined myself cradling my new grandchild. Andrea didn't have the right to steal that baby from me.

Later that afternoon I sat at my desk in the office. I'd just spoken to Sherry Henrick and had encouraged her to drive by a fixer-upper the couple had looked at several months earlier but thought needed too much work.

"The listing agent said the sellers are desperate," I told her. "They'll consider any offer. With the money you save, you can paint the interior and install new carpet. Remember, the house has a cute breakfast nook and is within walking distance of the elementary school." Sherry, speaking in monotone, said she would think about it.

I opened the Basetti file and called the listing agent for the home Mr. Basetti and his wife wanted, only to find I was too late. "We accepted an offer last night," the agent said. "But there's a contingency. The buyers are waiting for the sale of a piece of vacation property that's supposed to close in a few days. We'll look at your client's offer as a backup—as long as it's full price."

I cracked another of Lois's files and called the young man who hadn't given the lender verification of his income. He owned his own business—some sort of a consulting firm— and said he resented the bank treating him like a liar. "I've never needed verification before," he told me. "I took out a loan for a new car last month, and that bank was thrilled to lend me money."

I explained that any mortgage company would require copies of his income-tax forms as proof of earnings. "It's a matter of policy," I said. "I'd have to do the same thing."

As I hung up, Laurie straggled in unannounced. I'd left her a recorded message several hours earlier saying, "My dear friend, we need to talk."

Laurie collapsed onto the chair next to my desk. She looked bedraggled. Limp bangs hung across her eyes, and she wasn't wearing lipstick. I tried to remember if I'd ever seen her without lipstick. Once, I recalled, when she was in the hospital after giving birth, and once when she had strep throat.

"Something wrong?" I asked, pushing my paperwork aside.

"Dave was badgering me so much last night, I told him everything." She whispered so my coworker sitting on the other side of the partition wouldn't hear. "That I was attracted to a guy and had lunch with him, but nothing happened. That was a big mistake. Dave went ballistic and threatened to hire a private detective to follow me, get copies of my cell phone bills, and find out who I've been calling."

I heard voices approaching and glanced up to see two agents wandering past.

"Let's go somewhere more private," I said, getting to my feet. I led Laurie down a short hallway to the conference room. I scanned the room through the floor-to-ceiling windows to make sure no one was sitting at the hefty table that dominated the small space. On one wall hung a print of Mount Rainier, and crushed in a corner stood an artificial ficus tree. Once inside I closed the door, then swiveled two chairs so they faced each other.

"Did you two get a chance to speak again this morning?" I asked as we sat down. I knew Laurie wasn't the type to come groveling with an apology. She and I had suffered a spat several years before, and I'd been the one to call and patch things up.

"No. Dave slept on the couch." The corners of her mouth dragged down. "When I got up this morning, he was gone."

"Maybe this is a good time to make an appointment with a marriage counselor. Dave's feeling crushed, but I'm sure you two can resolve this issue."

She raked her fingers through her bangs, but they flopped back across her forehead. "I guess, but I don't know if Dave would go. He's acting so high and mighty, like he's never done anything wrong in his life." She worked her wedding ring up to her knuckle, then shoved it back down again. "When I think of all the nights he's stayed out late at supposed business meetings, and I haven't had a clue where he was, it makes me wonder what he was really doing. I'm always the one waiting at home like a cocker spaniel with his newspaper and slippers."

"That's not fair. I have meetings at night, and they're strictly business,"

She covered her mouth as she yawned. "I'm going home to take a nap," she said, standing. "We can talk more tonight on the way to class. What time shall I pick you up?"

Through the window, I watched several people walk by, their voices sounding as though they were submerged in a fish tank. "I'm not going," I said, avoiding Laurie's eyes.

"But tonight's our last class. Henry promised us a live model. You don't want to miss that."

"I can't go." I had little doubt Darla would follow through with her threats if I spoke to Henry again. And who cared about a dumb drawing class? I had more important matters on my mind.

She scrutinized my face. "You don't look so good." She slid back on the chair and scooted it close until our knees were touching. "What's wrong? Is it Tim?"

"We're not dating anymore."

"You poor little thing. What happened?"

"It was my idea, and it may have been the stupidest move of my life." I pictured myself dining alone at a restaurant at the age of ninety. "Tim was upset, but he seems pretty resilient." I affected a weak laugh. "When I called him this morning to make sure he was okay, he sounded happy as a clam. Seems he dropped by his old girlfriend's house on the way home from mine. Guess they got back together."

"That does it, you're coming tonight. You don't want to miss your last chance with Henry."

"All he wants from me is friendship—which is for the best." If that were true, why did it hurt so much to say it? "Thanks to Phil's big mouth, Henry won't even want me for a friend anymore." I stared at my hands in my lap. "Anyway, I'm not good enough for a man like him."

She tossed me a look of disbelief. "Not good enough? You're perfect."

"I'm anything but perfect. There's so much you don't know about me."

"I don't need to know any more about you. I love you just as you are."

Stephanie sauntered by and stopped short when she noticed me. She knocked on the door, then let herself in.

"A Darla Bennett just called for Lois," she said, handing me a slip of paper with Darla's telephone number written on it. "It sounded important. I told her the person who was handling Lois's sales would get right back to her."

I reminded myself of a lioness stalking its prey as I waited in my car for the source of all my problems—Phil. Parked in the lot behind his five-story apartment house, I turned off the engine and listened to it die. Sitting in silence, I recalled the day Phil and I attempted to reconcile—almost a year after our breakup. I'd felt naive optimism as I entered his slummy one-room apartment in the University District and thought how miserable he must be living there by himself. Scanning the open cupboards, I saw no trace of alcohol, and the room smelled as though it had been recently scrubbed. He'd prepared a lunch of tuna sandwiches served on paper plates, which I found sweet, and we dined sitting on the couch. He told me how much he needed me. "You're the only woman I'll ever love," he'd murmured in my ear, his breath feeling like a spring breeze.

After lunch he'd opened the couch into a double bed. He'd gently pulled me onto it, and I'd relaxed in his embrace, remembering how much I cared for him. I'd clung to him, never wanting to leave the safety of his arms. Several hours later as I prepared to go, I noticed something made of shiny black fabric lying on the floor between the crack of the couch and the mattress. I reached down to find a pair of women's panties. My hand shaking with fury, I flung them at him. Then I stormed out the door.

That pathetic scene still made my chest sink, as if Phil's barbed hook remained lodged in my heart after all these years, pulling me back in time. Maybe it was possible to be addicted to another person, I thought, but after today I would finally be free.

275

Phil's Saab sailed into the parking lot. He got out and, with a spring in his step, headed for the building's back door. The sight of him looking so cheerful ratcheted up my fury another degree. Eighteen years of harbored bitterness rolled back into place like an army deploying for battle. I vaulted out of my car and followed him.

"Phil!" I yelled.

His face showed friendly surprise. He pulled open the apartment house door, and I brushed by him, my elbow hitting his arm. I marched up the stairs and around the corner to his familiar door. I'd been to his apartment a few dozen times to pick up Rob, back before he could drive. Each time I'd been reminded of what a slob Phil was: dirty dishes stacked high in the sink and piles of cigarette butts collected in the huge ashtray he'd made in ceramics class in college.

As he fit the key in the lock, I felt like Mount Etna ready to spew off its lid.

He turned the knob and opened the door wide, as if welcoming a long lost relative. "After you," he said.

I felt disoriented—as if I'd never been here before. Instead of smelling a haze of secondhand smoke, I inhaled clean air enhanced with a hint of lemon. Ahead, the walls were freshly tinted buttermilk yellow, and cream-colored molding ran along the ceiling and floor. A Persian carpet led into the living room.

Phil grinned like a child showing his parents a straight-A report card. "Did I tell you my old landlord put the building on the market last year? All the tenants formed an association, and we turned it into a condominium. This place is mine."

Not noticing my scowl, he strolled into the living room, where two matching moss green couches stood at right angles to the marble-faced fireplace. A hand-blown glass bowl filled with shells sat on the sleek table between the couches. He relaxed into one couch and motioned me to the other.

I sat rigidly, my knees pressing against the table's edge. "Why did you tell Darla I tricked you into marrying me?"

His jaw dropped open. "I didn't mean to. It slipped out. But don't worry, she won't tell anyone."

"She was just at my house, and she threatened to."

"No way. She's not like that." He was showing himself to be as naive as I once was.

"She may have already blabbed to Henry." A tear trickled down my cheek and into the corner of my mouth. I was surprised I had any tears left inside me. "You promised never to tell anyone."

He got up and moved to my couch. Sitting next to me, he reached for my hand.

I yanked it away. "Don't touch me, you traitor!"

"I guess I've never been good at keeping secrets. Even when I'm sober, I talk too much." His arm eased over the back of the couch, then around my shoulder. "I'll call her and tell her to keep quiet."

That wouldn't work, I thought. Darla would always hold this information over me. My chest began shaking with my labored breathing. I tried to harden my melting features, but tears seeped out.

"Please don't cry." He pulled me closer. "You have nothing to feel bad about." He wiped my cheek. "I'm not sorry I married you. Marrying you and having Rob were the best things I've ever done."

"But I forced you to. And I almost aborted Rob." The words strangled me, closing my windpipe. I could never admit to anyone that I had later contemplated giving Rob up for adoption to a complete stranger. "I wasn't a very good mother."

He kissed my cheek. "That's all in the past." For a long moment, our eyes locked. His lips neared mine. Then he kissed me. I closed my eyes and allowed myself to be swept into his powerful embrace.

He pulled back a few inches and sighed. "You still taste good."

His lips brushed mine, but I pushed him away. "We can't do this," I said. "It's wrong."

"But this feels so right. What could it hurt?"

"Isn't acting impetuously what got us into trouble in the first place?"

"But we were married once."

"The key word is *were*." It would be like leaping out of an airplane to see if the ground was still hard.

Phil lifted a strand of hair away from my face and carefully tucked it behind my ear. "I've never met a woman who could satisfy me like you did."

My face was bathed in heat. "Not even Darla?"

"We don't ... I mean, she says we have to wait until after we're married."

I had to hand it to her this time; she had the right idea.

31

I found myself humming as I drove past the Seattle Asian Art Museum looking for a place to park. As my voice soared to hit a high note, I realized it was the Mozart piece I'd heard at Henry's studio. Not wanting to think about him, I turned on the radio, found an oldies station, and began singing along with Elvis: "I can't help falling in love with you." That was no good either, I thought. Switching off the radio, I tried to concentrate on my driving.

Circling the brick water tower on the south side of Volunteer Park, I found a spot at the side of the road. As I backed in, I tapped the car behind me, setting off its alarm. Listening to the car's siren beep and blare, I remembered Dad teaching me how to parallel park, but I'd never been very good at it. He'd taught me many things. I recalled his bringing the family to the park and climbing the water tower. We kids had scrambled up the stairs, our voices echoing as we dashed around madly, while Dad and Mom admired the view of downtown.

I hadn't spoken to Dad since our discouraging conversation at the restaurant, and I wouldn't do so until he and Mom reconciled, which could be never. Mom was beginning to worry me. I thought older people tended to suffer from depression, not incredible bursts of energy. But she'd sounded almost manic with her crazy talk about travel, and finding her roots, and signing up for a class called Independent Women and Finance. Was she really happier living as a single woman? Had she given up on reclaiming her marriage? No, I wasn't going to think about Mom either, I decided. Not for an hour anyway.

Trying to ignore the alarm of the car behind me, I got out, plugged my ears and took off with long strides. My toe hit a crease in the sidewalk, and I started to teeter forward. Flailing out my arms, I regained my equilibrium but felt foolish, even though no one was watching. Which was stupid. Who cared what others thought? I'd spent too much of my life trying to keep up an image, when in reality no one probably noticed. They were likely too busy worrying about themselves.

Up ahead stood the imposing stone-faced museum, with its panels of metal and white glass at the center. I heard running water from the fountains and inhaled the pungent smell of spent marigolds. Glancing toward the other side of the road, I could see Noguchi's *Black Sun*, a mammoth doughnut-shaped sculpture. Below it lay the reservoir, a round body of water.

Moving toward the front door, I saw the larger-than-life camel statues reclining on either side of me. A mother stood nearby as her son crawled atop one of them, and I recalled playing there as a child. Was I the reason my family came to the museum so often? Neither of my siblings had shown any interest in art.

I lugged the front door open and saw Emily waiting at the ticket booth, as we'd agreed. She'd called earlier that morning. "Are you available to see an exhibit of contemporary Japanese prints and paintings?" she'd asked in a voice I found impossible to refuse.

Emily's silver hair glimmered like a halo under the overhead lights. "I'm glad you could come," she said as I approached her.

"Thank you, it was nice of you to think of me." I opened my billfold and handed three dollars to the woman collecting admission. It was a nominal amount, I thought, and I decided to start visiting a different museum each month. Why not?

Emily and I ascended several steps and entered the first room as a couple was exiting through the passageway at the far end, leaving us alone.

On the near wall hung a sign, *Reflections of Water: Japanese Modern Prints and Paintings*, and I surmised the works all possessed an aquatic theme.

"It's a shame you missed the last class," Emily said. "A young woman from New Delhi dressed in a sari posed for us." She stopped before a print of four wooden skiffs moored on the banks of the Tone River. "Henry asked

Laurie and me if we knew why you weren't there. He seemed concerned."

"A conflict came up that made it impossible."

We moved to the next piece, a pen and ink drawing of a mist-enshrouded waterfall.

"Are you going to keep drawing?" she asked.

"I hope to. I painted something since we saw each other last."

"Good for you."

We migrated a few feet to view a print of rain slanting down upon a darkened Tokyo street.

My mind spun to my new marketing strategies: to send clients calendars at Christmas featuring remodeled homes with before and after photos, and a newsletter mentioning my latest sales and listings, and offering tips on creating intimate interior spaces using a coat of paint, existing furniture, and accessories.

"I'm not sure I'll have time to paint again until after Christmas," I added.

"I hope you will. You were doing something important. The way I see it, God gave us our talents to use whenever we can. He loves to watch us create."

I've got to tell you, her words sounded like gibberish to me. I couldn't see what God had to do with anything.

We continued into the next room to find a dozen high-school-aged students taking notes as their teacher explained a series of ten prints of Mount Fuji. We stayed a few minutes, then moved on to the next room, which housed a collection of kimonos affixed to the wall. Again, Emily and I stood alone.

"Exquisite," she said. Her eyes embraced the sapphire blue-and-caramel-colored geometric patterns of the fabric.

She turned to me. "Did I mention that I first met Henry at church? Over twenty years ago. I got to know his precious family, and my heart ached for everything he and his girls endured. I don't see him there anymore, but once you know the Lord, the relationship can never be severed."

I could understand how an old-fashioned woman might adopt such outmoded notions. It would be comforting to believe in a big father figure watching out for her, especially as she got on in years. But I had proof that fathers couldn't be trusted.

"Do you know Jesus?" she said.

All I could think about was ending this dreadful conversation. I thought about saying I needed to use the restroom and then never coming back. But I liked Emily too much to run out on her like that. I pretended to examine another kimono while my mind searched for a polite answer. "I went to church when I was young, but I haven't set foot in one for years—except when someone's getting married or buried. God and I don't get along all that well."

"I'm sorry to hear that, dear. Sounds like you feel he let you down?"

"Let's just say I gave the God thing a shot, and it didn't work out."

"There were times when I rejected God too. But he didn't give up on me." Her voice rang with certainty, as if she were citing a mathematical theorem, when in truth her beliefs were based on speculation. Fantasy, really. "He hasn't forgotten you either," she said. "You might give him another try."

"How can you be sure about something you can't even see?" I knew it sounded rude, but I was growing weary of this discussion.

Her eyes sparkled like a young girl's. "The same way I can be sure the sun's up in the sky even though I can't find it at night. I can see its light reflecting off the surface of the moon just as I see the Lord's reflected love shining in the lives of my friends, even if I can't observe it in my own."

The room felt suddenly cold; I hugged myself. "There was a time when I believed all things worked together for good for those who love God," I said. "But good things didn't come my way. And no matter how hard I try, bad things keep happening."

"Bad things do happen to good people," she agreed. "We'll have to wait until we get to heaven to ask God why he allows us to experience some hardships. Until then we must keep trusting him and asking for his wisdom and guidance."

"I stopped asking God for favors a long time ago, and it's been easier that way—one less thing to be disappointed about." I took a step toward the next room, but Emily remained where she was.

"God's timing isn't the same as ours, but he always has a reason for what he does," she said. "Even his allowing my Al to be taken away so soon. It's easy to become discouraged when he doesn't answer our prayers in a few days, or even years, but we must have patience." She sounded all too much like my mother, which made me feel defensive.

"I've lived the past eighteen years just fine this way." Thank you very much.

"Of course you have, dear. But remember, no matter what has happened in your life, God still wants to have a relationship with you. He's knocking at your door. All you have to do is open it."

God wanted to get to know me better? Fat chance. In a rash move, I said, "If God exists, he doesn't want me." There, the other half of the puzzle lay on the table.

She looked perplexed.

"I haven't been a very good person," I said. A woman like Emily couldn't begin to understand.

Her face glowed with sympathy. "We're all sinners."

I hated that word. "Not my mother. She's not a sinner."

"Dear, we're all cut from the same bolt of cloth. That's just the way we're made. The good news is, the Lord has promised that if we confess our sins and repent of them, he will forgive us and will wash us clean, the way I often whiten my wool before I spin it."

As we wandered into the next room to view an exhibit of Chinese ceramics, Emily started talking about a poetry class she'd taken, as if the previous topic had been the most natural in the world. "We should sign up for another art class together," she said. "Would you be interested?"

In spite of all her preachy talk about God, I longed to know her better. "Yes, I'd go if you were there." As long as there was a new teacher.

"Great, I'll look forward to it. When you're my age, you start losing your friends. It's hard to let go, but you have no choice. That's why it's good to have younger friends—like you."

"And I need a friend like you, too."

"Good, then it's settled." She clasped me in her arms, then stood back and said, "I'm afraid I need to be on my way. I'm babysitting the grandkids today."

"Sounds like fun, and I should get to work."

"We must do this again soon."

"Sure," I said. "We could try the Frye Museum, and have lunch afterward."

Strolling toward the exit, we passed a Ming Dynasty scroll and several earthenware statues we discovered were tomb attendants. We stepped outside the building and headed down the walkway. I'd intended to spend the afternoon at the office, but as Emily got into her car and drove away, I decided to take a closer look at the *Black Sun*. From the museum side of the street, I could see the far-off Space Needle rising behind the polished granite sculpture and through the nine-foot hole in its center.

A sporty roadster slowed to let me cross. In the middle of the street, my cell phone warbled. I quickened my pace while reaching into my purse, then pressed the phone against my ear and said hello.

"It's Lois." Her voice sounded fragile—no trace of its usual brassy self-confidence. She was the last person I expected to hear from.

"Marguerite, I need to tell you something you may already know."

A couple sat chatting at the base of the sculpture; I stepped out of their earshot. "You don't need to say anything."

"Yes, I do. No more secrets. I'm an alcoholic, an out-of-control drunk. The burden of keeping that fact hidden has been almost as bad as the booze. You know what I mean?"

"Yes." I knew what it was like to shoulder a secret weighing more than this massive sculpture. "How can I help?"

"If Stephanie gave you those files, you're already helping me."

As I walked around to the back of the *Black Sun* to view the reservoir below, I filled Lois in on what I'd accomplished so far. With my persuasion and some rather clever recommendations for carpet and paint colors, the Henricks had made an offer on the home they had viewed months earlier. Their offer accepted, the couple was acting like a pair of chickadees ready to build a new nest. Also, the Basettis had found themselves in first place for the house they wanted, and the man who needed to verify his income finally showed up with tax returns for the last three years, proving he was financially solvent.

"The only person I haven't spoken to is Darla Bennett." Speaking her name was like biting into rock salt, sucking the moisture right out of my mouth.

"I've learned a lot since I've been here," she said. "Life's too short to fawn over people who don't treat you with respect. If Darla bugs you, let someone else in the office handle her." She laughed, almost sounding like herself again. "I can't believe I said that." Her voice turned serious again. "By the way, if anything closes while I'm gone, I want you to keep the commission, one hundred percent."

"No, we'll split the money, just like we planned."

"You'd still want me for a partner?"

"As long as you stay sober." My vision traveled to the far-off horizon; I saw a slice of Elliot Bay, and behind it, craggy mountain peaks.

"When are you coming back to work?" I asked.

"I'm in here for twenty-eight days, so it'll be three more weeks, maybe longer. In the meantime please pray for me. Part of this process is admitting I'm powerless over my alcoholism and turning to God to restore my sanity."

"Good luck," I said, knowing it was unlikely I would be doing any praying. "Let me know if there's anything more I can do."

The sky was darkening, and the air tasted thick. I started back toward my car by way of a lily pond. The small body of water seemed the picture of tranquility. I envisioned Emily's peaceful face. Was it really God who gave her the courage to go on after her husband's death? If so, then why hadn't he shown up for me? I'd begged him to make Phil sober and to save our marriage. Where was he when my father cheated on Mom? Where was he the night my future grandchild was conceived? Why didn't he keep these terrible things from happening? A compassionate God wouldn't let good people suffer this way.

How many chances should I give you, God?

I shook my head. Even if I wanted to pray, my faith wasn't there anymore.

A drop of rain flicked my cheek. I looked to the clouds and saw a patch of blue. Was God still knocking on my door?

Visions of Rob holding a newborn, my parents battling in divorce court, and Phil marrying Darla swirled through my head. I wasn't strong enough to make it on my own, that much I knew.

God, I need you.

How I wished he could hear me.

∞

Three blocks from the office, I felt compelled to make a U-turn and drive the five minutes to Laurie's home. Coming down her street, I could see the two-story Georgian-style residence, which had recently been repainted a crisp white. Lustrous black shutters hung on each side of the windows, and two neat rows of boxwood lined the brick-paved walkway up to the snappy red door. From the outside everything looked perfect.

Laurie's Lexus sat in the drive. She hadn't shown up for the Mom's walk on Thursday. According to Erika, Laurie had called saying she was coming down with the flu and was going back to bed. But when I phoned her later that afternoon, she'd sounded fine—almost too fine. I'd asked about her situation with Dave, and she'd said, "Dave left town this morning for a week, and I refuse even to think about him until he gets back."

I strode to the front door and reached for the brass knocker. At that moment, the door swung open, and Laurie glided out.

She stopped short, her eyes widening with surprise. "What are you doing here?"

"I was worried about you," I said. She couldn't be headed to the beauty parlor. Her hair looked professionally coiffed, with glossy strands styled away from her face. A splash of scarlet accentuated her lips, and dark liner gave her eyes a seductive look.

Laurie zipped up her purse and hoisted the strap over her shoulder. "I'm on my way out."

I inhaled a whiff of Joy perfume, which I knew she saved for special occasions. "I came by to see how you're doing and to give you a hug." I put my arms around her, but she stood as straight as a broomstick, her arms dangling at her sides. I leaned back and appraised her outfit: a slim black knee-length skirt and a leopard-print top.

"Where are you headed?" I asked.

Avoiding my gaze, she said, "Downtown. I have an appointment in twenty minutes." She inched forward, but I blocked her path.

"A business meeting?" I asked, not budging.

She glanced at her watch. She was wearing the small gold one with the diamonds on the face. "No, just something I need to take care of."

My hands moved to my hips. "I'll go with you and keep you company. We can talk in the car."

"No, that won't work. I have to run a few errands afterward, then go to the grocery store."

A sedan pulled into the driveway across the street. Laurie waved at the driver, a woman, then took advantage of the diversion to sidestep me.

"I'll give you a call," she said over her shoulder. She scurried to her car and unlocked it with a remote key.

Where was she going? It was too late in the day for a lunch date. If she were meeting someone—

My mouth went dry. I wondered if I should beg her not to leave. But could I stop her even if I tried? Maybe there was no way to keep a boulder from rolling down a hill once it gained enough momentum.

"Laurie," I called after her, using the stern voice I employed when Rob was in trouble. The woman across the street turned her head.

Laurie's hand rested on the door handle; she waited for me to catch up with her.

"You're scaring me," I said. "Please tell me you're not meeting the person I think you are."

She wrenched open the door. "What if I am?" She raised her chin defiantly. "Are you going to turn on me too?"

"We'll always be friends, but that doesn't mean I like what you're doing."

"When did you get to be so high and mighty?" she asked, jangling her keys. Then she spun around, dove into the driver's seat, and slammed the door behind her.

I stood listening to the engine roar to life. I watched her back her car down the driveway and cruise halfway up the block. The car slowed, brake lights flickering. Then it sped away.

32

When I got home, Charlie met me at the door with a meager woof. It had taken several days for the dog to recover the strength in his legs, and he still moved like an old gentleman needing a cane. Hauling him up and supporting his weight on one hip, I listened to my phone messages.

"Honey," Mom's recorded voice said, "would you give me a call?"

I wanted to call my mother right away, but I waited for the next message to play.

"Do you think you could stop by my studio today?" Henry asked. "I want to show you something."

I played his message two more times. I couldn't imagine what he could possibly have to show me. A note from Darla? An article on morality?

"I'm not going," I told Charlie. There was no point in speaking to Henry Marsh about anything ever again. "I have my friends, my parents, and my son to keep me busy," I said. "And soon I'll have a grandchild. Wow." I was amazed to feel anything other than dread.

I deposited a kiss on the top of Charlie's fuzzy head, then set him down and fluffed his coat. He padded over to his basket, tucked his legs underneath him, and curled into a ball.

As I dialed my parents' number, I wondered what Mom had on her mind. Was she going to share the itinerary for her upcoming European voyage, or the news that she'd filed for divorce?

"Hello," my mother said in her usual way.

"Mom, how are you?"

"Oh, I don't know. Pretty good, I guess." The gaiety that I'd heard in her voice the day before had vanished. I pictured her camped out on the couch blotting her tears with a soggy handkerchief. I was about to offer to come over and keep her company, but before I could speak she said, "I know you were being sarcastic when you asked me what Jesus would say. But it got me thinking about God's unconditional love, how he keeps forgiving me each time I wander off course. Vern was over here pleading for forgiveness, wanting to come home. It's too early for him to move back, but I agreed to go to a marriage counselor with him on Friday."

"Wow." I felt like jumping for joy. "That's the best news I've heard all week."

"Now, don't get your hopes up too high. I don't know if I can forgive your father—I really don't."

"But you'll try?"

"Yes."

"Wonderful. And, Mom?" It felt odd giving my mother marital advice, and I proceeded with caution. "Remember, it took a long time for you two to get to this point. It might take awhile to get things back on track."

Minutes after I hung up, the phone rang. Hoping to hear Laurie's voice, I eagerly grabbed the receiver.

"I'm just checking to see if you got my message," Henry said.

My free hand moved to my collarbone. "I did, but I can't come over."

"How about tomorrow?"

"No, never." I told myself to stand firm. I'd taken the road of least resistance too many times. "If you have something to tell me, please say it now."

"You sound upset. And you have a right to be."

"No, I'm not. But it's better for everyone if we don't speak to each other again."

A long pause followed; the silence crackled in my ears.

"I've hurt you, haven't I?" His voice tapered to just above a whisper. "I'm sorry, I've only been thinking about myself."

"No, it's not you." Darkness threaded through my limbs as I realized I would never see him again. I felt myself beginning to crumble. "If you don't mind, I'd like to say thank you for the class and good-bye."

"I do mind. We need to talk."

This conversation hurt badly enough without prolonging the agony. I thought about hanging up on him, but my hand gripped the receiver. "Here, I'll make things easier for you. Someone's threatened to tell you everything about me. You'd be disgusted if you knew the whole story."

"I doubt it."

Anguish flooded my mind and spilled out in a tangle of desperate words. "What would you think of a woman who got herself pregnant on purpose, then threatened to abort her child if the father didn't marry her?" I felt like someone had knifed me open to expose my insides.

"I'd think she was young and foolish," he replied without hesitation.

The backs of my knees weakened. "You'd be furious at your daughter if she act liked that, wouldn't you?"

"Yes. But I'd forgive her, even if I disapproved of her actions."

I felt my throat close with anxiety. "I shouldn't be talking to you about this."

"It's all right, it's my turn to listen. I'll come over."

"No, I'll come there. But just long enough to make you understand."

As I drove toward Henry's studio, I wondered what in the world had made me agree to see him. How could I look him in the eye after what I just revealed? And what good could come of it? I needed to get over the storybook dream that a man—even a friend—was going to fix everything in my life. Another person couldn't do that for me.

Coasting down a side street, I saw a brownish orange shape out of the corner of my eye. I jammed my foot on the brakes just as a cat streaked in front of me. My tires squealed as the car jolted to a halt. The seat belt gripped my torso, and my head snapped forward, then fell back against the headrest. Oh, no! I thought. Please, no. I held my breath and waited. A moment later the cat skittered under a car on the other side of the road.

Someone honked. I checked my rearview mirror to see a UPS truck right behind me. I eased up on the brakes, and my car began to creep forward. My heart beat frantically—as if I were the cat running for dear life. What was wrong with me?

I turned onto Henry's block. Telling myself I would only be there for a minute, I rolled into a parking spot in front of his place, leaving more than a foot between the curb and my tires.

Henry answered his door on the first knock. "Come in."

"We can talk here," I said, backing down one step. "Say what you have to say."

"Please come in. I won't keep you long." He turned, and without glancing back, strolled around the corner into his studio.

I watched his wide shoulders, his easy gait. Feeling a tug deep inside, I followed.

He led me to a canvas sitting on an easel. "I've been working on this all week," he said, standing back.

I gaped at the full-length portrait. He'd painted me, of all people. I was shocked, as you can imagine. I'd never seen myself so realistically yet beautifully portrayed. Not even in a photograph. I was dressed in a long, flowing dress, the kind I might have worn in college. A gentle breeze seemed to flutter against the silky fabric, impelling me through an open door. The area outside the portal lay tinted with grays and sepias, but I was stepping through it into a lush, flowered meadow that stretched to snow-capped lavender mountains. My eyes were lifted toward the moon. Now here's the crazy part: He'd painted the same pearly moon and misty halo I had drawn.

"That's impossible," I said.

"I hope you don't mind that I painted you without asking your permission," he said from over my shoulder. "Do you like it?"

"It's the most incredible painting I've ever seen." He had captured a youthful innocence that had faded with time. "But I'm not that girl anymore."

"Yes, you are."

I turned to face him. "Didn't you hear what I told you on the phone?"

"Yes, I heard you. But all that took place over eighteen years ago. Why talk about it now?"

"Because we can never escape our past." My voice trembled, making me sound like Mom the day Dad moved out. "Someone's found out what I did and has threatened to tell everyone, including my son."

"That's blackmail." His voice became gruff, heated. "Who is it? I'll go set them straight."

"No. Please stay out of this. That would only make her madder."

"Her? Is it Darla?" The muscle along his jawbone flexed. "Phil must have told her how I feel about you."

So Darla was telling the truth? I wanted to hide my face. "But that was before you knew."

His hand came out to take mine, but I stepped back, out of his reach.

"Self-righteous people sometimes have secrets to hide themselves," he said. "I've known a friend of Darla's for many years."

"Vicki?" Thanks to Darla I knew her name. I wondered if Henry realized the woman carried a torch for him.

"Yes," he said. "She introduced me to Darla, and I introduced Darla to Phil. Vicki let a nasty fact about Darla slip out awhile ago. Seems she got mixed up with a married man a few years back." He shrugged, a small smile tugging the corners of his mouth. "We could call Darla and give her a taste of her own medicine."

"But then we'd be just like her."

"True. The best remedy would be not to care whether Darla tells anyone or not." He moved closer. "What's the worst thing that could happen if Rob finds out?"

I considered my son's distress, especially in the midst of his crisis with Andrea. "He'd be devastated, crushed." I would do anything to spare him that anguish.

"His feelings probably would be hurt, but your story illustrates an important lesson: Each life is precious. If Rob ever wonders whether he and Andrea did the right thing by keeping their baby, he could remember his own parents made the same choice. And it was a good one."

I felt light-headed, unsteady, as though the floor beneath me were swaying. "I can't risk it," I said.

"Do you think you're the only one in the world who's done something they regret?"

Of course I didn't. Everyone messed up now and then, but other people's mistakes were minor compared to mine. I had altered the lives of three people: Phil, Rob, and myself. And the repercussions continued to ripple outward.

"I'll share a story with you. I hate to admit this to any-one, but here goes." His weight rocked forward and his head bowed for a moment. Then he said, "You met my daughter Terry?"

"Yes, she's very pretty."

"After Barbara died, Terry was on my case about every-thing. Why didn't we have enough money to go to Disney World? Why couldn't she eat junk food in front of the TV instead of doing her homework? Why did she have to go to bed so early when all her friends got to stay up until mid-night? You name it, and it was my fault. Her grades plummeted, and her teachers called weekly. Then, when I didn't think things could get any worse, she was caught shoplifting." He rubbed one eye. "I called her a brat after the policeman brought her home and threatened to send her to a boarding school for juvenile delinquents."

I pictured myself in his place. After his wife's death it would be painful to be rejected by his daughter. I wanted to assure him that even the best parents lost their temper every once in a while.

His voice sounded strange, as though he were having trouble breathing. "Terry screamed, 'I hate you.' Then she slapped me in the face with all her might. Without thinking my fist flew out and stopped an inch away from her cheek."

As his arm swung out to demonstrate, I couldn't help recoiling. I abhorred violence and couldn't conceive of a man striking his own child.

When he saw me cringe, he bowed his head again and expelled a mighty breath. "The Holy Spirit must have grabbed my hand. At that time of my life, I honestly wasn't strong enough to do anything by myself.

"I'm not proud of that moment," he continued, sounding frail. "I'll never forget the horrified look on Terry's face as she cowered in fear. I still regret it. My girl could have ended up in the hospital."

"How did you both get past it?" Or had they?

"First, I apologized and promised that when I got angry I'd go somewhere to cool off. Never, never again would I allow frustration and resentment to govern my actions. Then I went in my bedroom and fell to my knees and begged for the Lord's forgiveness. I was so filled with shame it took awhile for me to accept his gift. But I finally found peace." He looked me squarely in the eye. "Do you think I deserved God's mercy?"

He answered his own question. "No, none of us deserves it. But God is generous beyond our comprehension, and his forgiveness is free for the asking. Now, have we got that all settled?"

"Yes." At least I wanted to understand. And I wanted to know his God and to be made whole, as he had been.

He glanced at his painting, his gaze coming to rest on my likeness. "I've kept myself isolated for so long, afraid of loving another woman who might leave me. I've been lonely."

"I know how that feels."

He slipped his arms around my shoulders with such gentleness and care—as if I were the most precious creature on earth. Then I felt my lips melt into his. The warm current flowing through my veins washed away all doubts and replaced them with happiness. I closed my eyes and let his strong arms support me. If he let go, I would fall to the floor. But I was willing to risk it. When our lips parted, we stood wrapped in each other's arms like entwined branches.

"Come on," he said. We sat down together on one of his chairs. I snuggled into his shoulder, closed my eyes, and let my head rise and fall on his chest. I didn't ask why he had painted me, or how he'd remembered so vividly what I looked like. I didn't even question his painting the same moon I'd drawn. None of that seemed to matter anymore.

When he stirred, I moaned. "Please don't get up. I want to stay like this forever." I couldn't believe I'd just bared my thoughts like a neon sign. But the moment passed and his breathing continued its steady refrain.

He said, "I have to get back to my work." Noticing my worried expression, he added, "I'm not going anywhere." He kissed my nose. "Look at this painting. It's obvious I'm smitten with you."

33

During the ride home, Henry's fragrant breath lingers in my nostrils, his sweet taste on my lips. My chest tingles with happiness, although that seems like a mundane word for the bliss I'm experiencing. I've never met a finer man, and he cares for me—skeletons and all. Imagine that.

And I'll tell you something else. Everything I pass looks alive with color and texture. The trees are ablaze with finery, the sky brilliant, iridescent, and even the telephone poles, arranged in endless repeating lines, invite me to capture their splendor on a canvas.

As I drive into my garage, I spy my forgotten easel up in the rafters, wedged between two-by-fours and plywood scraps. I use a stepladder to pull down my old friend, then haul it into the kitchen.

Glancing at the phone, I recall Mom's words, which still hum in my ears like a comforting lullaby. My parents will go to counseling. It doesn't guarantee reconciliation, I know, but it's a move in the right direction.

Maybe all things really do work for good for those who love God.

I lug the easel and the paints and canvases Henry gave me upstairs. A sense of hope lightens my steps. From what Henry said, God is compassionate, far more than I could ever be. With his forgiveness comes freedom from the past. As I embrace this truth, I feel the talons of shame and regret beginning to release their hold on my world.

I plant a foot on the landing, feeling rooted to my foundation, secure. I'm not alone anymore.

Breathing deeply, I expand my lungs, then pray: Dear God, please help me accept this situation with Rob. Watch over him and Andrea and my future grandchild.

I can't fathom how any good can come from the pregnancy, but maybe, somehow, God will turn it into a blessing.

As I enter Rob's room, I glance into the mirror above his bureau and find a radiant woman gazing back. The morning Rob left, I reeled in agony, tears cascading down my cheeks. Today I see vitality, confidence—and something stemming from deep inside me that lifts my features and brightens my eyes. At first I think this new Marguerite is Henry's doing, but I know he cannot transform me any more than a sculptor can fashion a living being out of clay. Then it dawns on me: What I see is God's love reflected in my face. Amazing. I wonder if Emily will notice the difference the next time we meet.

I feel as though I am in the eye of a hurricane, standing in the calm center. I open the easel. Tightening the screws, I give them an extra twist.

God, I'm not strong enough to face Phil and Darla by myself. I ask for your help in dealing with them, too. Whether I ever grow to like Darla doesn't matter; it's time to let go of bitterness, and of Phil.

A sense of peace washes over me.

I rest a canvas on the easel, and the northern light dances across its surface. A smile widens my lips as I visualize a new horizon of infinite possibilities. I open every tube of paint and squirt colors onto a plate.

I give my life to you, God. Please guide my hand.

I dip my brush into the cobalt blue. Then with a long, fluid stroke, I form the first bold line on the canvas.

READERS' GUIDE

*For Personal Reflection or
Group Discussion*

Readers' Guide

Over the course of this novel, Marguerite Carr struggles to recover her artistic passion and learns to forgive others and herself. Forgiveness is one of the major themes of *A Portrait of Marguerite*. As you answer the following questions, think about broken relationships in your life that could be healed by the power of forgiveness.

1. How does Marguerite feel the evening of her first drawing class, and how does her level of confidence compare to her college days? Why does Marguerite long for her instructor Henry Marsh's approval? What happens when a person bases his or her worth on the approval of others? How can pride and fear of failure keep you from using your God-given talents?

2. Why did Marguerite give up her dreams of becoming an artist? Who is Marguerite's biggest critic? When have negative voices in your head, calling you a failure, discouraged you from taking action? How did reading a book on recapturing creativity impact Marguerite? How can a person

reclaim his or her creative passion, whether it took root in the kitchen, the garden, or sitting at a piano? When you were a child, what was your greatest aspiration? How can you incorporate this dream into your adult life?

3. What does Phil represent to Marguerite? What positive and negative traits do you see in him? How does Marguerite's continued bitterness toward him hurt her and their son, Rob? How does she react to Phil's newfound sobriety and his accomplishments as a sculptor? Is it possible for people to change? Why does she feel the need to compete with him for their son's admiration?

4. Why does Marguerite fight her attraction to Henry? What is her attitude toward artists as potential spouses? In chapter 2, when Marguerite sees Henry's marvelous paintings in the gallery, how does she first react? How does this change when she realizes he painted them? Marguerite will never paint exactly like Henry; she brings her unique talents and emotions to the canvas. How is it possible to be a success without being the best?

5. Marguerite has relied on her son, Rob, to give her life direction. In chapter 3, how does she feel when Phil and Darla whisk him off to college? When have you experienced despondency and felt there was no end in sight? With an empty nest, how does Marguerite attempt to fill her days? How do her walking group friends attempt to bolster her spirits?

6. Fellow classmate Emily takes an interest in Marguerite. What do these two women have in common and how are

they different? What can Emily offer Marguerite that her girlfriends and mother cannot? In your own life, how has an older friend or mentor's wisdom affected you?

7. How does Laurie encourage Marguerite with her drawing? Who are your encouragers? In the second half of chapter 6, how does Marguerite react when Laurie says she's fed up with her husband and is interested in another man? Why do Laurie's musings strike home with Marguerite? How would you counsel her?

8. In chapter 9, how does Marguerite feel when she steps into her parents' home? The eldest child, Marguerite compares herself to her younger brother and sister. Do you think her parents would agree and why? What is Marguerite's reaction to her mother's questions about a new beau? Marguerite has placed her father on a pedestal. When her mother claims her father still meets with his former employee Alice, what docs Marguerite think? What is her reaction when her mother says God rescued her?

9. Why does Marguerite feel awkward visiting Henry's studio in chapter 10? Why is she unable to accept his compliments about her drawing ability? Henry mentions he works best in a studio with few distractions. In your home, where could you find a place to lay out craft and art projects, or set up a music stand? Why would having a workspace set up all the time make you more likely to start and finish projects?

10. Why does Marguerite finally agree to go on a blind date? What is Tim like and how does he compare to Henry?

Logic tells Marguerite that Tim embodies all the qualities she's looking for in a man, yet she doesn't find him attractive. Why do you think that is? In the past, why has she dated men she didn't really care for? What does her cairn terrier, Charlie, think of Tim?

11. In chapter 15, when Marguerite drives Henry home, why do you think he chooses to share his loss with her? How did his wife's death affect him? How did his two daughters force him to reenter the human race? How did his terrible loss eventually improve his painting? What is his house like and why does it surprise Marguerite?

12. What are some of the challenges of working at a commission-only job like selling real estate? In what ways is partnering with Lois a good business move? How does Lois let Marguerite down and how is their relationship later mended? When in your own life has a friend or family member, who appeared polished and successful, proved to be otherwise?

13. In chapter 22, when Marguerite creates her first painting since college, what are her emotions? Why does she choose to share her victory with Henry instead of Tim? Later that evening, when Phil calls to tell her about Rob, Henry assures her God can change darkness into light. When have you witnessed this in your life?

14. In chapter 24, how are Marguerite's images of her father shattered? Why did she go looking for him and whom does she confront? In chapter 26, when she finally tracks him down, what is his initial response? He once told

Marguerite, "A man's only as good as his word." What are your thoughts about this statement?

15. In chapter 28, Marguerite recalls the day Phil walked out on her and their infant son. When has a significant person in your life disappointed or abandoned you, making you wonder if God deserted you too? Do you believe that all things work together for good for those who love God? How is God's timing different than ours?

16. Why was Charlie's getting lost particularly frightening for Marguerite? Why does she blame his disappearance and Rob's situation on herself? At the end of the chapter, when Marguerite and Henry are in her kitchen, he gives her permission to paint badly. What does he mean? How does striving for perfection stop you from trying new things?

17. Marguerite has kept a part of her life a secret. Do past mistakes haunt you, keeping you from achieving intimate relationships because you're afraid friends and family members will think less of you if they find out? In chapter 31, how does Emily describe her faith in the God she cannot see but is sure exists? Do you notice God's love reflected in the lives of those around you? Why does Marguerite feel unworthy of God's forgiveness? What is Emily's response?

18. In the final chapter, Marguerite is shocked to find Henry has painted her portrait. How would you feel if someone painted your portrait? When has someone prepared a special meal, spoken words of encouragement, or given you a gift that demonstrated the same affection? In the painting, Marguerite is stepping from a drab world into a colorful

flowered meadow. What do you think the open door represents? How is her life transforming?

19. Why does Marguerite think she can't escape her past? How does Henry react when she reveals her darkest secret? What would you say to her? Henry tells Marguerite that God's forgiveness is free for the asking. How does he illustrate his point? What does Marguerite experience when she finally lets go of bitterness and resentment, and is willing to trust God? How does she feel mounting her stairs and setting up her easel? In your own life, how has God turned a heartache into a blessing? What is preventing you from creating your own masterpiece?

For information about Kate Lloyd visit her Web site at http://www.katelloyd.net.

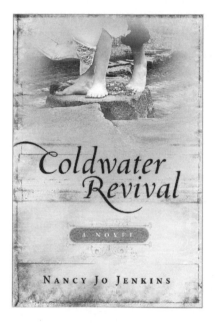

RiverOak . . .
Christ-Centered Fiction
in the Grandest Tradition

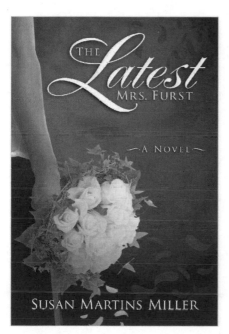

The Latest Mrs. Furst

Jayne knows a lot about inner suffering: She lost a child, and she lost her marriage. All too eager to lose herself in a new relationship, she meets and is immediately smitten by Mitchell, even though there's something a little . . . unsettling about him at times. Determined not to over analyze Mitchell and spoil the fairytale ending to her dream, she marries him.

But Jayne's dream is about to become a nightmare. She begins to suffer eerie visions at night as Mitchell's secrets begin to come to light. Along with her sense of well being, the marriage begins to fall to pieces. Will Jayne's blind love prevail? How long will Mitchell's inner demons haunt him and Jayne? This is a quest for redemption that only God can fulfill.

ISBN-13: 978-1-5891-9073-3
ISBN-10: 1-58919-073-4
Item: 104543 • $13.99
Paperback • 5.5 x 8.5

Pro-choice... pro-life.
It's still all about choices.

Dear Me

All of us have made choices, both good and bad, that have had a lasting impact on our lives. Many women spend their entire lifetime trying to cover up or undo the damaged caused by choices made earlier in their life. This is Vanessa's experience.

In *Dear Me*, Vanessa wrestles with the guilt resulting from an abortion. As she reflects on her life in journal style, Vanessa finds that she's constantly trying to repair her broken life on her own—until she discovers the grace of God.

ISBN-13: 978-1-5891-9024-5
ISBN-10: 1-58919-024-6
Item: 103663 • $12.99
Paperback • 5.5 x 8.5

Additional copies of *A Portrait of Marguerite*
are available wherever good books are sold.

If you have enjoyed this book,
or if it has had an impact on your life,
we would like to hear from you.

Please contact us at:

RiverOak Books
Cook Communications Ministries, Dept. 201
4050 Lee Vance View
Colorado Springs, CO 80918

Or visit our Web site:
www.cookministries.com